MURDER AT THE JOHN WORNALL HOUSE MUSEUM

A Culinary Mystery

by

Ruthie Wornall

Ruthie Wornall

-2010-

Jumbo Jack's Cookbooks
P.O. Box 247
Audubon, IA 50025
Phone: 1-800-798-2635

This book is part historical and part fiction and is the fourth book of the amateur sleuth Rhonda Winters series. All characters other than John Wornall, his family, the pastor at Wornall Road Baptist Church, and Dr. Prince Joseph are fictitious or used fictitiously. The other characters have no relation to anyone having the same name

Photographer—Ruthie Wornall
Photographs of the John Wornall House Museum, of John Bristow Wornall III and John Bristow Wornall V.

First printed by Jumbo Jack's Cookbooks August 2010

ISBN: 978-1-4490-7323-7 (e)
ISBN: 978-1-4490-7325-1 (sc)

Printed in the United States of America

This book is printed on acid-free paper.

ACKNOWLEDGEMENTS

Many thanks to Kandice Walker, director of the Wornall House Museum, and her assistant, Marguerite Milliken, for asking me to write a murder mystery about the Wornall House Museum. I've enjoyed writing it.

I also want to thank my husband, Jim Wornall, for editing this manuscript and for his constructive criticism. Thanks also go to our children, John Bristow Wornall V, Desiree Wornall Rivas, and to our friend, Gay Herndon, for reading the book and making helpful suggestions.

DEDICATION

This book is dedicated to the memory of my mother, Velora Davis Holt, and to my husband, James Frederick Wornall, who has put up with me for over thirty five years!

CAST OF CHARACTERS

RHONDA WINTERS	Amateur sleuth, retired teacher, writer, volunteer at the Wornall House
RICK WINTERS	Retired businessman, volunteer at the Wornall House, Rhonda's husband
NIKKI PRESTON	Former copywriter, Rick and Rhonda's daughter, John's wife
JOHN PRESTON	Homicide detective, Rick and Rhonda's son-in-law, Nikki's husband
JEREMY PRESTON	Nikki and John's son, Rhonda and Rick's six-year old grandson
JAMIE JACKSON	Director of the John Wornall House Museum
ANNA MARTIN	Assistant Director of the Wornall House Museum
BOB LANE	Owns Import-Export Co., Karen's ex-husband, Marianna's date, Volunteer
MARIANNA KELLY	Nurse, mother, widow, volunteer, Bob Lane's friend
KAREN LANE	Bob Lane's ex wife, Legal secretary

BART ASHLEY	Dentist, volunteer, Sally's husband
SALLY ASHLEY	Real estate agent, volunteer, Bart's wife
MANDY TODD	Restaurant chef, volunteer cook at the Wornall House
JEAN MURPHY	Web site designer, volunteer cook's helper at Wornall House
JASON VALORES	Police director of Guanajuato, Mexico, Rick & Rhonda's friend & neighbor
GREGORY GARSON	Polygraph examination expert, Rick and Rhonda's friend, Pat's husband
PATRICIA GARSON	Gregory's wife, Rhonda's friend
TIME	From Halloween to Christmas, 2009
PLACE	Kansas City, Missouri

PROLOGUE

At first after Bob Lane's death, the five volunteers sat frozen with shock at the dining table in the John Wornall House Museum. Then they began to ask questions.

"How could the spiced cider have killed Bob?" Sally asked, aghast. "He was just sitting at the table, talking and laughing. Then he gulped down that glass of cider and fell over dead."

"How could that have happened?" Rhonda asked. "All of us drank cider from the same pitcher and we're okay."

"Poor Bob. He must've had a heart attack," Marianna said.

"Or a stroke," Rick suggested.

"Well, it looks to me like he was poisoned!" Bart exclaimed. "Someone must've spiked his cider with cyanide!"

They were all wrong.

CHAPTER ONE

TROUBLE WAS BREWING AT THE John Wornall House Museum. Before long Rick and Rhonda Winters would be smack dab in the middle of a murder and a drug trafficking investigation.

Rick and Rhonda had just returned to Kansas City from Guanajuato, Mexico, where they'd spent four months vacationing and doing volunteer work at a Baptist church and an orphanage.

After Rhonda had finished unpacking, she went into the office of her publishing and book distribution company and booted up the computer to check her e-mails. She made copies of the cookbook orders she'd received. One order was from Jamie Jackson, the director of the Wornall House Museum, located in the Brookside area of Kansas City, Missouri.

Rhonda picked up the phone and called Jamie. "Hello, Jamie, this is Rhonda Winters. We've just gotten home from Mexico. I'm calling about your book order."

"Hi, Rhonda!" Jamie exclaimed, "I heard you've been solving murders in Guanajuato!"

"Well, I helped the police director catch a killer."

"I heard you were a suspect for awhile. Is that true?" Jamie said.

"Yes! All of the people at the party were suspects, including me," Rhonda replied.

"Isn't this the third murder you've helped solve? They say the homicide detectives are calling you 'Guanajuato's Secret Weapon'!"

Rhonda laughed. "How on earth did you hear that?"

"I have my ways!" Jamie joked. "To change the subject, our gift shop has sold out of your books. When you have time, can you bring us ten books of each cookbook and novel?"

"Sure. I'll be glad to. I have to go to Brookside in the morning. I can drop the books off around ten."

"Thanks. Be sure to come upstairs to my office and visit awhile. I want to hear about your most recent sleuthing adventures!"

Rhonda is fifty five, though she says she doesn't feel a day over twenty one. She has a quick smile and is a slender, green eyed brunette. Rick is sixty years old. He's average height and weight, and has brown eyes, and dark hair that's graying at the temples.

Five years earlier when Rick retired as vice-president of a manufacturing company, he and Rhonda built a vacation home in Guanajuato, Mexico. Guanajuato is a university town, located in the mountains, about two hundred and thirty miles north of Mexico City.

What Jamie said was true. Rhonda had stumbled into three murder cases while they were in Mexico, and she'd used her sleuthing ability to help solve all three.

The next day after Rick and Rhonda parked beside the beautiful brick museum at Sixty First Terrace and Wornall Road, they climbed the outside stairs up to Jamie's office and knocked.

Jamie opened the door and smiled. "Welcome! Thanks for bringing the books. Rick, would you take the boxes to the gift shop for me? Just set them on the floor by the desk. Rhonda, come on in and have a seat."

Jamie was a cute, blonde, blue-eyed woman in her thirties. Rhonda thought she was perfect for her job as museum director. She was perky, had a bubbly personality, and a love for this historic house.

"I'm glad to have company. I've been here by myself since eight," Jamie said.

When Rick came back into the office and sat down, Jamie asked, "Can I get you guys some coffee and cookies?"

"Not for me, thanks," Rhonda replied. "We've just finished breakfast."

"I'll have a cup," Rick said.

Jamie handed a cup of coffee to him, and he thanked her.

"Now, Rhonda, tell me about your sleuthing adventures in Mexico."

"A guy named Ted Saxon, and his wife, were visiting the minister's family, and we were invited to a dinner party at their home. When Ted died that night from arsenic poisoning, all the guests became suspects because apparently one of them had sprinkled arsenic over his dessert. To clear my name, I helped our neighbor, Police Director Jason Valores, solve the case."

Before Jamie could comment, Rick suddenly exclaimed, "I hear footsteps on the outside stairs."

"I'm not expecting anyone. Would you look out the window and see who's there?"

Rick got up and pulled back the curtain to look out. "I don't see anybody."

"Oh, well, it must be our resident ghost," Jamie said.

"Resident ghost!" Rhonda exclaimed. "I presume that's a joke since today's Halloween."

"No, it's not a joke. We hear him stomping up and down the stairs quite frequently. There's also the ghost of a Union soldier who guards the front door. I'm sure you know the Wornall House is haunted."

"We've heard that," Rick said.

"This house was used as a military hospital for the wounded soldiers during the Battle of Westport, which was fought nearby. Both the wounded Union and Confederate soldiers were brought here, and many men died in this house. We're hosting a ghostly gathering here tonight and tomorrow evening at seven. A lady from the Ghost Vigils and I will lead the tour through the house, and we'll tell stories about the various ghosts who've been sighted here. Why don't you come?"

Rick grinned, "That sounds like a fun way to learn more about your resident ghost, but we have plans to go to a party tonight, don't we, Rhonda?"

"Yes, and we have a church function tomorrow night, but we'll attend the next ghost tour."

Changing the subject, Rick asked, "What other tours are planned for the museum?"

"We have several school groups scheduled each month. Our next big tour will be the Christmas Candlelight Tour on the fourth of December. That reminds me, we need one more couple for the dining room scene. Could I talk you two into volunteering?"

Rick asked, "What do we have to do?"

"You'll wear clothing like those worn by the Wornalls in the 1860's and you'll sit at the dining table with two other couples and eat the dinner that will be served to you by the cook. You'll talk about what foods were served for Christmas dinner when the Wornalls lived there. We'll have a script for you. The tour group will gather in front of the dining room door to observe."

"Well, that sounds easy enough," Rick said. He turned to Rhonda. "Do you want to do it?"

"Sure. That sounds like fun."

Jamie added, "We're lucky to have a good cook who's had experience cooking in an open-hearth fireplace in an antebellum mansion in New Orleans. After the school children finish the tour of the house, they go to the kitchen and watch her bake cookies in the fireplace. Then each child gets to eat one. The cook explains to them that about one hundred and fifty years ago, Eliza and Roma Wornall used to bake cookies in this same fireplace."

"What a good learning experience for them!" Rhonda exclaimed.

"Yes, it is. The cook will also prepare the dinner for the Christmas candlelight dining room scene. I'll call you when we schedule the next ghost tour. I hope you'll be able to attend. Last year, Channel 9 sent a reporter over here with TV cameras to investigate the haunting tales. He and his crew filmed in the house, but no ghosts showed up while he was here."

Rhonda laughed. "Maybe the ghosts were shy."

"Apparently. The reporter talked about some of the ghost sighting stories such as the two little girls who've been seen in the children's bedroom and the white flowing figure that glides through the house at her leisure."

"Do you ever hear the ghosts rattling their chains?" Rick joked.

"No, but I really do think that was the ghost's footsteps we heard."

"Oh, Jamie, don't tell me you really believe there are ghosts here," Rhonda teased.

Jamie said, "Well, I'm beginning to wonder."

CHAPTER TWO

RICK AND RHONDA'S DAUGHTER AND son-in-law, Nikki and John Preston, had recently moved back to Kansas City from San Antonio with their three children, the twins Jeremy and Jeffrey, and their daughter, Jacquelyn. Each Friday night their grandkids took turns spending the weekend with them.

It was Jeremy's turn to stay this weekend. After a greeting and a hug, six year old Jeremy hopped onto Rhonda's lap and said, "Nana, my teacher told us she's going to take us on a field trip to the Wornall House and she wants some moms and grand moms to go on the trip with us. I told her that you'd go, but she said I had to ask you before I can volunteer you."

"She's a smart teacher. When's the school trip?"

"The tour is on December tenth. Can you go with us?"Jeremy asked wistfully.

"That's over a month away. Let me look at my calendar." She checked it and saw that she was free that day.

"Okay, Jeremy, you can tell your teacher that I'll go with you, but always ask me first before you volunteer me!"

"Okay, thanks, Nana. I'm glad you can go. We'll have fun!"

"Yes, we will. I always love to go places with you, sweetie."

Jeremy turned to Papa Rick and asked, "Will you play croquet with me in the back yard?"

They played until Jeremy was tired and hungry, then they went to George's Pizza for dinner.

As they sat at a table waiting for the salads and pepperoni pizza, Rick asked, "How do you like your new school?"

Jeremy replied, "I like it, and I like my teacher, too."

"How does your dad like his new job?" Rhonda asked.

"He loves it, but Mommy thinks it's dangerous. He's pretty good at catching killers."

"Yes, he is. The police chief told us that your dad is a top-notch homicide detective, one of the best in Kansas City."

"Dad said you're a sleuth, and you helped the police catch three killers in Mexico. I was really proud of you, Nana."

"Thanks. I've seen your report cards, and I'm proud of you for making straight A's."

The next morning, Rick took the three kids swimming in a nearby indoor pool.

After they left, Rhonda phoned Nikki and asked if she'd like to go to lunch at Andres.

"Oh, yes," Nikki exclaimed. "I'm hungry for Quiche Lorraine and a Napoleon."

While they ate lunch they talked about the upcoming Christmas Candlelight Tour that would be taking place at the Wornall House on December fourth.

"Your dad and I will be two of the volunteer diners. We'll be eating Christmas dinner in the dining room. Yesterday, Jamie asked Rick to make a talk about John Wornall before the tour starts. Why don't you and John come for the tour?"

"John might be working, but if not, we'll try to make it."

As it turned out, John was at the Christmas Candlelight tour, but NOT as a guest.

CHAPTER THREE

RHONDA WAS EXHAUSTED. SHE'D WRITTEN on her novel until two this morning, then she'd gotten up early for an eight thirty hair appointment at the Plaza. Since Rick was playing bridge and having lunch out, she decided to go shopping and have a Nicoise salad and a glass of iced tea for lunch at a favorite Plaza restaurant.

When Rhonda returned home, she sat down on the red sofa in the family room and turned on the TV. She was so tired, she kicked off her shoes and stretched out on the sofa to watch the news.

Her ears perked up when she heard the reporter say, "There's a breaking story about a drug trafficking case. The police have been aware for several months that a cocaine smuggling ring has been importing cocaine from Nuevo Laredo, Mexico, into Kansas City, Missouri. But until today, there haven't been any arrests.

"Federal investigators cracked this case today and arrested Mark Martin when they raided his Mission Hills home. After the investigators searched his house, they brought in a K-9 dog to sniff for drugs. The dog became very excited as he entered Martin's attic. He dashed over to some wooden boxes, and began sniffing at them. The narcotics agents opened the boxes and seized the neatly packed cocaine packets hidden inside the three wooden Boy Scouts boxes.

"Though cocaine was discovered and removed from the premises, agents haven't arrested the ringleader of this drug trafficking operation. Details will follow as more is learned about the case."

Rick arrived home from the bridge game not long after the news was over. He sank down in an arm chair and said, "I heard a sad story about one of my high school friends today. We were in the Boy Scouts together. He was busted for cocaine possession. I can't believe it! He was such a nice guy, an Eagle Scout, and an usher at his church."

Rhonda said, "I just heard some breaking news on TV about ten minutes ago that the police had raided a home in Mission Hills. They discovered a large stash of cocaine in three wooden Boy Scout boxes like the one you have."

"Oh, no! That must have been Mark's house. He's probably overextended himself financially. I know he lives in a large brick home and he has a vacation house in Martha's Vineyard. He drives a Hummer and his wife has a new Mercedes."

"Is he the one who's an executive for a firm that's laid off several employees? I hope he didn't lose his job and turn to crime to pay his expenses."

Rick said, "He always liked to keep up with the Joneses. It's a shame he got mixed up in drug trafficking. It would've been far better for him to have lost his house than to go to prison for smuggling cocaine."

"I guess he didn't think about that at the time," Rhonda said. "People don't believe they'll get caught."

Detective Preston called and talked to Rick, his father-in-law. "I was sorry to hear about your friend. An informant called and asked me to meet him in Loose Park. He was waiting when I arrived. He greeted me and slipped a folded note into my hand as we shook hands. Then we went our own way. According to the note, a cocaine shipment had been dropped off at Mark Martin's house in Mission Hills. I contacted the narcotics division and they took in a K-9 drug sniffing dog and raided his house."

"I wonder why the shipment was dropped off at his house?" Rick said. "I hope he wasn't set up."

CHAPTER FOUR

THE MONTH OF NOVEMBER PASSED by quickly. Thanksgiving with the family was a fun time with turkey, football, and a trip to the Plaza to see the turning on of the Christmas lights. Before long, it was time for the Christmas Candlelight tour at the Wornall House Museum.

The tour began in the carriage house. The carriage house docent stood on the make-shift stage behind a podium. The tour group sat in the folding chairs, surrounding the stage.

The docent said, "Thank you for joining us for the John Wornall House Museum's annual Christmas Candlelight Tour. Before we start the tour, I'd like to introduce you to one of our volunteers, Mr. Rick Winters. He'll tell you about John Bristow Wornall, the man who built this house. Then after his talk, we'll take a candlelight tour through the Wornall House.

"Rick Winters is a retired executive of a manufacturing company here in Kansas City. He has volunteered at the Wornall House for twenty years. Here's Rick!"

Rick went up to the podium and took the mike from the docent. He began, "Thank you for inviting me.

"In 1858, John Bristow Wornall built this house in the Greek Revival style of architecture with bricks that were hand-fired on his property. The house originally sat on the Missouri frontier, in the center of his farm. Now, it's engulfed by Kansas City's Brookside neighborhood, and is listed on the National Register of Historic Places.

"Wornall was descended from Roby and Edyth Wornall. Roby was born in England and he was a colonial resident of Virginia. Roby died in 1784. His son, Thomas Wornall, was the first member of the Wornall family to move to Kentucky. Thomas Wornall became a Kentucky state representative and a colonel when he fought in the War of 1812.

"It was Thomas Wornall's son, Richard Wornall, who moved to Missouri in 1843 when he was forty four years old. Richard and his wife, Judith Ann Glover, had owned a large farm in Shelbyville, Kentucky. They sold their land, and took their two sons, John Bristow Wornall, age twenty one, and George Thomas Wornall, age nineteen, on the six hundred miles trip to Westport, Missouri. Richard Wornall purchased five hundred acres of land and a four room log cabin for twenty five hundred dollars from John Calvin McCoy. He paid five dollars per acre for the land that stretched between present-day fifty ninth and sixty seventh streets, to State Line and Main Streets, in what is now Kansas City, Missouri. Wornall made enough money from the crops that first year to pay the entire purchase price of the farm.

"Wornall successfully farmed the land there for six years until 1849 when both his wife and his son, George, died. He was so sad that he gave his surviving son, John, the farm and the cabin and he returned to Kentucky to live. In Kentucky, he married a wealthy widow named Mary Harrison.

"John Bristow Wornall, born on October 12, 1822, remained in Missouri and farmed his land. He grew wheat, corn, and oats. In 1850, he married Matilda Polk, but she died childless one year later. Three years later, when he was thirty years old, he married Sarah Eliza Johnson, daughter of Thomas Johnson, for whom Johnson County is named.

Thomas Johnson was born in Virginia in 1802. He and his wife, Sarah, had thirteen children, but several of them died young. He was a Methodist minister and missionary to the Shawnee Indians. He founded the Shawnee Indian Mission in 1831. During the Civil War, union troops occupied the mission. On January 2, 1865, Johnson was murdered, shot on his front porch.

Soon after John Wornall's marriage to Eliza Johnson, John began building this house which took four years to complete.

John commissioned his friend, the famous artist, George Caleb Bingham, to paint his and Eliza's portraits.

John and Eliza had seven children during their eleven year marriage, but five children died. Both Fannie and Sallie died when they were only one year old. Edna died at the age of three. Eliza Johnson Wornall died in 1865 from childbirth complications one week after Thomas's birth. She was only twenty nine years old. She was buried by her five children. Her son, Thomas, became a Missouri state senator in 1904.

"In 1866, when John was forty four years old, he married twenty-year old Roma Johnson, Eliza's first cousin. Four years later, in 1870, John became president of the Kansas City National Bank and was elected a Missouri state senator.

"Hugh Ward, for whom Ward Parkway was named, was Wornall's closest neighbor. The two families were lifelong friends.

"John and Roma were active in the Baptist church where John served as treasurer and moderator. Also, John became president of the board of directors of William Jewell College. A building at the college was named Wornall Hall in his honor, but this building later burned to the ground. Wornall's Lane, the street running in front of his house, was named for him. Today, that street is Wornall Road.

"During the Civil War, after General Ewing issued Order Number 11, John Wornall was forced to leave his new brick home. He moved his family to a house at Ninth and Main.

"The Battle of Westport was fought near the Wornall house, and the home was used as a hospital for the wounded soldiers of both sides. The Wornalls continued to live there until after Eliza's death. When he married Roma Johnson in 1866, they moved to Ninth and Delaware.

"Roma and John had two more sons, John Bristow Wornall Junior and Charles Hardin Wornall. It was their son, John Bristow Wornall Jr.'s line that has carried on his name. The Reverend John Bristow Wornall V, an ordained Baptist pastor, is presently living in Texas and working as a hospital chaplain. He has been married for four years, and his father hopes there will soon be a little John Bristow Wornall VI!"

The audience chuckled.

Rick continued, "In 1874, John Wornall moved his family back to the home he had built in 1858, and they lived there for thirteen years, until he decided to build Roma a new home at Thirty-Ninth and Baltimore. He sold the Wornall homestead, and they moved into the new house where they lived until his death on November 24, 1892. He was buried at Forest Hills Cemetery, in Kansas City, Missouri.

"John's widow, Roma Wornall, said she had always loved the Wornall House and she wanted to live there the rest of her life. She said it felt like home, so she bought it back. She moved in and lived there until her death in 1933. She was buried beside her husband."

Rick smiled at the audience and wound up his talk. "When you go on the tour, the docents will give you more information about the family's experiences during the Civil War and about the Battle of Westport. You've been a wonderful audience. Thank you."

The group applauded politely, and Rick stepped down. The docent took the floor.

"Thank you, Mr. Winters, for telling us about the life of John Wornall," she said. "Does anyone have a question?"

A man raised his hand. "Where did John Bristow Wornall get his middle name? Is Bristow a family name?"

Rick replied, "He was named for John Bristow, his father's friend and neighbor in Kentucky. He was also the guardian of Judith Ann Glover Wornall, John's mother."

The docent glanced at her watch. "I'm sorry, but we won't have time for any other questions. It's time for the tour to begin. Thank you, Mr. Winters. Now, we'll walk up to the House. Please follow me. To get us all in the holiday spirit, let's sing 'Jingle Bells' as we walk along."

She turned to Rick and asked, "Would you lead the singing, Mr. Winters? I've heard you sing, and I know you have a good baritone voice."

Rick smiled. "Of course." He began singing and the group chimed in. When they reached the porch of the house, the Parlor Docent stood on the porch between the large columns. The group stood in the yard in front of her. She said, "Hello, everyone! In a moment we'll enter the parlor. Let's pretend that this year is 1858, the first Christmas that the Wornalls celebrated in their new home. As you enter each room, you will pretend that it is another year, from 1858 until 1864. Now, let's walk into the entrance hall and go inside the parlor, where you will see Eliza and her mother, Sarah Johnson, putting the finishing touches on the Christmas tree."

Eliza turned to her mother and said, "I'm so happy you and Father could spend Christmas with us."

"It's our pleasure, my dear."

"Isn't it great that after running the Shawnee Mission for over twenty years, Father has decided to retire and let Alexander take over?"

"Yes, I'm happy about that. It's time for him to relax and enjoy life," her mother replied.

"I'm sure Alexander will do a good job," Eliza said

"Yes, he will. I love your new home, my dear, and I'm sure you do, too."

"Oh, Mother, it's like a dream come true! It's wonderful to live here after being crowded in that small cabin for the past four years."

"This is a great place for entertaining. Look at the children. They're having such a good time, especially Frank."

The men soon joined the ladies, and Rev. Johnson said, "We should be going home now. Thank you for the delicious Roast Duck and Plum Pudding dinner and for the enjoyable evening."

"We were happy to have you," John assured them. Then he said, "Before you leave, could we sing a hymn?" John sat down at the piano and began playing, 'Hark, the Herald Angels Sing'.

They sang the Christmas song together, then the Johnsons put on their coats, hugged everyone, and went out to their waiting carriage.

The Family Room Docent came into the parlor and led the group across the hall to the twin parlor or to the room we would call the family room. She said, "Two years have passed. This is the year 1860. The Wornall and Johnson families are happy to celebrate Christmas together again this year, but the men are upset that Abraham Lincoln has been elected president. They worry that he will lead the country into war. Already South Carolina has seceded from the union."

"Do you think Missouri will leave the union, too?"Rev. Johnson asked.

"I hope not," John muttered, "but I'm afraid they will."

"Many people are angry with Lincoln. He'd better be careful. Someone might try to assassinate him."

Eliza turned to the men and said, "We're here to celebrate the birth of Christ. Let's be joyous. Dinner is ready. I've prepared baked ham and all the trimmings for us this year."

The docent said, "After the family finished their dinner, Eliza played the piano and the family sang Christmas songs. After the sing-a-long, John asked if they'd like to play a parlor game, but Rev. Johnson said, "It's getting late. It's time for us to leave." He hugged his daughter and said, "You're a wonderful cook, my dear. What a delicious dinner!"

Eliza's mother and father wished them a Merry Christmas, before they left.

The Bedroom Docent entered the room and said, "We'll now skip to the year 1863. The Wornalls are NOT having a Merry Christmas this year. The Civil War is raging. At that time, their home was located in the Missouri frontier and was referred to as the most pretentious house in the area. Colonel "Doc" Jennison and two hundred of his Kansas Jayhawkers commandeered their home and used it for eight days as his headquarters. Jennison used their parlor as his office and he slept in their bedroom. Eliza had to cook for him. His soldiers killed their livestock for food and destroyed their crops.

Jennison said, "I might've killed the Wornalls if they hadn't been so hospitable to us. They fed us well and were always courteous."

The docent added, "General Thomas Ewing issued the infamous Order eleven, which forced many families, including the Wornalls, to leave their homes. Ewing did this to put a stop to the food that farmers had been providing for the Confederate soldiers.

The Wornalls did not celebrate Christmas in their home in 1863."

The Kitchen docent entered the room and said, "Please follow me downstairs to the kitchen. The year is 1864. After part of Order Number Eleven was repealed, the Wornalls were allowed to return to their home and plant their crops.

In the year, 1864, the Wornalls had another terrible experience. The Civil War was still raging and the bloody Battle of Westport was fought very close to their home. John Wornall had been forced into a Minutemen unit to aid in defending the area, and was not home during this battle. Eliza and ten-year old Frank hid in the cellar under the kitchen floor, but they were found by the soldiers. Eliza was told that her house was going to be used as an emergency military field hospital for both the wounded Confederate and Union soldiers. Not only did Eliza cook for the soldiers, she also bandaged their wounded.

One day, Eliza cooked breakfast for the Confederates and dinner for the Union soldiers.

The wounded soldiers were carried into the Wornall House and laid on pallets on the floor. Surgeries took place in the family room. So many soldiers died during this battle that their bodies were stacked in the dining room, near the window. Their bodies were passed out through the window to men who loaded them onto wagons and took them for burial."

By Christmas of 1864, the soldiers were gone and John and Eliza were living in their house again. This was the last Christmas the Wornalls celebrated in their home for ten years. This year, they invited Eliza's parents and her aunt and uncle, Mr. and Mrs. Rueben Johnson and their daughter, Roma, from Fayette, Missouri, to celebrate Christmas at their home. Rueben Johnson was Rev. Thomas Johnson's brother, and Thomas had invited them to spend Christmas at the mission with his family. Eliza served turkey and dressing and all the trimmings to their guests. After dinner, John played the piano and they sang Christmas carols. They also played a parlor game before the evening was over.

Roma Johnson was Eliza's first cousin, and Eliza loved her very much. Roma was impressed with Eliza's lovely new home and her handsome husband.

When it was time to leave, the Johnsons thanked the Wornalls for the delicious food and for a lovely evening. John and Eliza hugged their relatives and wished them a very Merry Christmas before they returned to the mission."

A volunteer asked, "May I tell this group why 1865 was the saddest year of John Wornall's life?"

"Certainly," the docent replied.

"Not only had John Wornall's father died on June 10, 1864, about six months earlier, but in January, 1865, John's father-in-law, the Reverend Thomas Johnson, was murdered on the front porch of his house. The Civil War ended a few months later in April of 1865, and the Missouri slaves were free at last to start new lives. A little less than three months later, John and Eliza's seventh child was born. The baby boy was named Thomas Johnson Wornall in memory of Eliza's father. Eliza died at the age of twenty nine, on July 5, 1865, due to serious complications after Thomas' birth, leaving John with two motherless children to raise. Eliza had only lived in the Wornall House for about seven years.

The Side Porch Docent came into the room and said, "Come with me to the side porch and I'll tell you about John Wornall's third wife, Roma Johnson Wornall."

The group followed her to the porch.

The docent began, "After Eliza's death, John was left with two motherless children to care for, and Eliza's cousin, Roma, was asked to take care of the children for him.

"A little over a year after Eliza's death, John Wornall married Roma Johnson on September 25, 1866. Roma Johnson, who was born on August 31, 1846, had just turned twenty years old one month before her wedding to the forty-four year old John Wornall. She was his third wife, and she outlived him by about forty-one years.

"John took their entire wedding party on their honeymoon to Baltimore, Maryland. While there, he bought Roma an ornate mahogany quarter tester bed with a matching marble-topped dresser and night stand, which is still in the family today.

"When they returned home, John took Roma to live in Kansas City at Ninth and Delaware. He commissioned the famous Missouri artist, George Caleb Bingham, to paint Roma's portrait in her wedding gown. Bingham's invoice for the work was dated October 15, 1867, and it still exists. Today Roma's portrait can be seen at the Nelson Art Gallery in Kansas City, Missouri.

"Roma and John had two more sons, John Bristow Wornall Jr. and Charles Hardin Wornall. Roma was a good mother to all four of John's sons. She said she loved Eliza's sons like her own.

"Roma's youngest brother, Francis Johnson, was killed in the Battle of Wilson Creek, one of the early battles of the Civil War. Roma's sister, Lucilla Johnson, lived with Roma and John, and she helped with the cooking, the housekeeping, and taking care of the four boys. Lucilla was described as tall, lanky, and stern while Roma was said to be small and sweet.

"In 1874, Christmas was celebrated once again in the Wornall House. John and Roma had moved back to the mansion that John had built in 1858. This Christmas, two of their neighbors and good friends, Alexander Majors, who started the Pony Express, and Hugh Ward, a former frontier trader on the Santa Fe Trail, but who was now a banker, joined the Wornalls for a turkey and dressing Christmas dinner.

"John and Roma lived in the Wornall House for thirteen years, until John built a home nearer downtown for Roma. When it was finished, he sold the Wornall House and moved his family to their new home. They gave parties at both homes, and John was an excellent host. They lived there until his death on March 24, 1892. Roma and John had been married for twenty five years.

" After her husband died, Roma sold their home and bought back the Wornall House. She said it felt like home to her, and she lived there for the remainder of her life. Adding together the thirteen years she and John had lived there plus the forty years she lived there after John's death, Roma had lived in the Wornall House for over fifty years. Eliza had only lived there for seven years.

"In 1909, Roma helped organize the Robert E. Lee Chapter of the Daughters of the Confederacy, and she served as its first president. She was later elected to the office of state president.

Eventually, Hugh Ward and Roma Wornall sold much of their farmland to J.C. Nichols. Before long, houses began to spring up in what used to be their wheat fields.

Roma donated land for a church and construction was begun on the Wornall Road Baptist Church, located on the corner of Wornall Road and Meyer Boulevard, and she became one of the charter members.

"Roma remained active and continued to drive her electric car from her home to Westport until she was eighty years old.

"Before Roma's death, one of her friends wrote that 'Roma's gracious bearing and sympathetic heart made her one of Kansas City's most beloved citizens.'

"Roma lived in the Wornall House until her death in 1933, at the age of eighty seven. She is buried beside her husband at the Forest Hills Cemetery, in Kansas City, Missouri."

The docent ended her recitation about the life of Roma Wornall by asking the group to sing, 'Silent Night', one of Roma's favorite Christmas carols.

CHAPTER FIVE

THE DINING ROOM DOCENT CAME out to the side porch and said, "Please come inside to the dining room where the Wornall family celebrated their last Christmas with Roma Wornall before her death. Six volunteers will reenact their Christmas feast.

Since all of the participants were volunteers at the Wornall House Museum, Rick and Rhonda were acquainted with Bob, Marianna, Sally, and Bart. They were all dressed in costumes.

Bob was a tall, blond, blue eyed guy who owned an import-export business. Marianna, a registered nurse, had beautiful brown eyes, curly brown hair, and a curvy figure. Sally was a petite red head with hazel eyes. She worked as a realtor, and her husband, Bart, was a dentist. He was an overweight, bald man with blue eyes and a thin mustache.

The blonde, blue eyed cook, Mandy Todd, and her efficient helper, brown haired, gray eyed Jean Murphy, were both dressed in long dresses, aprons, and bonnets. They carried in a platter of roast duckling, and bowls of dressing, mashed potatoes, gravy, salad, vegetables, and biscuits, and set them on the table.

The cook spoke to the tour group. "All of the foods served tonight are from recipes that Eliza and Roma Wornall cooked in the open-hearth fireplace in the kitchen of this home. I will also be serving two desserts, Concord Grape Pie and Christmas Plum Pudding, that the Wornall ladies used to prepare."

As the cook spoke, Jean, her helper, went back to the kitchen and returned with a pottery pitcher full of chilled spiced cider. It was full of aromatic seasonings and it smelled divine. She poured cider into each of the six glasses, then the cooks returned to the kitchen.

Bart picked up his glass and asked, "Shall we make a Christmas toast?"

"Yes, of course!" Bob exclaimed enthusiastically.

Bart continued, "Merry Christmas and Happy New Year! May you all have peace and plenty!"

The six of them raised their glasses in a toast and drank.

Bob must've been thirsty. He drank down his full glass of cider in one gulp.

Just as Rhonda looked over at Bob to wish him a Merry Christmas, the words stuck in her mouth as she saw his empty glass tumble to the floor. Bob's handsome face had contorted as if he was having a convulsion. His eyes were bulging, and he was clutching his throat with both hands. The stress on his face increased as he gasped for breath. He frantically began to dig at his jacket pocket. His eyes looked wild as he gasped, "Epi. Pen. Help!"

Sally said, "Bob, I don't understand what you're saying."

Bob repeated, "Epi," but Sally felt helpless. She had no idea what an epi was.

Bart asked, "Do you want me to get something out of your pocket?"

Bob mumbled a word that sounded like 'nut'.

Just as Bart started to reach into the pocket of Bob's jacket, Bob clutched at his throat again and suddenly crumpled to the floor. His body shuddered, then he lay still.

Marianna and Bart both dropped to their knees beside Bob and tried to help him.

Rhonda stood and shouted to the audience, "Is there a doctor in the house?"

Until then, the audience had thought Bob's actions were part of the skit.

Just as Marianna was taking his pulse, a doctor from the audience rushed to Bob's side and she moved out of his way. The doctor felt Bob's pulse, but there was none.

The doctor shouted, "Somebody call 9-1-1. Tell them he's not breathing and to bring a defibrillator. ASAP!" Then he started CPR on Bob.

Sally whipped out her cell phone and dialed. "Send an ambulance to the Wornall House ASAP!" she yelled excitedly into the phone. "Emergency! Man not breathing! Bring a defibrillator!"

Marianna asked the doctor, "Shall I start mouth-to-mouth resuscitation? I'm a nurse."

"Yes," the doctor replied, as he continued CPR.

Marianna began mouth-to-mouth on Bob and the doctor continued CPR until the ambulance arrived. The paramedics ran in with oxygen and the rest of their gear, then they took over. They used the defibrillator on Bob, but after several tries, one of them shook his head and muttered, "He's gone."

The police dispatcher sent early responders, two officers from the patrol division and a medical examiner to the scene. Rhonda heard one officer say to the other, "We'll treat this as a crime scene until we know for sure what happened to him. You know the rules. Don't touch anything, isolate the witnesses, and write everything down."

Until that moment, it had never occurred to Rhonda that this could be a crime scene.

"Did the spiced cider kill Bob?" Sally asked. "One minute he's sitting at the table, happy, laughing, and talking. Then right after he drank the cider, he fell over dead!"

"We all drank cider from the same pitcher, and we're okay!" Rhonda exclaimed.

"What happened to him?"Rick asked. "His speech was garbled. Maybe he had a stroke."

"Or it might've been a heart attack," Marianna murmured sadly.

Bart shook his head. "No, I think he was poisoned. He died so fast, the cider must've been spiked with cyanide!"

The first patrol officers who arrived warned everyone, "In case this is a crime scene, don't touch the glasses, the plates, or the pitcher! The witnesses must not talk to each other."

After the patrolman isolated the witnesses who were sitting at the dining table, he made sketches, then began taking photographs of the table, the glasses, the pitcher, and of the entire scene. He took copious notes about what had happened.

The second officer worked at controlling the scene by keeping unauthorized people away. The group who had come for the tour were still standing by the dining room door, gaping at Bob. The officer took out his notebook and pen. He asked each person for his name, his address, and phone number, and wrote down the information.

The officer told them, "All of you are witnesses, and we'll want to talk to each of you. Don't leave. More officers will be here in a few minutes to interview you while your recollections are fresh. Now, I'm going to separate you. Do NOT talk to each other."

As soon as the medical examiner arrived and saw Bob lying on the floor, he raced over to him and began to examine him. When there was no response, he pronounced Bob dead at the scene.

The doctor from the audience came to the medical examiner's side and introduced himself as Dr. Mike Trotter. He said, "The victim's symptoms started almost immediately after he finished his drink. I was observing him and I thought he was having a convulsion. Mr. Lane grabbed his throat like it was swelling shut and he appeared to have difficulty breathing. As I ran to his side, he was frantically trying to find something in his pocket. Before he could find it, he gasped for breath and tried to say something, then he seemed to pass out and fell out of his chair. By the time, I reached him, he was lying on the floor and two of the diners were on the floor beside him, trying to revive him. I think he was dead by the time his body hit the floor. When I examined him, there was no pulse and he wasn't breathing. I started CPR and one of the women diners did mouth-to-mouth. It was all to no avail."

"Those symptoms sound like a life-threatening food allergy reaction to me," the medical examiner said.

"Now that you mention it, I believe that's exactly what happened," Doctor Trotter said.

"If that diagnosis is correct, he was probably carrying an epinephrine auto injector in his pocket in case of an emergency and maybe some antihistamine pills, too. I'll check his pockets." The medical examiner, or the ME as he is often called for short, pulled out an item about the size of a magic marker and a bottle of pills from Bob's pocket. He held them up, and exclaimed, "Here are his epi pen and his pills!"

"I wonder what he was allergic to," Dr Trotter said. "Maybe one of the people sitting at the table with him could tell us."

"Good idea. I'll talk to one now." The medical examiner turned to Dr. Trotter. "Thank you for your assistance."

"Glad to help," Dr. Trotter said before leaving.

The medical examiner asked one of the officers if he could talk to a person who'd been at the table with the victim.

"Sure. I'll bring someone to you," the officer said. "By the way, what do you think about Mr. Lane's death? It was a suspicious death. Do you think it was an accident or murder?"

"Your guess is as good as mine until after the autopsy and the lab reports are in," the ME replied.

The officer took Rhonda to the medical examiner.

She said, "Hello. My name is Rhonda Winters. I was told you wanted to talk to me."

"Hello. Would you tell me how Mr. Lane reacted just before his death and what he said and did?"

"Right after he drank the cider, he grabbed his throat and began gasping for breath. He asked for something that sounded like 'epi', but I had no idea what that was."

"Did this reaction occur directly after he drank the cider?"

"Yes. He was fine before he drank it. Jolly, even. There must've been something in the cider that Bob was allergic to."

"Do you know if he had allergies?"

"No, I don't. Maybe Marianna, or Karen, his ex-wife, or the cooks would know."

"If they knew, they would've probably mentioned it. Okay, thanks. I imagine Preston will be talking to everyone tonight."

Rhonda suggested, "There's always a chance that somebody knew what Bob was allergic to, and they stirred that ingredient into the cider on purpose."

"Anything is possible," the medical examiner said as he pulled out his cell phone. "Thanks for your help. You can go now."

As Rhonda walked away, she tried to eavesdrop on the ME's phone call. She heard him say, "Send a crime lab tech to the Wornall House.

ASAP. Better send that new homicide detective, John Preston, over here, too, and another detective, if one is there. I have a funny feeling about this case. It might be a homicide."

As the Medical examiner talked, he looked up and saw Rhonda dawdling. She hurriedly ducked around the corner and returned to the room where she'd been assigned.

Since the police station was only five minutes away, the homicide detectives arrived quite soon. Detective Preston introduced himself and consulted with the officer in charge who filled him in on the situation.

The crime lab tech and his assistant arrived, and Preston asked him to get prints off the glasses, the pitcher, and the plates at the table, and to take samples from each. He told the tech to bag Bob's glass and the pitcher, and take all of these items back to the lab for analysis.

Preston told the tech assistant to take all of the witnesses' finger prints. "And that includes everyone who was sitting at the table, the cook, her helper, the docents, the witnesses, and all of the members of the tour group."

When some extra officers arrived, Preston told them to start interviewing each witness who'd been in the house when Bob Lane died, to take their written statements, and have them signed. "I'll interview the five people who were sitting at the table with Lane, as well as the cook and her helper."

Preston asked Kirk, the other homicide detective, to supervise the fingerprinting and questioning. He reminded Kirk that nobody should leave the house until they'd been fingerprinted, interviewed, and had written and signed their statements."

The crime lab tech also took DNA samples from the saliva left on the diners' glasses. After he finished that, he swabbed everyone's mouth for additional DNA tests.

Detective John Preston murmured, "It's better to run too many tests than not enough."

Preston was married to Rick and Rhonda's daughter. Since everyone who sat at the table with Bob was now considered a suspect, including Rick and Rhonda, he didn't want anyone to know he was their son-in-law while he was working on this case.

Preston took out his notebook and pen. He told the officers, "Witnesses must be questioned separately. I'm sure you already know what I want, but a reminder never hurts."

Preston next talked to the medical examiner who told him, "I've pronounced the victim dead at the scene. I'm almost sure he died from an anaphylactic shock due to a food allergy. We don't know yet what Lane was allergic to and if his death was an accident or murder."

Preston said, "His death could be an accident, but we can't take a chance. For the time being, we'll treat it as a homicide."

"I think that's a wise decision," the ME agreed. "Now, I need your permission to take the body to the morgue."

Preston gave the medical examiner permission to remove the body from the scene.

The ambulance attendants put Bob's body into a body bag, loaded him onto a gurney, and placed him in the ambulance. An ident officer was called to ride with the corpse to the morgue. He was told to take any necessary additional photographs, including some close-ups, and also to take possession of the victim's clothes and his personal effects.

The medical examiner told Preston that an autopsy would be performed the next morning and a report would be faxed to him.

"Thank you," the detective said. He then turned to the other detective. "Now, I'll start questioning the people who sat at the dining table with the victim and take their statements. I'll talk to them one at a time in the parlor, starting with the woman who was with Lane tonight. Please send her in."

CHAPTER SIX

MARIANNA WALKED INTO THE PARLOR, which was furnished with antiques from the 1850's and 1860's, and introduced herself as Marianna Kelly to Detective John Preston.

"I'm glad to meet you. Have a seat, please, and tell me why you were chosen to be one of the diners at this Candlelight tour."

"Bob Lane invited me as his guest."

"How long have you known him?"

"I've been seeing him socially for about a month. Tonight was our fourth date."

"Did he ever tell you he had a food allergy?"

"No, he didn't."

"Have you ever been to dinner with him?"

"No. Tonight would've been our first dinner together. We went skating on our first date, to a movie on our second, and to a ballgame on our third. He and I were both watching our weight, so we didn't eat or drink anything during or after these activities."

"Mrs. Kelly, how did you meet Bob Lane?"

"We were both volunteers here at the Wornall House. I met him at one of their socials."

"What's your occupation?"

"I'm a registered nurse. I tried to help Bob by administering mouth-to-mouth resuscitation while Dr. Trotter performed CPR, but we weren't successful."

"It was kind of you to try to resuscitate Lane. What can you tell me about him?"

"He's been divorced for about a year. There were no children. He owns an import-export business, which apparently was pretty successful. He was Catholic. I think he spoke Spanish, and he made trips back and forth to the Mexican border each month. He was a volunteer at the Wornall House. He was a nice man, friendly, and good company. I'll miss him."

"Tell me about your life."

"I'm a widow and I have two children to support, so I have to work. My children and I attend church each week. I like to be home with them as much as possible, so I only volunteer here twice monthly."

"How did your husband die?"

"He was killed in a car accident," Marianna replied.

"Since you're a RN, maybe you can tell me how six people could drink cider, which didn't faze five of them, but might've killed one?"

"Bob must've had a life threatening allergy to one of the spices in the cider."

"That sounds plausible. You said Mr. Lane was divorced. Do you know his wife's name? Presumably, she'd know if he had a food allergy."

"Her name is Karen Lane, and I have her phone number. Bob wrote down her number on the back of his card and said if anything ever happened to him, I should call her. Isn't that odd? It's like he was psychic." Marianna reached into her purse and pulled out her billfold. She thumbed through some cards, extracted one, and handed it to the detective.

Preston took the card and looked it over. "What do you know about Mrs. Lane?"

"Bob didn't say much about her. I don't know why they were divorced or where she works. I think he gave her their house."

Preston asked, "If it's okay with you, I'm going to call her right now."

"Sure. Go ahead. I'd like to know what his allergy was."

Preston took out his cell phone and dialed Karen Lane's number. The phone rang several times, but nobody answered. He left his name and number on her answering machine and asked her to call him.

Detective Preston turned back to Marianna. "Do you know if Mr. Lane had any enemies?"

"Last night he phoned me and said he thought somebody was out to get him. When I asked who it was and why, he said it was a long story, and he'd tell me about it after the candlelight dinner, but he died before he could tell me."

"Did Mr. Lane give a hint about who was angry with him?"

"No. He said he was in a hurry and didn't have time to talk about it."

"Do you know of anyone who was angry with him?"

"No. During the times we were out together and he saw people he knew, they acted glad to see him."

"Where did Mr. Lane live?"

"In the Brookside area. He'd recently bought a house and had furnished it himself. He was proud of it. He invited me over to see it last weekend. It was really nice. It was a Spanish style house and was decorated with Mexican furnishings. He told me he'd imported the furniture from Mexico. He said his trucks had hauled the furniture to Kansas City."

"Tell me what happened to Mr. Lane tonight."

"Bob was in such a good mood. Then he drank the cider and suddenly his face became flushed, his eyes bulged, and he clutched his throat like he couldn't breathe or was choking. He tried to talk, and I heard him say the word 'nut'. Then he gasped for breath and fell onto the floor. The doctor started CPR and I began mouth-to-mouth. An ambulance arrived, and the paramedics tried to revive him with a defibrillator, but nothing worked. I can't believe Bob is gone. It happened so fast." A tear ran down her cheek, and she wiped it away.

"So you think Lane said something about a nut? Do you think he was trying to tell you what his allergy was, what was causing these symptoms? Do you think he could be allergic to peanuts or to such nuts as pecans and walnuts?"

"Oh, Detective Preston, I'll bet that's it! He must've been allergic to nuts. In retrospect, he had the symptoms of a person having an anaphylactic shock. I feel terrible that I couldn't help him. I'm a nurse and I should've picked up on those symptoms, but I didn't. That must've been what he was trying to tell us. Here's something important to know. If he was allergic to nuts, he would've carried an epinephrine auto injector and antihistamine pills everywhere he went. Do you know if an epi pen was found on his body?"

"What's an epi pen?" Preston asked.

"That's short for epipherine auto-injector. If Bob could've reached it, he could've given himself a shot and saved his life. Oh, my lands, I've just had a thought. Rhonda said she heard Bob say the word 'epi', but she didn't know what he was talking about. I didn't hear him say that. He must've been trying to get the epi pen out of his pocket. I remember seeing him grabbing at his pocket. How I wish he'd told me about his allergy. If I'd known, I could've given him an injection and saved his life."

Just then Preston's cell phone rang. The caller said, "Hello, Detective Preston. This is Karen Lane. I'm returning your call."

"Thank you for calling back, Mrs. Lane. Can you tell me if your ex-husband had a food allergy?"

"Yes, he's allergic to peanuts. Is he in the hospital?"

"I'm sorry to tell you that he died tonight, possibly from an allergic reaction to peanuts."

"Oh, no! I can't believe it!" Mrs. Lane exclaimed. "Thank you for telling me. I'm sorry to hear it. He's always been extremely careful about eating anything that had peanuts in it. What happened?"

"He drank a glass of spiced cider and apparently had an anaphylactic shock," Preston said.

"Then someone must've put peanuts in his drink. Are you telling me he was murdered?"

"I didn't say anything about murder, Mrs. Lane. What would cause you to ask that?"

"Bob must've eaten peanuts if he died from an anaphylactic shock. The only way peanuts could've gotten into spiced cider is if somebody put them in it."

"We haven't ruled out death by accident. We'll know more after the autopsy."

"Bob always carried his epi pen with him. Why didn't he give himself an injection?"

"Apparently his symptoms occurred so rapidly and were so painful, he wasn't able to get the pen out of his pocket in time."

"Poor Bob. His allergy was so severe than even one peanut dropped into his drink could've caused an anaphylactic reaction."

"Thanks, that's what I wanted to know. Who knew about his allergy besides you?"

"His brother and sister knew about it. He probably told the women he's dated since our divorce."

"What were the women's names?"

"I think he worked with one of them. I believe her name started with a J, but I can't remember it. The other one's name was Amanda. The most recent woman was a nurse. Bob has told various chefs about his allergy. Before we went out to eat at a new restaurant, he'd call and talk to the chef to make sure there were no peanuts, peanut butter, peanut oil, or any kind of nuts in the kitchen. He was so allergic, he couldn't eat in a restaurant that had peanuts or any nut products in their kitchen."

"That's interesting," Preston mumbled. "Did he have any enemies?"

"I don't know. He usually got along with people. You might check out the employees in that new import-export business of his."

"What do you know about his business?"

"Nothing. He started it after our divorce was final."

"Thank you for your time, Mrs. Lane. You've been very helpful. If you think of anything else that might help my investigation into Mr. Lane's death, please call me at the number I left on your answering machine."

"I'll do that. Thank you for telling me about Bob."

After she hung up the phone, Preston turned back to Marianna. He handed her one of his cards. "Please call me if you think of anything else about Mr. Lane that would be helpful."

Marianna took the card and put it into her purse. "I will."

"You've been helpful and I appreciate your time. Please go across the hall into the family room, sit at the round table, and write and sign your statement. Give it to Detective Woods before you leave."

She nodded.

"Also, would you please ask Rhonda Winters to come in next?"

"I will. Goodnight, Detective."

"Good night, Mrs. Kelly."

When Rhonda entered, she had a big grin on her face. Detective John Preston, her son-in-law, stood and said in a low voice, "Well, Mom, it looks like you're in the thick of another murder."

John's mother had died twelve years earlier, and he'd called Rhonda mom ever since he and Nikki were married ten year ago.

Rhonda asked, "I assume Bob's death was suspicious since he seemed to be perfectly healthy, and then he just suddenly keeled over dead. Is that why you're treating it as a murder?"

"That's one reason. The autopsy will determine how he died."

"Maybe he was allergic to an ingredient in the cider."

"He was allergic to peanuts."

"Now John, even you know enough about cooking to be aware that peanuts are not an ingredient in spiced cider!" Rhonda teased.

"I was told that Bob's allergy was so severe that even one peanut dropped into that pitcher of cider could've finished him off."

"What a shame! How did you know that?" Rhonda asked.

"I just talked to his ex-wife and she told me."

"Well, I guess she ought to know. I wonder who else knew that Bob had this allergy besides his ex-wife and his family," Rhonda said. "If he was murdered, someone must've gone into the kitchen and dropped some peanuts into the pitcher."

"If the cook left the kitchen door unlocked when she went to the bathroom, anyone in this house could've gone in and spiked the cider with peanuts. Or stirred in some peanut oil."

Rhonda said, "The scary thing is that one of the volunteers here at the Wornall House must be the murderer. I guess your suspects are the diners who sat at the table with Bob tonight, as well as the docents and the cooks. Oh, good grief! That means Rick and I are suspects, too."

"Even one of the witnesses in the tour group could've done it," John said. "We know the cause of death and we know what weapon was used. I think the cider was just setting out in the kitchen. Everyone in the house had an opportunity to go in there, and anyone who had peanuts in his pocket had the means."

"The problem is finding out who had a motive," Rhonda said. "Who had an ax to grind with Bob?"

"Have you heard if he had any enemies?" John asked. "Who could've been angry enough with him to kill him?"

Rhonda shook her head. "I don't know. I hardly knew him."

"If a peanut was accidentally dropped into the cider, his death was an accident," John said.

"Do you believe it was an accident?"Rhonda asked.

"No. I think he was killed, but why? This case will take a lot of investigation.

Rhonda said, "You'll probably be finding out tomorrow who Bob's beneficiary is. If he hadn't changed his will and if his ex-wife is still his beneficiary, then she's a suspect. Bob might've ditched a previous girlfriend when he began dating Marianna, and she could've killed him out of anger and jealousy. A girlfriend would probably know about his allergy. Or there's always the chance Bob had made an enemy at his new job."

"Those are good ideas, and they're possible motives. So, Mom, are you going to help me investigate?" John teased.

"Can I?" Rhonda asked with a big grin.

"Officially, no. Unofficially, yes! This has to be our secret. I don't want to get into trouble with the police chief, but I'd like to have your help and also use you as a sounding board."

"What do you want me to do first?"

"You can talk to the suspects. Just have lunch with them and chat about Bob. They might tell you something they wouldn't tell the police."

"Okay, I can do that. I'll invite the suspects for dinner or take them to lunch. I'll mention Bob's name if they don't bring up the subject, and I'll tell you every word they say."

"Good. Use that mini tape recorder Jimmy gave you. Put it in your pocket and turn it on when the subject turns to Bob's death."

"Hey, I'm starting to feel like Mata Hari! By the way, I'm glad you mentioned Jimmy. He and his wife are coming home for Christmas. We'll have all the relatives over for Christmas dinner so he can visit with everyone."

"Nikki, the kids, and I will be happy to see him."

"So will I. That six foot guy is still my baby, you know!"

They chuckled.

"Let's get back to the case," John said.

"This case is going to be a tough nut to crack!" Rhonda said. "Pun intended."

John laughed. "Mom, sometimes you're so funny!" He leaned over and kissed the top of her head.

Rhonda smiled at him. "I'm so glad Nikki married you, John."

"So am I!" he replied, grinning. "I'm going to need your help. We have a big puzzle to solve. We have to prove whether or not Bob was murdered, and if he was, what was the motive?"

"What do you want me to do besides talk to the suspects?"

"For starters, would you research peanut allergies on the internet and fax the info to me?"

Rhonda grinned. "Sure. I'll Google it when I get home tonight and FAX the FACTS to you!"

He smiled. "I'll appreciate your help."

"What's your strategy?"she asked.

"For starters, we'll get Bob's medical records, the autopsy and the lab reports, then we'll run background checks on all of the suspects, track Bob's movements, try to find out if he had any enemies, if anyone had a beef with him or a motive to kill him. Was anyone stalking him? We'll interview all the people who knew him, starting with the suspects and the witnesses, and we'll get search warrants for their homes and conduct searches if there's possible cause. I definitely want to search Bob's home."

"You've really got your work cut out for you! Do you think there's anything helpful on the surveillance cameras?"

"We'll make a DVD of them and find out. We'll download everything from the time the volunteers arrive in the house until the police came. Do you know where the surveillance cameras are located?"

"I think there are four. One is in the foyer, aimed at the front door, and the other three are by the exit doors."

"Tell me the last name of the other couple who sat at the dining table with you."

"Ashley. They're Bart and Sally Ashley."

He jotted down their names in his notebook.

"What's the first thing you're going to do in the morning?" Rhonda asked.

"Run background checks on the suspects and the witnesses."

"I hope you plan to share what you learn with me."

"Don't get your hopes up. There's only so much I can tell you."

"I was afraid of that. Well, I wonder who Bob's beneficiary is," Rhonda said. "He's divorced. No kids. Maybe he has a relative listed in his will who desperately needs money."

"I'll get a copy of his will in the morning and also I'm going to call his ex-wife and make an appointment to talk to her again."

"I liked Bob and I'm sorry he died," Rhonda said, "but I have a feeling that his death is connected with his import-export business."

Oh, those 'feelings' of yours!" John teased. "You may be right about that, and I plan to check it out. Well, Mom, write out your statement, sign it, and give it to Kirk. Tell Dad to come in next. I'll talk to him for five minutes, then you two can go on home."

"Thanks, John. Goodbye and good luck with the case." She went to the room across the hall and did as requested.

Rick came into the parlor and he and John shook hands. "Hi, Dad. Do you have any ideas about this case?"

"I've heard some talk."

"Like what?"

"That Bob might've been mixed up in the drug trade. Somebody said they thought Bob was involved in the cocaine drug bust in Mission Hills last week."

"Who told you that?"

"Bart. If Bob was involved in drugs, I wonder what the motive for his murder was."

John made a note of it. "Some motives for murder are jealousy, anger, hatred, money, fear, revenge "

"The motive is probably jealousy if a woman's involved."

"Did you hear that a woman is involved?"

"That's just a feeling."

John laughed, "You've been around Mom so long you're starting to sound like her!"

Rick chuckled. "Actually, it's not just a feeling. I played golf one day about a week ago with Bob, and his cell phone rang. The call was from a woman and she was yelling so loud, I could hear every word she said. She was angry because Bob was seeing another woman and she threatened him. She said, 'I could kill you for that'!"

"Now, you're talking! Thanks for that information. Do you know the woman's name?"

"No. Bob didn't say and I didn't ask."

"Of course, people often make remarks like that when they're angry. They don't mean it."

Before Rick could comment, they heard a commotion outside. They looked out the window and saw that several newspaper and TV reporters and TV cameramen had arrived.

"I'm curious about who contacted the media," John complained. "Of course, most people carry cell phones. Any one of them could've called."

"It's inevitable."

"True. Well, Dad, write a statement and sign it. Then you and Mom can go on home."

"Good luck with the case, John."

"Thanks. Please tell Mandy Todd to come in here next."

"Will do." Rick left the room.

Mandy walked in. "Detective Preston, my name is Mandy Todd. I was told you wanted to see me."

"Yes. Have a seat, please. Who made the spiced cider?"

"I did. I just stirred a package of spices into the cider and refrigerated it."

"What ingredients are in the spiced cider?"

"I don't remember. The spices came in a sealed package. Shall I go to the kitchen and get a package for you to see? There's some extra ones."

"When we finish talking, I'd like to have one of those packages to take to the lab. Were there peanuts in the mix?"

"I doubt it. I've never heard of peanuts in cider."

John asked, "How well do you know Bob Lane?"

"I had a few movie dates with him."

"Did he tell you he had a peanut allergy?"

"No, he didn't."

"It's difficult to believe a man who had a severe allergy that could kill him didn't discuss his allergy with you before the dinner tonight."

"I agree that was foolhardy. Maybe he discussed it with my assistant, but if so, she didn't mention it to me."

"I'll talk to her after we're finished. Do you have peanuts in any form in the kitchen? Any peanut butter, peanut oil, or nuts of any kind?"

"No. We were told because people are sometimes allergic to peanuts, we shouldn't have any nut products in the kitchen. I guess Bob knew that, so that's probably why he didn't mention his allergy to me."

"That's a possibility. Can you think of any way peanuts could've gotten into the cider?"

Mandy shook her head. "When we're out of the kitchen, somebody could've brought in some ground peanuts and stirred them into the pitcher."

"Why did you mention ground peanuts?"

"Because ground peanuts would mix better with the spices than whole ones."

"Are there times when nobody's in the kitchen?"

"Yes, there are. Tonight, Jean and I both carried food into the dining room at the same time, and nobody was there. The cider was still in the kitchen. Jean returned to the kitchen for the cider and carried it into the dining room. Sometimes only one of us is here, and when we go to the bathroom, the kitchen is not staffed."

"Here's my card. If you think of anything else, please call me."

She thanked him and put the card in her pocket.

"When I have more time, I'll call you for an appointment and we can finish our discussion. Would you bring a packet of spices to me now and ask your assistant to come in?"

"Yes, I will."

"Thank you for your time. Please write and sign your statement before leaving."

A few minutes later, Jean Murphy came into the parlor and introduced herself. She handed a spice packet to John. "Mandy asked me to bring this to you."

"Thank you. Have a seat, please. Did you make the spiced cider?"

"No. Mandy prepared it."

"Who carried the pitcher of cider into the dining room?" John asked.

"I carried it in and I poured the cider into the glasses," Jean said.

"Did you know about Mr. Lane's food allergy?"

"No, I didn't. What was he allergic to?"

"Peanuts. Were both you and Mrs. Todd out of the kitchen at any time when the cider was still in the kitchen?"

"Yes. Mandy and I both carried platters and bowls of food into the dining room at the same time. The cider was in the kitchen while we were in the dining room. I returned to the kitchen and picked up the cider, brought it into the dining room, and poured it."

"Did you see anyone in the kitchen when you returned for the pitcher?"

"No, I didn't."

"Had anyone else besides you and Mrs. Todd been in the kitchen while you were preparing dinner?"

"No."

Preston asked, "If peanuts had been stirred into the cider, would they've been added whole or ground?"

"I think the peanuts should've been finely ground to mix better with the spices."

"Mrs. Murphy, I appreciate your time and information. Time is short tonight, and I want to talk to you and Mrs. Todd again when I have more time. I'll be calling you. Here's my card. Please call me if you think of something that can help this case."

"I will." She put the card in her pocket.

"Would you ask Mrs. Ashley to come in next?" John asked. "Please write and sign your statement before leaving. Thank you for your time."

Sally Ashley came in a couple of minutes later.

"Hello, Mrs. Ashley, please have a seat."

"What can you tell me about Bob Lane?"

"He has a fairly new import-export business and he buys products in Mexico."

"Do you have any idea why anyone would want to kill him?"John asked.

"No, not unless he was mixed up in the drug trade."

"Do you think Mr. Lane was mixed up in drug trafficking?"John asked.

"Yes. One time he gave me two marijuana cigarettes. When I asked if he'd like to smoke one of them, he said, 'I never get high on my own supply'!"

Preston grinned. "He's a poet! Thanks for telling me. Did you know that Mr. Lane had a severe peanut allergy?"

"No."

"Did you see anyone put peanuts or any other ingredient in the spiced cider?"

"No."

"How well did you know Mr. Lane?"

"We both were volunteers at the Wornall House. We had a friendly relationship, but we didn't socialize. I'm a realtor and I sold him a house. He was a pleasant man and I liked him."

"Time is short tonight, but I want to talk to you again. I'll call one day soon for an appointment. Here's my card if you think of anything else you want to tell me. Please ask your husband to come in then write and sign your statement before leaving. Thank you for your time, Mrs. Ashley."

When Doctor Ashley came in, John greeted him, asked him to be seated and said, "I don't have much time tonight, but I'll want to talk to you and your wife again sometime soon."

"That will be fine."

"How well did you know Bob Lane?"

"We were both volunteers here at the Wornall House and I've played golf with him twice. We saw each other at activities sponsored by this museum. That's about it. He was an affable guy and I enjoyed our golf games."

"Did he tell you he had a food allergy?"

"No. He might've told me if we'd had a meal together."

"Didn't you guys ever have lunch together after the golf game?"

"No, I invited him for lunch once, but he said he had an appointment."

"Did you see anyone put any ingredient into the cider?"

"No. I wasn't in the kitchen where the cider was."

"Did Mr. Lane have any enemies?"

"Not to my knowledge."

"Was there anything about Lane's lifestyle that wasn't aboveboard?"

"When my wife said she didn't feel well, he offered her two marijuana cigarettes."

"Have you seen him associating with unsavory characters?"

"No, but I usually only see him when I'm here at the Wornall House."

"Here's my card. If you think of anything else, please call me. Write and sign your statement before leaving. I'll call you for an appointment in the next few days. Thank you. I appreciate your time."

John went into the room where the docents were waiting. He said, "I'd like to have a few words with each of you tonight, then I'll call you soon for an appointment so we can talk longer."

He talked to each one, but didn't learn anything of significance. They all said they'd only seen Bob Lane at the Wornall House. Nobody knew about his peanut allergy. Nobody knew if he had an enemy. Nobody had been into the kitchen the entire day. Nobody knew anything about Bob's business, and everybody was sorry to hear about his death. So John got their names, phone numbers, and addresses, and then he called it a night.

The police had held the reporters and cameramen off until all the suspects and witnesses had been questioned. When the police chief was notified that several reporters had arrived, he came to the Wornall House and ran interference for the cops with the press. He met with the press on the front porch where he answered some of their questions.

One reporter asked, "Why would anyone want to kill Bob Lane?"

The chief replied, "His death was probably an accident. We won't know until after the autopsy and lab reports are in."

Another reporter asked, "I heard Mr. Lane was deathly allergic to peanuts and that he died after drinking some juice. Were there peanuts in the juice? Who had access to the kitchen?"

"We won't know the cause of death until we receive the reports. Just about anybody who was in this house tonight had access to the kitchen. Anyone could've gone into the kitchen after the cook stepped out."

"Who had motive, opportunity, and means?" asked a tall brunette reporter.

And on it went. The chief knew the story would be on the news channels that evening and that it would be splashed across the front pages of tomorrow's papers.

As Rhonda and Rick rode home in their van, Rhonda's mind raced back to something that their friend and neighbor, Jason Valores, the director of police security of the Mexican state of Guanajuato, had once said to her, "The investigator has the best chance of determining how the crime was committed and finding a suspect in the first twenty four hours. Clues and evidence are collected at that time and the witnesses' memories are fresher."

Rhonda closed her eyes and prayed that God would help John solve this case. She believed that God works in mysterious ways, and she hoped He'd use her to help John find out WHODUNIT!

CHAPTER SEVEN

THE NEXT MORNING, RHONDA HAD a phone call from Jamie, the director of the Wornall House. Jamie came right to the point. "My assistant, Anna, and I were just now talking about you and how you'd helped solve those murders in Mexico. We're hoping you'll do some sleuthing on the case of THE MURDER AT THE JOHN WORNALL HOUSE MUSEUM."

"The Brookside Police Department won't know if Bob was murdered or not until they receive the autopsy and lab reports. Besides, they might not be too pleased to have me meddling in their case," Rhonda replied.

"If they determine that Bob was murdered, couldn't you do some unofficial sleuthing?" Jamie persisted.

"I suppose I could."

"I heard a new homicide detective has been put on the case. I don't know if he has any experience or not."

"What's his name?" Rhonda asked, pretending she didn't know.

"Detective John Preston."

"You're in luck. I've heard all about him. He's had ten years of experience in San Antonio, and he has an excellent record of solving murder cases. In fact I heard he's considered to be one of the best detectives in Kansas City, so you don't have to worry about him."

"That makes me feel better, but we'd still like for you to snoop a little. It will be our little secret!"

"Then you've got yourself a snoop!"

"Thanks a lot. Talk to you later. Bye."

"Bye, Jamie."

Rhonda told Rick about Jamie's call, and he offered to help her. She was pleased because he often had good ideas.

Rhonda then called Detective Preston, her son-in-law. "Hi, John, I thought you might want to know that Jamie called and asked me to do a little sleuthing."

"Good for her. I presume you agreed to help."

"Of course."

"I'm glad you called. I wanted to tell you that we finished questioning all of the suspects and witnesses last night. Unfortunately, we didn't learn much. Nobody admitted knowing that Bob had a peanut allergy, but it's apparent that somebody knew it."

"Bob's ex-wife knew it."

"Yes, and I have an appointment with her."

"Have the background checks been done?"Rhonda asked.

"Yes, but I can't give you that information."

"I was afraid you'd say that."

He laughed. "I know, but it can't be helped."

"What did Sally have to say about Bob?"

"She said she's a realtor and she sold him a house. She said she and Bart didn't know Bob very well and they had no idea he had a peanut allergy."

"Did Bart contribute any helpful information?"

"No, just a repeat of what Sally told me."

"Did you learn anything from the cook or from her helper?"Rhonda inquired.

"I checked the cider recipe with Mandy. She said the spices came from a mix, and that peanuts are not one of the ingredients. She's surprised Bob hadn't told her about his allergy, and I agreed that was curious."

Rhonda said, "I suspect that either Bob had told her or else he hadn't planned to eat the dinner. Maybe he was only going to have the drink because he thought it would be safe."

"That could've been his plan."

"Did you question the cook's helper?"

"Yes. She knows Bob, but didn't know about his peanut allergy. She said Mandy made the spiced cider."

"Did you learn anything from the docents and the witnesses?"

"Not much. Nobody admitted knowing about Bob's peanut allergy."

"So there's no prime suspect, so far?" Rhonda asked.

"There might be. Bob's ex-wife knew about his allergy. Also, I've just learned that Bob didn't change his will before his death, so she's still his beneficiary."

"That certainly makes her a suspect," Rhonda agreed.

"I'll know more after my appointment with Mrs. Lane. I have one more thing to tell you. Last night after everyone had left the Wornall House except Jamie and Anna, I asked them for permission to search the entire house. They were cooperative and while I had a whole crew of cops in the building, I took advantage of the situation and had them search every inch of the place. They took more fingerprints and samples. There was one thing that might interest you. One peanut was found on the floor in the kitchen."

"Just one peanut?" Rhonda asked, surprised.

"Just one, but that tells us somebody brought peanuts into the kitchen. A suspect must've dropped it. I was told that peanuts weren't allowed in the kitchen."

"I checked out several web sites devoted to peanut allergies. I hope you received the fifteen pages I faxed to you," Rhonda said.

"Yes, I got them, but I haven't had time to read them. Can you tell me the gist of what you learned?"

"Sure. The gist is that peanut allergy is the most common cause of death from food allergy. Strict avoidance of peanuts is the only way to prevent an allergic reaction. About one third of peanut allergy patients have severe reactions, and these reactions can begin and proceed rapidly. In extreme cases, a person can die within minutes. These sufferers must use an epi pen to give themselves an injection at once. If used in time, the injection can reverse the condition. After the patient gets the shot, he should go immediately to the hospital emergency room for further treatment.

Some people with peanut allergies can react when someone merely opens a candy bar containing nuts. Some peanut allergic people could not sit at the same table with a person eating peanuts. One person touched a peanut butter and jelly sandwich that had been set on the table where he was eating. His touch caused the peanut oil to be absorbed through his skin and caused a major reaction. It took an injection with his epi-pen and a trip to the emergency room to save his life.

Peanuts show up in foods you wouldn't expect, such as in Chinese food, Thai foods, Indian, and African foods. Sometimes people even thicken chili with ground peanuts. One article said people with peanut allergies shouldn't ever eat anything without reading the labels, and that they shouldn't eat any food that was processed in a plant containing peanuts. Another thing they have to be careful about is restaurants that fry their chicken in peanut oil. Some people only have mild reactions to peanuts, such as hives or stomach problems, while others with severe allergies who eat peanuts could have a life threatening reaction and could die in minutes if they don't get a shot."

John said, "Most people have no idea what to do when a person has a severe reaction to peanuts. I read the anaphylactic shock often sets in within two minutes after the person eats peanuts or peanut products. Bart had a point when he thought Bob had been poisoned with cyanide since it kills so rapidly."

Rhonda said, "I heard a true story today about a man who had a peanut allergy. He took his girlfriend to a Chinese restaurant and she ordered a dish that contained peanuts. After eating it, she leaned over and kissed him on the lips, and his lips swelled up!"

"Great Scott! That allergy is powerful!"

Rhonda asked, "Who would stir peanuts into the cider?"

John replied, "Somebody who knew Bob had a severe allergy to peanuts and wanted to make him sick or kill him. The spouse is always considered a prime suspect until cleared. Because of that, Bob's ex-wife would be my suspect if she'd been at the Wornall House last night."

"Karen might've been here," Rhonda said. "Remember she wasn't home when you called her the first time and left your phone number."

"You're right, she could've been. Karen has the most to gain from Bob's death since she's his beneficiary. She has the motive and she could've obtained the means very easily. She could also have had the opportunity if she'd been there that evening."

Rhonda asked, "Who do you think is the most likely suspect?"

"At first, I thought it was Karen, but I'm about to change my mind."

John asked, "Whodunit in your opinion?"

"I think it was either Karen or Sally, but it could've been one of the cooks. Both Mandy and Jean had opportunity and means, but for the life of me, I can't imagine what their motive would be."

CHAPTER EIGHT

Detective John Preston had asked a fellow officer to follow his prime suspect for two days. On the second day, the officer called in sick, so John took his place. In an unmarked car, John followed the suspect to the Forest Hills Cemetery.

John saw the suspect drive a blue Ford into the cemetery and go to the Wornall Monument where all the Wornalls had been buried since the death of John Bristow Wornall Senior in 1892.

Detective Preston had parked some distance away from the monument in an area hidden by bushes and trees. He opened the glove compartment and took out high powered binoculars. He watched the suspect with a great deal of interest, and saw the person carrying a spade as he walked to John Bristow Wornall's grave. The suspect knelt beside the tombstone and used the spade to dig a hole directly in front of it, then placed a small box in the hole. The spade was used to cover the box with the dirt that had been scooped out, and the top was tamped with a shoe. The suspect then looked around, walked back to the Ford, got in, and drove away.

Preston was indecisive as to whether he should dig up the package or follow the suspect. He decided to call for back up. He radioed a description of the car, the license plate number, and the location to the dispatcher. John asked him to send whichever officer was closest to the cemetery to follow the Ford and report to him where it had gone.

Preston then drove to the grave of John Bristow Wornall and noticed that there was a clear partial shoeprint on top of the hole that had just been dug. He went to his car and raised the trunk door. He took out some dental stone to make a cast of the shoe print and he set about casting it.

Preston put the shoe print in a card board box and set it on the floor in the trunk of his car. He then returned to the tombstone where the hole had been dug. He picked up a strong twig that had been lying nearby and used it to dig up the small package. He pulled on latex gloves and opened it. He saw a key nested there, then put the top back on the box and re-buried it.

Then Preston got back into his car and drove it a distance away where he was again partially hidden by trees. He patiently waited to see if somebody would come to the cemetery to dig up the "buried treasure." Finally his patience was rewarded. A black Buick drove up the rutted road to the monument and parked.

As soon as the man arrived, Preston radioed the police station and asked the dispatcher to send reinforcements to the cemetery. He gave the car's description and license plate number. By the time the man had finished digging the hole and had removed the box, Preston saw two unmarked cars drive through the cemetery gates.

Preston continued to use his high-powered binoculars to watch the man. He noticed that the man didn't bother to open the box. He just put it in his shoulder bag, got into his car, and drove away.

Preston watched as the man drove slowly up the lane to the entrance. Before he could drive through the gates, the two police cars blocked his exit, then another police car pulled in. One of the patrolmen used a bull horn to tell the perpetrator to get out of his car with his hands up. The man opened his car door and climbed out, his arms raised.

The officer handcuffed the perpetrator, and had begun to search him when Detective Preston drove up to the entrance, parked his car, and took out his keys. Preston introduced himself and thanked the policemen for their quick action. He then walked to the perp and took over. Preston read him the Miranda rights, and asked, "What's your name?"

"Ray Carter."

"What's your occupation?"

"I'm a pilot."

"Why were you in the cemetery with a spade? What were you digging?"

"I don't want any trouble, sir. I'll do what you tell me to do and tell you whatever you want to know. I was hired to go to John Wornall's tombstone and dig up a little box, and that's what I did."

"Who hired you?"

"I received a phone call from the person who did not give me a name. I was asked to dig up a small box buried by Mr. Wornall's head stone and take the key to a storage locker. I was told somebody would meet me there to retrieve some boxes. After I agreed to run this errand, Fed-Ex delivered a box to my house with a cash payment and the name and directions to the storage locker. That's all I know."

"What did you dig up?"

"Just a box. Do you want it?"

"What's in it?" Preston asked.

"I don't know. I didn't open it."

"What's supposed to be in it?"

"A key."

"What's the key for?"

"To open a storage locker."

"Do you know where the locker is?"

"Yes sir."

"Let me have the box, then direct us to the locker."

The man gave the box to Preston, then one of the officers guided him into the back seat of a cruiser.

Another officer said, "He left his keys in his car. I'll move the car to a parking space and get his keys for him."

Preston thanked the officers again for their fine work and asked them to follow him in case trouble was waiting at the storage locker."

Preston climbed into the front seat of the cruiser that held the perp, and asked the officer to drive them to the storage locker. He instructed the man to give them directions. The man was frightened, and he did exactly what he was told to do. They were at their destination in less than fifteen minutes. The perpetrator pointed to the right door. The officer stayed in the car to keep his eye on the man.

Preston's phone rang. The dispatcher informed him that the suspect he had originally been following, the one who had dug the hole and put the box in it, had returned home. Preston did not want to make an arrest yet. He wanted to give the suspect enough rope to hang herself.

Detective Preston dusted the key for fingerprints before he had to use it to open the storage room. He got out of the car and used the key to open the door of the storage unit. He had trouble opening it, but the door finally opened. He walked inside and saw several boxes neatly lined up along the walls. He took the top off of one of the boxes and said aloud, "We're in luck!"

Preston inspected the rest of the stash, then took out his cell phone and called his chief. "We've found a shipment of cocaine. It could be connected to Bob Lane's death or to that Mission Hills cocaine bust last week. Should I turn this over to the Narcotics Division or to the DEA?"

He listened a moment and said, "Thanks. Yes, I'd appreciate it if you took care of it. We'll wait here until they arrive. There's some other officers with me and the perp is in the back seat of a cruiser. He's been very cooperative, and he'll be brought in after this is over."

After Preston disconnected his cell, he asked the perp, "Where's the man who was supposed to meet you here to pick up the boxes?"

The perp grinned, "When he saw the police cars, he probably took off like a bat out of Hades!"

CHAPTER NINE

THE NEXT MORNING, JOHN CALLED Rhonda. "Hi, Mom. I've been so busy I haven't had time to call you about the autopsy and lab results. There was nothing toxic found in Bob's stomach so that rules out poison. The autopsy report mentioned he had edema of the glottis, a swollen throat, which could indicate an allergic reaction. The upshot was that Bob died of an anaphylactic shock from his peanut allergy."

"So the autopsy confirmed your suspicion that Bob was murdered, didn't it?" Rhonda asked.

"Yes, that and one lab report. According to the lab results that I received yesterday, peanut residue was found in the pitcher and in the glasses, but none was found in the spice packet. We're investigating Bob's death as a homicide because somebody put peanuts in the cider, and we're pretty sure it wasn't Bob! Somebody at the Candlelight Tour knew about his allergy."

"Thanks for telling me. What about the suspects' DNA and fingerprints?" Rhonda asked.

"They were clean," John said.

"All of them? How could that be?"

"None of the suspects had a record"

"What a surprise!" Rhonda exclaimed.

"I have some more information for you. A policeman had been following a suspect for me. This afternoon, we hit pay dirt. The officer became ill so I took his place and followed the suspect to the cemetery where all of the Wornalls were buried. To make a long story short, a guy named Ray Carter was arrested there and a great deal of cocaine was found hidden in a storage locker. The narcotics agents picked it up."

"Why do you think the suspect went to the cemetery and buried the key in a box? Why wouldn't he or she just give it to the drug peddler?"

"Maybe the suspect didn't want the perp to know her identity."

"Why didn't you arrest the suspect?" Rhonda asked.

"I'm playing a waiting game with this one. There's more to be learned, which I wouldn't learn if I made an arrest now. I'm waiting and watching," John said. "Talk to you later."

At lunch, Rick reminded Rhonda, "Don't forget, we're going on the ghost tour at the Wornall House tonight."

"It should be a SPOOKTACULAR evening!" Rhonda joked.

"Do you believe in ghosts?"Rick asked.

"I'll believe they exist when I see one. I'm from Missouri, the 'Show Me' state."

Rick said, "Since we don't know anything about ghosts, I looked them up on internet. I'll tell you what I learned. Ghosts may be earthbound spirits of human beings, in both the physical and spiritual realm. One author said they're alive, and they retain the mind of the person they were when they were living. He said shadow ghosts are the most common of all ghosts. Another author says ghosts are transparent, and that the spirits of these people who've died can't enter into rest or peace. Ghosts may haunt places where they used to live. Those who manifest are seen wearing clothes they once wore on earth. Some ghosts are trouble makers who haunt the physical world with negative energy. They move objects, flip light switches on and off, and even cause electrical disturbances. The houses they inhabit are called haunted houses."

"That was interesting, Rick. Thanks. I have to get busy on my novel now." She went into her office, booted up the computer, and wrote four chapters before it was time to leave.

That evening when Rhonda and Rick arrived at the Wornall House, they were ushered into the parlor and seated with the other tour members. Jamie, the director, welcomed the group and gave a short talk about the history of the Wornall family, then she introduced a woman from Ghost Vigils who does paranormal investigations.

The lady from the Ghost Vigils spoke about the way ghosts communicate mind-to-mind with humans. She passed around an EMF, an Electromagnetic Field Detector, so each person could look it over. She talked about how it was used to detect the presence of ghosts. She said people who see ghosts say they don't see their feet. She also talked about an EVP, an Electronic Voice Phenomena, and said, "The reason ghosts' voices can't be heard is because they talk above human hearing." She then turned the tour over to Jamie.

Jamie began, "I'll lead you on a tour through the house and tell you about all the ghosts who have been sighted. There have been several sightings of ghosts here in the parlor, where the Wornall family received their guests. Several people have reported seeing a dark-haired lady in this room who wore her hair pulled back in a bun and was wearing a blue dress. This 'Lady in Blue' has been seen sitting in the arm chair where I'm sitting now. At times she's taking china out of a box. This might've been a new set of china dishes that she'd ordered. She appeared to be happy about receiving the china."

At this point, one of the tour members said, "I'm assuming the 'Lady in Blue' is Eliza. I remember reading that some of Eliza's china dishes were stolen during the Civil War. Maybe her husband had ordered a new set for her to replace what was taken."

"That's possible." Jamie continued, "Also, this woman has been seen in the parlor playing the piano, which was purchased the year after the house was built."

Next, there was a discussion about houses that had ghosts in them. One person said the ghosts might've returned to this house because they were happy here or because they had unfinished business they wanted to take care of.

Jamie led the group out to the entrance hall. She pointed to the stairs at the far end, and used a flashlight to show the spot at the landing where she said the ghost of a Civil War Union soldier guards the front door. "Several people have said they've seen the ghost of this sentry. According to another story, a lady was walking down the stairs. When she reached the landing where the sentry stands, she stumbled and almost fell over the railing. She said she felt someone reach out and pull her back, but there was no other person on the landing except the ghost soldier. The lady believes the ghost saved her life."

Rick glanced at Rhonda and rolled his eyes toward the ceiling.

Rhonda merely grinned.

One of the men on the tour said his cousin saw a ghost in a long flowing white gown walk down these stairs.

A woman added, "There have been sightings in the gift shop of a woman in a long white gown."

"Yes, several people have reported seeing this ghost," Jamie said.

Rick jokingly whispered to Rhonda, "If you see her, give her my regards!"

Jamie said, "Please follow me into the family room across the hall." She pointed to the fireplace. "On several occasions, two little dark-haired girls, about two or three years old, dressed in nineteenth century clothing, have been seen warming themselves in front of this fireplace. They've also been seen playing outside on the front lawn, and upstairs looking out their bedroom window. They may be two of John and Eliza's daughters who died before they were three years old."

Jamie also told the group that when the Battle of Westport was fought nearby, both armies turned the Wornall House into a hospital for their wounded soldiers. Many died in this house.

Jamie changed the subject and asked, "Have any of you smelled cherry scented pipe smoke as we've walked through this house?"

Four people raised their hands and said they'd smelled it.

Jamie told them, "One of the ghosts in this house is a man who smoked the cherry scented pipe tobacco. Sometimes the scent is especially strong where the sentry stands on the stairs, guarding the front hall. I smell the smoke quite often."

Jamie took the group through all of the rooms except her office. The last room they visited was the master bedroom where John and Eliza slept. "There have been sightings of Eliza sitting up in bed, drinking a cup of tea. Notice that her china teapot, teacup, and saucer are still setting on a tray on her bed. Other times, when people have been in her bedroom, they've heard Eliza groaning. Since she had seven children, she could've been groaning from the pains of childbirth."

The tour ended in the gift shop where people were invited to look at the gifts and books that are for sale there.

Rick and Rhonda thanked Jamie for an interesting tour.

Jamie said, "Can I talk to you both in my office for a few minutes?"

"Sure," Rick said.

When they were seated, Jamie said, "I heard that Bob was involved in drugs. I'm afraid that's going to give the Wornall House a bad name."

"I don't think so," Rick said. "There might've been one or two bad apples in the barrel of volunteers, but people won't believe the Wornall House had any part in that."

"I hope it won't hurt the museum. You see, the Wornall House survives entirely on donations, admissions, and membership dues. People won't donate if the museum is involved in a scandal."

Rhonda said. "Don't worry. Hopefully the killer will be arrested in a few days."

Jamie stood, and so did Rick and Rhonda. Rick said, "Thank you. We enjoyed the tour. Goodnight, Jamie."

When they climbed into their car, Rhonda asked, "Well, Rick, how many ghosts did you see tonight?"

Rick joked, "Only Bob Lane! I think he was smoking a joint!"

CHAPTER TEN

THE NEXT MORNING, RICK AND Rhonda were lying in bed watching a Matlock re-run on TV. When a commercial came on, Rick teased, "Haven't you and John found out who killed Bob yet? It only takes Matlock an hour to catch a killer. You guys have worked on this case for four days."

"We haven't found a motive yet. We have to find out who hated Bob enough to make him suffer and die in front of a group. The killer must be someone connected with his volunteer work or with his business."

Matlock resumed so they stopped talking. They didn't want to miss the courtroom scene.

When the next commercial came on, Rhonda said, "I'm going to call Jason in Guanajuato and tell him about this case. He might have some suggestions."

"Good idea. He's had a lot of experience solving murders and working with drug dealers."

"Before I call Jason, I think I'll call Bart and Sally and invite them over for barbecue, and hope they'll talk about Bob. Maybe they'll tell us something they haven't told the police."

"It's worth a try," Rick agreed.

After Matlock solved the case, Rhonda phoned Sally and invited them over.

"We'd love to come and we both love barbecue," Sally said.

"Great! How about Thursday at six?"

Sally checked her calendar and said. "We're busy then. Any chance we can come today or tomorrow at six? Don't go to any work. We'd be happy with pizza."

"Today's good for me," Rhonda said. She was delighted they could come so soon. The sooner the better, she thought.

"Great! We'll be there. What can we bring?"

"Just your appetites. We'll look forward to seeing you at six."

Mission accomplished, Rhonda thought to herself.

Rhonda said, "Rick, the Ashleys are coming today. After I put a brisket in the oven, I think I'll phone Jason and tell him about Bob's death and the suspects. I was a pretty good sleuth when I was helping him, but I've not been worth a hoot on this case."

"I remember John helped you and Jason in that last case you worked on. I think Jason would be glad to return the favor."

As soon as Rhonda finished her breakfast of a bowl of Cheerios with sliced bananas in milk, she phoned Jason. When he answered, she said, "Hi Jason. This is Rhonda. Are you busy?"

"Hi, Rhonda! I always have time for you. What's up?"

She told him that John was investigating the death of a man named Bob Lane. She explained about his peanut allergy and what had happened and added he'd been dating a nurse who was sitting next to him when he collapsed and died.

Jason suggested, "Check out his love life and find out whom he'd been dating before he met the nurse. This could be one of those 'hell hath no fury like a woman scorned' type of murders. I guess John has already investigated Bob's business. He might've had an enemy there."

"That's possible. He owned an import-export business and he dealt with people on the Mexican border."

"I'm working on a case involving a couple of men from Guanajuato who are mixed up in drug trafficking at the border. I've been talking to a snitch who told me this guy was involved in an import-export business in Nuevo Laredo, Mexico. Where was Bob's business located?"

"In Laredo, Texas, but that's just over the border from Nuevo Laredo."

"Isn't it interesting that Bob and my two smugglers were in the same area? There might be a connection. Could you fax me the name and Laredo address of Bob's business and tell me what products he imported and exported? I've been working with the police in Nuevo Laredo and on both sides of the border. I'll do some checking around and let you know what I learn."

"Thanks. John and I will appreciate that."

"Glad to help."

"Thanks for your time, Jason. It was good to talk to you."

That night, Bart and Sally arrived on time. They sat on the rose velvet antique sofa in the living room and ate an artichoke dip that Rhonda served with crackers. They drank freshly-made lemonade, and chatted about their children, their grandchildren, and their hectic schedules.

Sally changed the subject to say, "Would you give me the recipe for this delicious dip?"

"Of course. It's very easy. Only three ingredients."

"That's my kind of cooking."

Rhonda refilled their glasses, and excused herself to put dinner on the table. She returned to the living room. "I hope you're hungry for barbecue."

"We certainly are."

They moved to the dining room and were seated at an antique mahogany table, and dined on barbecued beef, scalloped potatoes, and coleslaw. They had chocolate cake and ice cream for dessert.

"Dinner was delicious," Sally complimented her.

"Thank you."

"You have some lovely antiques. Are you planning to attend the Antique Roadhouse at the Wornall House?"

"Oh, yes, I'm looking forward to that!" Rhonda exclaimed. "I've never been to it. Is it like the TV show?"

"Somewhat. It's a money making project. For twenty five dollars, you can bring three antiques, and an antique appraiser will be there to tell you their approximate value."

"That sounds like fun. I love to watch the Antique Roadhouse on TV. We'll definitely plan to go. Wouldn't it be great to discover we have a piece that's worth a fortune?"

Sally smiled, "I wish you luck."

"Thanks. By the way, have you always lived in Kansas City?"

"No," Sally said. "We're from Tucson, Arizona. Our son still lives there."

"How long have you lived in Kansas City?"

"Five years. Don't you have a home in Mexico?"

"Yes, in Guanajuato. It's in the mountains, about two hundred and thirty miles north of Mexico City," Rhonda replied.

"I'll bet the weather is great there."

"It's the Garden of Eden. We love it, but we're thinking about selling the house. It's too far to drive and I don't like to fly."

Bart changed the subject. "I wonder how the investigation into Bob's death is coming along?"

Rhonda was glad that he'd brought up that subject. She reached in her pocket and clicked on the tape recorder. "I've been wondering about that, too. I can't imagine why anyone would want to kill Bob. He seemed like a nice man."

"How well did you know him?" Sally asked.

"We hardly knew him at all. I only saw him at the Wornall House a few times."

"I'm going to tell you something in confidence," Sally said. "I don't think he was a very nice man. I think he was mixed up in drugs."

"Oh, what a surprise!" Rhonda exclaimed. "I guess we never really know a person."

"I think Bob was a crook," she said bluntly.

Rhonda was interested to hear Sally's remarks. She asked, "What do you know about him?"

"Not much, but It would be easy for his trucks to bring drugs back with his imports from the Mexican border to Kansas City. He could pack drugs inside the pottery or in the furniture."

"You're smart to think of that," Rhonda said, complimenting Sally.

"I imagine the police have already thought of it."

"I hope so, "Rhonda replied.

"Do you have any proof?" Rick asked.

Sally said, "I was working as a tour guide one day at the Wornall House and I overheard some woman talking to Bob. She sounded angry. She asked him when he was going to get his drugs out of her house. He told her to be quiet, that someone might hear. She repeated in a lower voice that she wanted him to get them out of her house today."

"What did Bob say?" Rhonda asked curiously.

"He said he'd be over that night and get them. That was all I heard."

"Did you see the woman Bob was talking to or recognize her voice?" Rhonda asked.

"No."

"Do you think it was Marianna?"

"I don't think so, but Marianna was there."

"Who was in the house when you heard Bob talking to that woman?"

"Let's see." She thought a minute. "Jamie, Bob, Marianna, and two women whose names were Polly Jeffries and Darlene Martin were there. The cook and her helper were there, also. The woman who was fussing at Bob probably left before I finished with the tour."

"Maybe she was talking about medicine," Rick suggested.

Sally laughed at that suggestion. "No. There was too much anger in her voice for her to be talking about Tylenol!"

Rhonda said, "This could be significant information. I hope you'll tell the police what you've told us."

"I don't want to get involved."

"Sally, if Bob was involved in drug trafficking and you know something about it, but don't tell the police, you might get in trouble for withholding evidence."

"I hadn't thought about that. What's the name of that detective who appeared to be in charge of the case?"

"His last name was Preston. Rick, do you remember his first name?" Rhonda asked, pretending not to know him well.

"John Preston. I've heard he's very good at his job." Rick replied.

"That's good to hear," Sally said.

Hoping to get more information, Rhonda asked, "Who do you think killed Bob?"

"I have no idea," Bart said.

Sally said, "I think it was that woman Bob was talking to about the drugs."

"Why would anyone kill him because he left something in her house?" Bart scoffed.

"This is going to be a tough case to solve," Rhonda said. "So far, nobody has admitted that they stirred peanuts in the cider, and nobody has said they saw anyone do it, so how will the detectives ever figure out who did it?"

"Perhaps it was an accident. If the cook was eating a hand full of nuts and she passed by the pitcher, some could've fallen into it."

"That's a possibility, but I don't think it happened that way," Rhonda argued. "Since Bob was so allergic to peanuts, surely he'd talked to the cook about it. If so, she shouldn't have allowed peanuts or any nuts products in the kitchen."

Bart said, "Let's change the subject and talk about something more pleasant. Rick, why don't we play golf on Saturday?"

"Sounds good to me."

Before they left, Rhonda jotted down the recipe for artichoke dip and gave it to Sally.

Sally thanked her. She glanced at the recipe. "My, this looks easy." She put it in her purse.

"Thanks for the delicious dinner. We enjoyed the evening. Our turn next."

"We'd like that." Rhonda replied, smiling. She hugged them good night.

After they were gone, Rhonda and Rick discussed what they'd heard about Bob. "Do you think Bob really was selling drugs?" Rick asked.

"Hard to believe, but it's a possibility," Rhonda replied. "I'm going to call John and tell him what Sally said about Bob."

"Do you want to hear a story I read about two grandmothers who were recently busted for selling drugs?"Rick asked.

"Sure."

"I read about it in a magazine. These two grandmas were neighbors and they were in cahoots. They'd been selling drugs, until a snitch tipped off the police about them. The cops went to their homes with search warrants and searched the premises. They discovered hundreds of bags of heroin in one of the grandmothers' homes and nearly two thousand dollars hidden in a cookie jar. Then they went to the other granny's house and ransacked it. There they found a stash of one thousand baggies of heroin and also some cocaine. They found six thousand dollars of cold cash hidden in her freezer in empty boxes of frozen vegetables!

"The gray-haired grannies had originally peddled cocaine, but they'd recently started selling heroin. They were grossing between five to ten thousand dollars each week.

"Their supplier was also busted and charged with possession and intent to sell a controlled substance, and he's still in jail.

"The two grannies faced charges of possession and selling, but they were released on bail since they cooperated fully with the investigators."

Rhonda exclaimed, "I'll bet they sold that supplier up the river!"

ARTICHOKE DIP

1(14 oz.) can artichoke hearts, drained and chopped

1 cup grated Parmesan cheese

1 cup mayonnaise

Combine the three ingredients in a mixing bowl and mix well. Pour into a greased baking dish.

Bake at 350 degrees for 20 to 30 minutes.

Serve with crackers, chips, or fresh vegetables.

CHAPTER ELEVEN

RHONDA CALLED HER SON-IN-LAW. "I have news for you. Sally and Bob were here for dinner. When Bart started to talk about Bob, I clicked on the tape recorder." She told him everything that they'd said about Bob. "It sounds like Bob was running drugs, doesn't it?"

"We've been investigating that possibility. I've talked to the DEA about him."

"What's the DEA?"

"An acronym for Drug Enforcement Administration."

"It sounds suspiciously like Bob was involved in drugs since the mystery woman told Bob to get his drugs out of her house."

"That's just hearsay. The conversation could've been misinterpreted. I have a search warrant for Bob's house, and that's on my agenda for tomorrow."

"That's good. By the way, I phoned Jason in Guanajuato about Bob, and asked if he had any ideas. She told him what Jason had suggested, and that he'd said he'd call when he had news.

"Thanks for the update."

"You're probably busy, so I'll talk to you another time. Bye, John."

"Thanks for calling. Keep up the good work, Mom."

Before she went to bed, Rhonda e-mailed Jason and told him about the autopsy and lab reports. She also wrote about the cemetery caper, and how the key unlocked a security locker filled with cocaine, and that Sally had overheard a woman telling Bob to get his drugs out of her house.

The next morning, Rhonda called Marianna and invited her to lunch.

"I'd love to have lunch with you," Marianna replied. "Do you like Panera's Restaurant?"

"Yes, I do. Would you like to eat there?"

"It's across the street from Shawnee Mission Hospital where I work. I have an hour for lunch, so I could meet you there today at one, if that's okay?"

"Fine. I'll be there at one. Bye, Marianna."

Rhonda went into the office where Rick was balancing the check book and told him about her plans for lunch. She said she was glad Marianna could go today. If she has any information, John needs it as soon as possible. Rick said this was his day for lunch with the ROMEO'S, an acronym for 'Retired Old Men Eating Out'.

Rhonda and Marianna met at Panera's and gave their order. Marianna ordered broccoli-cheese soup and a Fuji Apple Chicken Salad. Rhonda ordered tuna salad on Asiago bread and a Greek salad. Both had iced tea. Rhonda paid for lunch with her Mastercard.

They carried their trays to a booth and sat down. "Thank you for lunch," Marianna said. "I'd like to cook dinner for you and Rick one evening soon."

"We'd like that. I'll bring dessert."

"I'll bet it will be a good one. I heard you're a cookbook author. Tell me about your cookbooks."

"The recipes are all fast and easy." Rhonda reached into her purse and pulled out a copy of her very first book. "Here's a copy for you. It's so easy your kids can use it to cook dinner."

"Thank you very much." Marianna took the book and thumbed through it. "Just what I need! The recipes look so easy." She laid the book on the table and ate another spoonful of soup.

"How many books have you written?"

"Twenty cookbooks and four novels."

"I didn't know you write novels, too. Are you writing one now?"

"At the moment, I'm writing a children's cookbook and a three-act play." Rhonda took a bite of her sandwich. "Umm… Delicious! How old are your children?"

"Jerry is fourteen and Caroline is twelve. You'll meet them when you come to dinner."

"I'll look forward to it."

"They're good kids if I do say so. Maybe I'll invite Bart and Sally to dinner, too. You like them, don't you?"

"Yes, very much."

When Marianna brought up the subject of Bob's death, Rhonda reached in her pocket and clicked on the tape recorder. She'd started carrying it with her everywhere she went.

Marianna confided, "I'm terribly upset about Bob's death. He was the first guy I'd dated in some time who I really liked. He seemed fond of me and the children, too."

"I'm sorry for your loss," Rhonda said. "I liked Bob, too, but to be perfectly frank with you, it's starting to look like he wasn't the good guy we thought he was."

"I'm afraid you're right, but I still miss him."

Rhonda said, "I don't know much about import-export companies. Did Bob talk to you about his business?"

"A little. He said he had to fly to Laredo, Texas, each month to buy Mexican products such as lawn furniture, pottery, copper pans, silver jewelry, and Mexican candy and cookies. His trucks hauled the products back to Kansas City, where he sold them to gift shops, Mexican grocery stores, and restaurants. Other times, his trucks hauled products made in Kansas City to Laredo. I guess these products were sold in both Texas and Mexico. I don't know much about his business, but I assume he made pretty good money. He showed his house to me last weekend and it was quite nice."

"Was his office and his warehouse in his home?"Rhonda asked.

"I think they were in the basement. He didn't show them to me."

"Did you say he transports the imports in trucks?"

"Yes, and sometimes by air."

"So he was a pilot? He must have been doing well if he owned a house, a car, two trucks, and an airplane," Rhonda said, bluntly. She was feeling a little guilty at being so inquisitive. But all's fair in love, war, and crime solving!

"He had a partner who owned the trucks and the plane, but he also owned a rental house. Someone lives there now, but he said he stored imports in it when it's not rented."

"How long did you say he'd owned this new business?"

"About a year," Marianna said.

"Just a year? Either he's making a fortune or he's got the best credit in town. Sorry I shouldn't have said that."

"Yes, you should. I realize something wasn't kosher. I'm worried that he was involved in something illegal. That thought keeps coming to me, but I keep putting it out of my mind."

"He might've been. Where did he keep the plane?"

"Bob said he had a friend who has a hangar and a landing strip on his ranch near Laredo. Sometimes he kept the plane there when he had to fly into Mexico to pick up Mexican products."

"Marianna, did you ever hear Bob arguing with a woman when you were volunteering at the Wornall House?"

She replied, "Yes. She told him to get something out of her house."

"What did she want him to get out?" Rhonda asked.

"I'm not sure I heard her correctly, but I think she said to get his drugs out."

"That's interesting," Rhonda said. "Somebody else told me the same thing."

"Do you know if he'd dated anyone exclusively before he met you?"

"He told me he used to date a woman who helped him get started in his import business. He said they still worked together, but they were having problems and he wished he could fire her."

"I don't guess he could fire her if she's his partner," Rhonda commented.

"No, he couldn't," Marianna said, "I hope he wasn't involved in drugs."

"I hope he wasn't, too."

"I'm so glad I can talk to you about Bob. I've kept my worries bottled up. I don't think he was making enough money to pay for his possessions. Before he started this new business, he'd been out of work for quite awhile, so he probably didn't have any savings. When he was divorced, his wife kept their house. He hadn't received an inheritance, so where did his money come from? The thought occurred to me that when he took the plane into Mexico to pick up imports, he could've picked up drugs there and flown them back to sell in Kansas City. Also, the Mexican truck drivers could've brought drugs back from the border with his imports."

"That's entirely possible. Have you mentioned your suspicions to Detective Preston?"

"No, but I think I should."

"I think you should, too. Now, I want to change the subject. I know you've grieved for Bob, but I don't think he's worth it. When this is all over, I want to introduce you to a nice pediatrician from my church who's about your age. His wife died about a year ago from cancer. You two have a lot in common, and I have a feeling you'll hit it off."

"That's nice of you."

"I'm a good matchmaker," Rhonda bragged. "I've introduced five people who have gotten married."

"Hey, you are good!" Marianna exclaimed. "You've brightened my day and given me something to think about besides Bob and this murder case." She glanced at her watch, and jumped up from the table. "I have to leave right now or I'll be late to work. Thanks so much for lunch, for the book, and for any future matchmaking. Work your magic, Rhonda! I'll call you soon about dinner. Bye."

When Rhonda returned home, she e-mailed all the information she'd learned about Bob Lane from Marianna to her son-in-law. She typed, "Did you know Bob had a rental house? Have you searched it? Who's his renter? Where was Karen, Bob's ex-wife, the night he was killed? Have you searched her house? Who was Bob's partner in the import-export business?"

Rhonda glanced at the clock. It was time for Judge Judy. Just as she started to turn on the TV, the phone rang. It was John. "Hi, Mom, I wanted to thank you for the informative e-mail. I told you that people would tell things to you they won't tell the police. This is one of the ways you're helpful to me."

"I'm glad I've helped you."

"This morning I picked up some search warrants that the judge had signed, so you can guess what I'll be doing this afternoon and tomorrow."

"Good luck. Have you talked to Bob's brother and sister yet?"

"I have appointments with them in one hour."

"Have you talked to Bob's neighbors?"

"Yes, but he'd only lived in that neighborhood about six months, so none of them knew him very well. His next door neighbor said he heard Bob and some woman having a loud argument about a month ago, and that it seemed to be a jealous rage about another woman. As for his other neighbors, all of them thought he was a nice man and they seemed to like him."

"They say the killer is usually someone the victim knows," Rhonda said. "That's probably right in this case since Bob knows all of the suspects. Have you finished their background checks? Does anyone have a criminal record?"

John laughed. "What's this, the inquisition? That's privileged information, but I'd tell you if I could."

Rhonda shrugged. "Nothing ventured, nothing gained."

Rhonda liberally sprinkled adages and clichés in her speech. She'd noticed that John had picked up a few of them.

"That's true. I have an appointment with Karen for tomorrow, but I think I'll talk to her today. In your e-mail, you suggested I search her house and find out where she was when Bob died. After I interview Bob's brother and sister, I'm going to stop by Karen's house without calling and see if she has an alibi for her whereabouts that night. I'll take the search warrants with me. While, I'm there, I'm going to search her house. Bob might've left something of significance in her home. Also, I'll ask her if she knows the name of Bob's renter and who his business partner is. Maybe she'll know the name of Bob's former girlfriend, the one who's been calling him and screaming at him."

Rhonda said, "I bet she'll know. I really like Bart and Sally, but I'm getting a little suspicious of them. Sally has been trying too hard to connect Bob to the drug trade. Maybe she's right about him. Maybe she knows things about him we don't know. But I wonder if she's doing that to divert suspicion from herself and her family. I've even wondered if Sally and Bob had a thing going when she was showing houses to him, and maybe he ditched her for Marianna, so she's angry with him now."

"Who knows? I'm taping our conversation."

"One of the volunteers at the Wornall House, whom I know, called and asked if I thought it was safe for her to continue to volunteer there. I told her that Bob's death was an isolated incident of violence, and it was very safe there."

"You're right. People scare easily. Thanks for your help and for being my sounding board. Got to go interview three people! Bye, Mom."

When Rick came home from his golf game with Bart, she told him about her lunch with Marianna and her chat with John. Rick told her what Bart said about Bob. He said Sally had been working on a project with Bob at the Wornall House. Sally told him she wasn't feeling very well, and Bob told her all she needed was a little weed. Sally was surprised, but pretended not to be. She said she didn't know where to get it. Bob said he had some in the trunk of his car and he'd get her a couple of reefers. She said he went out to his car, got something out of the trunk, and came in with a small envelope. He handed it to her. She opened it, and found two marijuana cigarettes in it. She thanked him and asked how much she owed him. He said they were a gift, and he hoped they'd make her feel better. She thanked him, said she couldn't smoke it until she got home, then she put the envelope in her purse."

"Bart said Sally came home and showed the reefers to him. He told her she was lucky the police hadn't stopped her for a traffic violation. If they'd searched her purse, she might've been charged with possession. He said she grabbed them and threw them into the toilet stool."

Rick added, "I asked Bart if he thought Bob had been running drugs from Mexico to Kansas City. Bart nodded, and said Bob might've been killed over a drug deal that went bad."

Rhonda muttered, "If he'd only owned his company for one year, he couldn't afford the major purchases he'd made unless he'd been moonlighting big time."

CHAPTER TWELVE

THAT AFTERNOON, JOHN ARRIVED PROMPTLY at Bob's brother's home for their appointment. He rang the doorbell, and Bob's brother came to the door. He was a tall, slim man, who had thick blonde hair shot with gray and blue eyes like Bob's.

John said, "Hello, I'm Detective John Preston. I'm looking into the circumstances of your brother's death. Please accept my condolences."

"Thank you. My name is Tim Lane. It's nice to meet you. Thanks for coming. Please come in and have a seat. Can I get you a cup of coffee?"

"Nothing to drink, thank you." John sat in a comfortable arm chair and took out his notebook and pen. "Do you mind if I tape our conversation?"

"That's fine with me."

John turned on the tape recorder and laid it on the table beside his chair.

Tim said, "Before you ask me any questions, I want to tell you what a wonderful brother Bob was to me after I lost my job. He paid off my house mortgage so my wife and I wouldn't lose our home, and every month until I got another job, he sent us a five hundred dollar check."

"You had a kind and generous brother. I know you miss him very much."

"He certainly was, and I'll never forget what he did for me. I told him often how much I appreciated him. When I got a new job, I offered to make monthly payments to pay him back, but he said what he did was a gift to me. He wouldn't accept any money."

"Not many brothers would do that," John said. "What business was Bob in?"

"He was in business for himself."

"What kind of business?"

"Import-export. He invited my wife and me over for dinner last month and told us about it. He showed us around his new home, which was furnished with Mexican furniture he'd imported. He showed us his new car and his rental house. We're proud of him. He's done well."

"How long has he owned this new business?" John asked.

"About a year, I think. My wife is a bit nosy. She asked him how he could afford so many new things. He told her he needed them for his business and that he could deduct much of it from his taxes. He told her not to worry, that he had a good tax attorney."

"When we returned home, my wife quoted, 'the guilty flee when no man pursueth.' She has a suspicious mind. Bob was a good man."

"Did you know about Bob's allergy?"

"Yes, he's had that peanut allergy most of his life. He always had to be very careful what he ate. We couldn't have peanuts, peanut butter, or peanut oil, or any other nuts in the house."

"How did Bob feel about his ex-wife?"John asked.

"He loved her. The divorce devastated him. At first, he hoped Karen would take him back, but after she began dating her divorce attorney, he gave up. I think he called her fairly often though, to keep in touch. When he realized she was getting on with her life, he decided to do the same. He met a woman who helped him get started in his new business, and they began dating."

"Do you know her name?"

"I don't think he ever told me her name. I never met her. When he spoke about her, he called her his business partner."

"Did she own the trucks and plane?" John asked.

"I think so."

"Is there anything else you can tell me about Bob?"

"No, but he was a great guy. I'll never stop missing him."

"I'm sorry for your loss."

"Thank you."

John reached in his pocket and took out his billfold. He extracted a business card and handed it to Tim. "If you think of anything else, please call me at the number on this card."

Tim nodded. He took the card and put it in his billfold.

John said, "Thanks for your help." They shook hands, then John gathered up his tape recorder, notebook, and pen, put them in his attaché case, and left.

John's next stop was at Bob's sister's house. She answered the door bell right away. He introduced himself and said, "I'm sorry about your brother, Mrs. Travers."

"Thank you. He was a great guy. We really miss him."

Polly Travers was a tall woman. She had curly blonde hair with gray streaks and blue eyes. She was dressed in a denim shirt, blue jeans, and tennis shoes. Her home was clean and comfortable.

She took him into the living room and said, "Have a seat." John sat on the blue sofa, and she sat on a matching blue chair, next to him.

He asked if it was okay to tape their conversation and she said that was fine.

John asked, "Were you aware of your brother's allergy?"

"Oh, yes, he'd been allergic to peanuts as long as I can remember. He'd had some close calls. He knew exactly what he could eat and what he had to stay away from. He'd been in the hospital several times due to reactions. He carried an epi pen with him all the time. What I don't understand is why he didn't give himself a shot with his pen at that dinner the minute his throat started to swell?"

"I think he tried to reach his pen, but the symptoms came on too fast."

"I have a peanut allergy, too, but it's a mild allergy in comparison to Bob's. I'm careful about what I eat, but I'll be even more careful now that I've heard what happened to Bob"

"That's wise," John commented.

"Do you have time for me to tell you about a close call I once had?"

"Of course."

Polly said, "One evening I ate dinner at someone's house. She served chili that had been thickened with ground peanuts. I'd told the lady about my allergy, but I can only assume she'd forgotten. I didn't hold any ill will against her because of it. Anybody could forget when they're stressed and trying to cook a quick supper. We were each served a bowl of chili with our choice of a variety of toppings. After I ate two or three bites, I suddenly felt a throbbing pain in my throat. Within a minute, my lips, tongue, and throat began to swell. I couldn't swallow. I realized that somehow I'd eaten peanuts, and I knew what was happening. I grabbed the epi pen out of my pocket and pushed off the top. I jabbed the needle in my stomach, then I closed my eyes and lay back in the chair until the epinephrine kicked in. My heart started beating fast and the swelling in my throat started to go down. I knew I had to get to the hospital pretty fast because the medicine I injected only lasts thirty minutes. One of my friends drove me to the emergency room. I got there before my throat started swelling again. I was scared that I'd suffocate. The doctor immediately took me in and administered the meds I needed. I thanked God I made it there in time. If I hadn't, I'd probably have died."

"I'm thankful you made it on time, too. Your story helped me understand more about the seriousness of a peanut allergy. By the way, where did Bob work?"

"He owned an import-export business. I was proud of him. He was very successful. In just one year he'd bought a new house, a car, and a rental house. I've heard that often people don't make much money the first year they're in business, but Bob was a hard worker," Polly bragged. "He was also very generous. Did you notice the blue Cadillac parked in my driveway?"

"Sure. It's a beautiful car."

"Bob gave it to me for my birthday last month. He knew blue was my favorite color. He also gave me a box with twenty five thousand dollars in cash in it. He said that was my early Christmas present. I think he knew he wouldn't be with me at Christmas."

"What wonderful gifts!" John exclaimed. "Not many people have a brother like that."

"That's for sure. He also gave our son a thousand dollars, and he needed it. He's at the university, studying to be an engineer like Bob."

"Was he close to his nephew?"

"Yes. He was Bob's only nephew. Tim has two girls. They're both married now."

"Do they have children?"

"Not yet. They've just been married a year or two."

"I wish I'd done more for Bob. Everytime I drive my new car, I think of him."

"He was a great brother, and I'm sure he loved you, but I have to ask you a question that I hope won't make you angry. Was Bob ever involved with drug trafficking?"

Polly shook he head. "I swear Bob would never get mixed up in something like that. He was a good man."

"Then where did he get so much money? According to the records we've seen, Mr. Lane paid cash for both of his houses and his car."

CHAPTER THIRTEEN

After John left Bob's sister's house, he had lunch, then he phoned Kirk Woods and asked him to go to Karen's home with him. The two homicide detectives spent the rest of the day searching Karen's and Bob's homes.

They arrived at Karen's house without an appointment. They showed her their badges and introduced themselves. Her large green eyes widened in surprise when she saw them. John told her he was the detective who had called to tell her about Bob's death.

She invited them inside and asked them to have a seat in her attractively furnished burgundy and champagne living room. The detectives sat in the two burgundy wing back chairs on either side of the cream sofa.

Karen was an attractive red head. Her shoulder length hair was arranged in a pretty, curly style. She was average height and weight, and had a nice smile and friendly personality.

Preston offered his condolences, and she thanked him.

"I realize we had an appointment tomorrow with you, but since we were out this way today, we thought we'd take a chance that you'd be home. Please forgive us for any inconvenience. We'd like to ask you a few questions about Mr. Lane, and if you don't object, I'd like to tape our conversation." Before she could object, he continued, "First, will you tell us about the jobs Mr. Lane had after your marriage?"

"Bob was an engineer. Before we were married, he'd worked at the same job for two years. He worked there for one more year, then he quit. I wasn't working at the time, so needless to say, I was upset with him. Before long, he got another job, but he only worked there a year and a half before he quit. He was out of work four months before he found another job. But he finally got a pretty good job, and he worked there for four years. After he quit that time, it took him six months to find another job, and we got behind on our house and car payments. Eventually, he got another good job and he worked there for five years.

"This time when he quit, I told him I was fed up with his instability. I wanted him to find a job and keep it until he retired, like my father did, and by now I knew he never would. He got bored after he worked at a place for a couple of years, and wanted to get something new. He couldn't or wouldn't keep a job, and he was a poor money manager. He spent more money than he made. This time, he didn't even try to get a job, and we had a lot of arguments. He lay around and drank booze that we couldn't afford, which caused more fights. This time, he seemed to be too lazy to interview for jobs. I don't know what was wrong with him. Maybe he was depressed.

"This time when I realized he wasn't even trying to get a job, I decided I'd have to go back to work. I was a legal secretary when I met Bob. I put my application in at a law firm and I was hired right away. It was lucky that I made a decent salary because I was our sole support. I'm a good money manager, and eventually I was able to pay off most of our debts. Bob still wasn't looking for a job. He was content to lie around and let me support him. Finally, I told him I couldn't live this way and I wanted a divorce. He told me he loved me and tried to talk me out of it, but I filed anyway. I kept the house, and after our divorce was final, I started dating my attorney.

"Since I was no longer supporting Bob, he decided he'd have to go to work or starve. He went into business with some woman, and apparently he had done very well. Money started pouring in, and he bought himself a new house and a new car."

"Where do you think he got the money to start a new business?" Detective Woods asked.

"For all I know some drug lord bank rolled him."

"Are you serious?" Woods asked, curiously.

Karen laughed. "No. I'm joking. I'm not sure if he went to work for that woman or if they were partners. I'm sure she owned the trucks and the airplane. For all I know, he might've rented his house and car from her."

"Doesn't he also own some rental property?" Preston asked.

"Yes, he does. I quizzed him about where he was getting so much money, and he said he had good credit."

"Has he dated anyone since your divorce?"

"For awhile he dated his partner, the woman who helped him start his new company. He called her his 'silent partner'. I think he'd dated a blond chef a few times, too. I don't remember her name. It was something like Marge or Amanda."

"Do you know where the chef worked?"

"No, I don't know anything about her. I guess they broke up because last month he started dating a nurse."

"How do you know so much about Mr. Lane's girlfriends?" Woods asked curiously.

''Bob usually called me about once a week and he'd tell me about the women in his life. I don't know why. Maybe he thought that would make me jealous."

Preston asked, "Do you remember the first time I phoned you?"

"Yes, of course."

"You weren't home when I called, so I left my number, and when you came home you called me back."

"That's right."

"Where were you that night?"

"My attorney friend and I were having dinner at Houlihans."

"Did you stop by the Wornall House anytime that evening?"

"No, we didn't."

"Will you please get your date on the phone? I need to verify where you were that night."

Karen looked irritated, but she picked up the phone and dialed. She had a speaker phone. When her friend answered, she said, "There's somebody here who wants to talk to you."

John said, "Hello, this is Detective Preston. To whom am I speaking?"

"Bill Wyman."

"Do you remember where you were the night Bob Lane died?"

"Yes, Karen and I went to dinner at Houlihans, then we returned to her house."

"Did you stop by the Wornall House on your way home?"

"No. I've never been there."

"Thanks for your time. Goodbye, Mr. Wyman." John hung up the phone.

John turned to Karen and said, "We realize that you could've cooked up this alibi with your friend, but I think you're telling the truth." He pulled a document out of his case. "Detective Woods and I would like to conduct a search of your home while we're here."

"Why?"

"We're looking for some of Mr. Lane's records. If you have them, we want to see them."

"I guess you sprung this surprise on me so I wouldn't have time to hide anything," she said.

John grinned. "You've caught me!" He handed the search warrant to her. "This is your copy."

She took it and began to read it.

"May we start now?"Woods asked.

"Okay, go ahead. Search the house. I have nothing to hide. You're wasting your time. I'll be in the family room if you need me."

"Fine. We'll join you there and search that room first."

The detectives pulled on latex gloves and went to work. They searched every drawer, checked the furniture for secret hidden drawers, looked through every book in the bookcases, removed pictures to see if there was a wall safe behind them, and rolled up the Oriental rugs to see if there was a hidden safe under the floor. They were thorough, and it was a time-consuming job.

Karen had sat in a recliner, reading a novel during the entire search of that room. From there, they searched the living room, kitchen, dining room, then the three bedrooms in the house. They were especially interested in her office and spent a great deal of time going through the desk, bookcase, and file cabinets.

After searching Karen's house from top to bottom, they were about to give up when Preston found a large sealed manila envelope in a bottom drawer. Bob Lane's name was written in black magic marker at the top of the envelope. Under his name, were the words, "Not to be opened until after my death."

Detective Preston took it to Karen and asked, "What's this?"

"I don't know. Bob gave it to me about two months ago. He told me to keep it in a safe place and not to open it until after his death. As you can see, I have not opened it."

"Can I open it now in your presence?"John asked.

"Go ahead."

John opened it, reached inside it, and pulled out a variety of legal papers. There was a will, a title to Bob's car, deeds to his two homes, and a contract with a woman named Jeannette. Her last name wasn't listed. There was also a set of keys. The keys were labeled 'home, rental house, office, and storage room.' John put everything back into the envelope except the keys. "I need to take this envelope to the lab for fingerprints."

"Okay, but I'll want it back."

"Of course, I'll return it," John promised. "I'll give you a receipt for it right now." He took a receipt book out of his attaché case, wrote down what he was taking, and signed it. He handed it to her.

She thanked him.

"We also have a search warrant for Mr. Lane's home," Preston said as he handed her a copy. "Will you go with us now to his house so we can search it, his office, and his storage room?"

"Certainly," Karen replied almost eagerly. She seemed interested in seeing for herself what might be there. She grabbed her purse, Bob's keys, and her novel. She stood, "Shall we go now?"

"Yes, please. You can ride with us. We have an unmarked police car in your drive way."

She gave them the directions. Bob's house was less than a mile away. John pulled into his driveway and parked. Karen took out the key labeled "home" and opened the front door.

"May I have the keys, please?" John asked.

Karen handed them to him. John put them in his pocket, then the three of them went inside.

"Shall I walk through the house with you?" Karen asked, hopefully.

"Why don't you just sit in the living room and read your novel while we look around?" John suggested.

Karen sat down in an arm chair by the front window, turned on the floor lamp, and opened her book.

The detectives searched through each room, but found nothing of interest, so they went downstairs to the basement, which was divided into locked rooms. John used the key marked 'office' to open the first door.

The office was a large room with white walls and a red Oriental rug on the floor. At the far end, there was a large walnut desk, a desk chair, and a matching credenza. There were two red chairs for visitors in front of the desk. Hanging on the wall above the desk was a large framed painting of a Mexican courtyard surrounded by columns, a splashing fountain, red flowers, and tropical plants.

The office also contained three wooden file cabinets and two bookcases at one side of the room. There was a long mahogany table with six matching chairs around it at the other side.

"Perhaps this is the board room," Woods joked.

Preston said, "I'm going to take several things from this room to the police station so the experts can check them out. Who knows what all we might learn!" He picked up Bob's computer from his desk and set it on the floor near the door. He set the printer beside it, then gathered up the telephone, Bob's answering machine, his address book, his calendar, and his cell phone.

"The specialists will check these very carefully," Preston said.

Next the two detectives searched through all of Bob's file cabinets and removed several of his business records and laid them beside the computer.

"Here's a ledger that you'll find interesting," Detective Woods said, picking it up and handing it to Preston.

Preston skimmed it. "You've found a gold mine!" he exclaimed. He thumbed through it and read some parts. "This shows what a successful drug trafficking operation has been going on under our noses here in Brookside." He placed it on top of the records they were taking to the station.

After they'd finished looking through everything, they carried the items they planned to take to the station upstairs to the front hall and set them on the floor near the door.

"What are you going to do with all of those things?" Karen asked.

"We're taking them to the police station, but we'll give you a receipt for them, and they'll be returned."

"Why are you taking them?"

"We'll want to listen to Lane's answering machines on both the phone and cell phone and read his e-mails to determine if anyone had made threatening calls to him or left angry messages. We'll check the calendar to see what appointments he had, and with whom. We'll turn our expert loose on Lane's computer, and we'll ask the phone company to pull up his recent calls. Other specialists will go over his business records."

"I hope you'll find clues to who killed Bob," Karen said.

"That's what we're looking for. I've written a receipt for these items. Please sign your name at the bottom of the page, giving us your permission to take them," Preston said. "They'll be returned as soon as we're finished with them." Preston handed the receipt to her, and she signed her name and returned it to him. He gave her a copy.

"As soon as we put these things in the trunk of the car, we'll be back in to search the basement, which we assume Lane used as a storage room for his imports."

When they returned and went downstairs to the basement, Preston used the key labeled "storage" to open the locked door. This was where Bob warehoused his imports. Woods made an inventory of the products and searched each item to see if drugs were hidden inside them. They didn't find anything that shouldn't have been there.

"Are you ready to search the second storage room?" Woods asked.

When they entered that room, the detectives thought it was interesting that there were two large portable steel storage containers in there. Kirk opened each container and saw that the interior was beige and spacious. They included patented door and locking security systems. The storage units had a drill resistant container guard lock.

There were several pallets of packaged Mexican cookies in each of the containers.

"How many of these should we open?" Woods asked.

"All of them. What an ideal place to hide small bags of cocaine!" Preston exclaimed.

Woods took out his knife and cut the tape on the first box. He opened one, took out a package of cookies, and handed it to Preston. "This cookie package seems pretty heavy."

"It sure is." John opened the first one and removed the cookies. Tucked into the bottom of the bag were several small packages. He looked at Woods and exclaimed, "Guess what this is!"

"Cocaine?" Woods guessed.

"Right on! Just what I thought we'd find!" Preston exclaimed. After they'd opened about half of the packages and found each one stuffed with cocaine, Preston took out his cell and dialed the chief of police's number. He told the chief what they'd found. "What do you want us to do with it? Should we turn this over to the narcotics agents or to the DEA?"

He listened to the chief's reply and said, "Okay, thank you for calling them. We'll wait here until they arrive."

Preston turned to Woods and said, "I suspect there are a lot more 'Mexican imports' in these security units. Let's check them out."

When they'd finished their search, the detectives went back upstairs to the living room and John asked, "May we sit down, Mrs. Lane? I want to talk to you."

"Of course. Have a seat."

"Thank you." They sat on the sofa. "We have to wait a few minutes for some people to arrive, and while we're waiting, I think you should know that at this moment, you're the prime suspect in your ex-husband's murder."

Karen was surprised. "Why?" she sputtered. "I'd never kill Bob or anyone else."

"You're Mr. Lane's beneficiary. He never changed his will," Preston told her.

"Bob didn't tell me he hadn't changed it."

"His will was in that package he asked you to hold for him until his death. Didn't you open the package and read the will?"

"No, I did not open it. I had no idea he hadn't changed his will."

"If you opened it, your fingerprints will be all over the pages of the will. It will be sent to the police lab today and checked for your prints."

"If the will is the original one, my prints will be on it because I've read it, but if it's a new will, they won't be there. You won't find my prints on any of the other documents because I didn't open the package."

"Most women would've opened it out of curiosity."

"I've been too busy with my new job and going out with my attorney friend to have time to be curious. I'd forgotten about it."

"Are you surprised that Bob was murdered?" John asked.

She shook her head. "Not really."

"Why not?" John asked, surprised.

"Bob was making too much money. I thought something fishy was going on."

They talked a few minutes. Finally, John heard a car pull into the driveway and stop. Then Preston said, "The agents are here from the DEA."

"What's the DEA?" Karen asked.

Woods said, "The Drug Enforcement Administration."

CHAPTER FOURTEEN

JOHN PHONED RHONDA AFTER HE got home. "Hi, Mom. I have some news for you. We searched Bob's house and found cocaine in his basement."

"How much?"

"A lot! The DEA came and picked it up. They were sure happy to get it, too!"

"What was it stored in?" Rhonda asked.

"You'll love this! It was packed in cookies!"

Rhonda laughed. "A cookie Caper!"

"Very good! The DEA called it 'Operation Cookie Caper'!"

"Drug smugglers are creative, aren't they?"

"Too bad they don't use their creativity in legal ways. Well, I knew you'd want to hear the latest. You and Sally were right about Bob being mixed up in drug trafficking."

"Thank you for telling me," Rhonda said.

"You're welcome. Got to go. Bye."

That evening at dinner, Rhonda told Rick about 'Operation Cookie Caper.'

After they'd finished discussing Bob and his stash of cocaine, Rick said, "Don't forget we're going to the Wornall House Antique Road Show fundraiser tomorrow morning."

"That should be fun. I think it's similar to the PBS Antique Roadshow on TV," Rhonda said.

"We're supposed to take some antiques for an appraisal. How many can we take?"

"Probably as many as we want to take. They're charging ten dollars each or three items for twenty five dollars." Rhonda added.

"What should we take?" Rick asked. "Taking furniture is out of the question because it's too heavy. Let's walk through the house and choose a total of three small pieces."

That's what they did. They chose three paintings in antique frames that they thought might have some value. Rick took a Currier and Ives print in an antique frame that his mother had given to him when he was twelve. Rhonda took a signed painting a cousin had willed to her thirty years earlier. She also chose an original oil painting that she'd bought at a garage sale.

As Rick drove down State Line Road, he said, "I heard there's going to be an outstanding group of antique dealers and appraisers who will give a good estimate of their value."

The Roadshow opened at nine, and Rick and Rhonda arrived Saturday morning at nine. Since they came early, they didn't have to stand in line very long.

Their paintings were appraised, and Rick was told that his Currier and Ives was a copy of an original, but that its frame was an antique that placed its value at three hundred dollars. Rhonda's picture of Princess Charlotte was signed by the artist and was in an antique frame, making it worth four hundred dollars. The three dollar garage sale original oil painting was estimated to be a hundred years old, as was the frame, but the appraiser said the painting was not particularly well done. He appraised it at one hundred dollars.

As Rhonda and Rick loaded their pictures back into their van, she grumbled, "Well, there went my dream of having a masterpiece worth a fortune!"

CHAPTER FIFTEEN

A COUPLE OF DAYS EARLIER RHONDA had told John some of Sally's stories about Bob, so he decided to have a talk with Bart and Sally. John phoned Sally and asked if he and Detective Woods could stop by her home for a short talk. He explained, "The night of Bob's death, we didn't have much time to talk to the diners and docents. Now, we'd like to talk to everyone again."

"Would tonight at seven work for you?"Sally asked.

"That would be fine. Thank you."

The two detectives arrived promptly at seven. Sally took them into the living room, and they sat on the emerald green sofa. She sat on a matching chair.

"What can I get you to drink?" Sally asked.

"Nothing for me, thank you," Kirk said.

"Nothing for me, either. Thanks." John replied. "Is it okay if I tape our talk?"

Sally nodded.

"Do you want to talk separately to Bart and me?"

"Yes, please. We'll start with you." John laid the tape recorder on the coffee table and took out a pen and notebook. "Please tell me how you met Bob Lane."

"All of the diners and docents were volunteers at the Wornall House. We first met him at the Patron's Party a year ago and we've seen him at various other social events. Sometimes we were both volunteering at the Wornall House at the same time. In fact, not long ago, he and I worked together on a project."

"I know your husband is a dentist. Are you his nurse?"

"No. I'm a real estate agent. I sold Bob's house to him."

"Then you had a chance to get to know him. Did he tell you about his peanut allergy?"

"No he didn't tell me about it. We never had dinner together, so the subject didn't come up. Most of our conversation was about houses."

"I'm interested in learning everything I can about Mr. Lane, no matter how insignificant it might be. What can you tell me about him?"

Sally got right to the point. "I think I've told you he might be involved with drugs."

"Yes, you mentioned it when we first spoke. Why do you think that?"

"Once when I was leading a tour through the Wornall House, I heard a woman tell him to get his drugs out of her house."

John asked, "Do you know the woman's name?"

"No. I didn't see them. I just heard their voices."

"Why haven't you called and given us this information?" Woods asked. "Didn't you know that withholding evidence from the police is a serious offence?"

"I'm sorry. I'll tell you everything else I know."

"Did you ever hear Mr. Lane talking to anyone else?" Kirk asked.

"I overheard him talking on his cell phone to someone. He said, 'Will you get out of my life and stay out?' I assumed he was talking to a woman."

"Do you think he was talking to Marianna Kelly?" John asked.

"I doubt it," Sally said. "He seemed to really like her. I imagine it was some woman he'd dated before he met Marianna."

"Do you know the names of any women he used to date?"

"No. We didn't know Bob very well. When I showed him a house, he met me there and we walked through it. Our conversation was always about houses. He never mentioned a woman's name to me."

John asked, "Is there anything else you can tell us about Mr. Lane?"

"He paid cash for his house."

"That's interesting." John made a note of it. "Do you have any idea why somebody might want to kill him?"

"No. I've told you all I know about him. I have no idea who'd want to kill him unless it had something to do with drugs or jealousy."

"Thank you for your time, Mrs. Ashley," John said. "Here's my card. Please call me if you hear anything about Bob that might help our investigation. Now, may we speak to your husband?"

Sally took his card and put it in her pocket. She stood. "I'll tell Bart to come in." She went to the hallway, and yelled, "Bart, come into the living room, please."

When Bart entered the room, he shook hands with the two detectives. Sally left the room. Bart sat down in the chair Sally had vacated. "What can I do for you?"

"We're interested in learning everything we can about Bob Lane. Is there anything you can tell us about him or anything you've heard others say about him?"

"I've told you that my wife thought he was running drugs."

"Does she have any proof?"Woods asked.

"I doubt it."

Woods laughed. "Did Bob ever talk to you about his business?"

"When we played golf, he said he had to make a lot of business trips to Mexico, but he didn't mention drugs, of course."

"Did you ever see him smoking pot?" Woods asked.

"No, but one day I saw him sitting in his car and I thought he was snorting coke."

"Were you close enough to see that the substance he was using was cocaine?"

"No. I shouldn't have mentioned it," Bart said.

"It isn't evidence, unless you know for sure. It wouldn't hold up in a court of law."

"I realize that."

"Here's my card. If there's anything else you hear or remember that you think would help us with this case, please call me."

"I will." Bart put the card in his billfold.

Preston thanked him for his time, and he and Woods left for their next appointment.

CHAPTER SIXTEEN

Rhonda always read her e-mails around nine o'clock at night. She enjoyed the jokes and laughed heartily at many of them. She also enjoyed reading notes from friends. Tonight there was an e-mail from Patricia Garson, whose husband, Gregory, was a lie detector specialist. She and Pat had become friends when they were neighbors in Guanajuato, Mexico, and they had kept in touch by e-mail.

Pat wrote that she and Gregory were going to Kansas City in two days and they'd like to invite them out for dinner one evening while they were there.

Rhonda wrote back and asked them to stay at their home while they were in town. "We'll have the guest room ready for you and a roast in the oven. Will you be flying in or driving?"

Pat accepted the invitation and said they'd be driving. She added, "I know you've been volunteering at the Wornall House. You said you were scheduled to make a talk there about 'Quick & Easy Cooking,' so that gave me an idea. Do you think the director would invite Gregory to speak about polygraph exams?"

Rhonda replied, "I'll e-mail Jamie right now and ask her. I'll bet she'd like that. I'll get back to you as soon as I hear from her. I'm so glad you're coming." Rhonda also wrote all the details to Pat about Bob Lane's murder and told her she was unofficially trying to help her homicide detective son-in-law with his case.

Pat wrote that Greg would have all of his lie detector equipment with him. He said he'd volunteer to test John's suspects if he wanted him to."

Rhonda was quite excited about that and she wrote to thank them. Patricia wrote back that John would have to get permission from the chief of police before Gregory would be allowed to test anyone.

Rhonda wrote a quick e-mail to John about the offer of polygraph tests, and forwarded Pat's e-mails to him.

Before reading her other e-mails, she wrote Jamie about the expert polygraph examiner who was willing to make a talk about lie detector tests, and told her which days he'd be in town.

When Rhonda climbed into bed beside Rick, she told him all about Patricia's e-mails. She belatedly asked, "Is it okay with you if they stay with us?"

"Sure. It will be fun to have them here."

Just then the phone rang. It was John. "I hope I didn't call too late."

"I'm awake. What's up?"

"I just read your e-mails from Pat about the poly exams. I think it's a great idea. I'll have to talk to the boss in the morning and see what he says. I'll call you after he and I discuss it."

"Okay. Thanks."

"See you later. Bye."

Within minutes the phone rang again. It was Jamie. "Hi, Rhonda. I just read your email about the polygraph expert. I think it would be great to have Gregory speak about lie detector tests, especially since we've just had a murder in the house. Ask him if he could speak Thursday evening at seven. Maybe he can bring his machine and give you a poly exam!"

Rhonda laughed, "Not me! Let's ask for a volunteer."

"When he lets you know if Thursday is good for him, I'll send out emails, make phone calls, and put it on Facebook. We won't have time to mail cards or advertise it in the paper. I'll try to get all of the suspects and the witnesses to attend his lecture."

"That's a great idea."

"You can tell Gregory that I'll be his guinea pig. He can wire me up and give me the test at the end of his speech so everyone can see how it's done."

"Good way to end the talk. I'll tell him."

"Thanks for the idea. Goodnight, Rhonda."

"Goodnight."

Rhonda glanced over at Rick. He'd slept through both phone calls. She slipped out of bed and went to her office. She booted up the computer again and e-mailed Pat that the talk was on, and to wind it up, Jamie had volunteered to take the lie detector test.

As luck would have it, Pat was still reading her emails. She replied to Rhonda that Gregory said Thursday was fine.

Before going back to bed, Rhonda e-mailed Jamie. She wrote that Gregory and Pat would be at the Wornall House on Thursday night at seven o'clock with the poly machine in his hand.

Two days later, Gregory and Pat arrived at their home. They hugged Rick and Rhonda.

"I'm so happy you could come," Rhonda said.

"You were nice to invite us," Gregory said, smiling.

Pat handed Rhonda a box. "This is for both of you."

Rhonda exclaimed, "Godiva Chocolates! My favorite! Thank you very much."

"My favorite, too," Rick said. "Thanks."

Pat looked around and said, "We're planning to build a new home next summer, so I'm paying special attention to houses. I love your center hall plan, with the living room on the right of the foyer and the dining room on the left."

"Thanks. Come on in and make yourselves at home. I'll show you around later. Right now you probably want to take your suitcases upstairs to your bedroom. First room on the left and the guest bathroom is next door. When you come down, I'll have a snack in the family room to tide us over until dinner."

While they were upstairs, Rhonda went into the family room and fluffed the pillows on the red sofa. Red was her favorite color. Her kitchen walls were painted red and she carried that color scheme on into the family room. A red and ivory Oriental rug covered the hardwood floor. The Eastlake sofa, loveseat, and chairs were upholstered in red velvet. Framed pictures of hunting scenes with men in red jackets hung over the fireplace and decorated the paneled walls. Ivory and red chairs set on either side of the fireplace.

When Gregory and Pat came downstairs, Rick and the two poodles joined them. Rhonda handed everyone a glass of freshly made limeade, with a scoop of lime sherbet and a maraschino cherry floating in it.

Pat took a sip. "Oh, this tastes yummy. So refreshing."

"There's a sandwich shop called Winsteads at the Plaza that serves great hamburgers and they make their limeades like this." Rhonda placed a platter of Brie cheese, red seedless grapes, and crackers on the large round marble-topped coffee table. There were red napkins, silver coasters, and four small Wedgewood plates on the table so they could serve themselves.

Gregory sliced off a wedge of cheese and placed it on a plate with some crackers and a clump of grapes. Before he took a bite, he looked around the room and said, "Red is a lively color. It energizes me."

"It energizes me, too," Rhonda replied, smiling.

"It's fortunate that I like red, too, since we have a lot of it!" Rick said with a grin.

"Your poodles are so pretty," Pat said. "I remember the black dog, but isn't the champagne poodle a new one?"

"Yes, and he's a sweetheart. We're crazy about him. We adopted him in Guanajuato. His owner had to go into a mental facility and her brother was going to have him put to sleep. We were asked if we'd take him, and we're sure glad we did."

Patricia asked, "Have there been any new developments in the peanut murder case since I last talked to you?"

"Yes. We learned that Bob was mixed up in the drug trade."

"What a shame! Who was involved in it with him?"

"John doesn't know yet," Rhonda replied, "but he has some suspects."

"Greg, that's where your poly machine may come in handy, though large city forces often have their own examiners. What did John say?"

Rhonda said, "He seemed excited about the idea, but he has to ask the chief for special permission to use Greg's services."

"Greg is the crème de la crème of polygraph examiners!" Patricia bragged.

Rhonda grinned, "Then let's hope the chief agrees."

Gregory smiled. "Patricia is prejudiced. I imagine both the chief and John will want to discuss it with me."

"When can you talk to John?"

"Anytime."

"Well, I'll call him right now while I'm thinking about it, and tell him you're in town. Don't want any grass to grow under my feet! Excuse me." Rhonda picked up the phone and dialed.

John answered on the third ring. "Hi, John. I thought you'd like to know that Gregory and Patricia are here. Would you like to talk to Greg about the poly tests now? You would? I'll give him the phone in a minute. First, I want to tell you you're invited to come over and eat roast beef with us and talk to him after dinner, if you wish. I know you love roast."

Rhonda listened to his reply, and said, "You will? Great! I'll give Gregory the phone. He's right here. Talk to you later." She handed the phone to Gregory.

After Gregory finished talking to John, Patricia asked, "Is he coming for dinner?"

"Yes, he said he can't pass up a roast beef dinner. He isn't going to bring Nikki and the kids, though. They had other plans. Some church activity."

After eating a dinner of beef, mashed potatoes and gravy, salad, green beans, and cherry cobbler a la mode, Greg and John moved to the office for their talk. Rick offered to do dishes so Patricia and Rhonda could take the dogs on a walk through the neighborhood.

As they walked, Pat said, "Greg is in his element when he's giving polygraph exams and solving crimes."

"Didn't you tell me he's also a homicide detective?"

"That's right."

"Then he and John will have a lot to talk about. John has only been working at the station for about six months, and he wants to quickly solve this crime to impress them."

"That will do it!" Pat replied with a chuckle.

"Would you and Greg like to go for a tour of Kansas City with us tomorrow and then out to lunch?" Rhonda asked.

"That sounds great. I've heard that Kansas City is a beautiful place."

CHAPTER SEVENTEEN

On Thursday night, Gregory, Patricia, Rhonda and Rick arrived at the Wornall House for Greg's speech. They were a few minutes early. There were about twenty people seated in folding chairs in the family room. Rhonda looked around the room to see how many of the suspects were present. She counted six.

Jamie offered each person coffee or punch and Patricia was asked to pass around a platter of hors'douvres.

At seven, Jamie introduced Gregory as Rhonda and Rick's friend. She added, "He's a homicide detective and a lie detector genius. She added, "He's a highly respected and nationally recognized expert polygraph examiner. He's administered thousands of polygraph exams during his twenty five years of lie detection experience."

There was a polite applause.

Gregory came to the front of the room and smiled at the audience. He turned to Jamie and said, "Thank you for your kind introduction and for having me here tonight."

He began, "Another name for the lie detector test is the polygraph examination. Some people call it the poly, for short. The word 'polygraph' literally means 'many writings,' which refers to the method of recording several physiological activities at the same time.

"Polygraphs, often called lie detectors, are instruments that monitor a person's physiological reactions. They do not detect lies, as the name implies. They can only detect whether a person is displaying deceptive behavior.

"A polygraph machine records the body's involuntary responses to an examiner's questions in order to ascertain deceptive behavior. The test measures physiological data from three or more systems of the human body, generally the respiratory, cardiovascular, and sweat gland systems.

"Polygraph testing is mainly done for law enforcement, judicial, and private business sector purposes.

"The polygraph technique is highly accurate, but errors can occur. According to the American Polygraph Association, over 250 studies have been conducted on the accuracy of polygraph testing. Recent research reveals that the accuracy of the new computerized polygraph system is close to 100%. Errors that occur are usually due to inexperienced polygraph examiners. Just as one doctor can look at an x-ray and not see a problem, a more experienced doctor can look at that same x-ray and see exactly what the problem is. So it is with polygraph charts.

Gregory told several anecdotes about how polygraph tests helped find a suspect guilty. One of the stories he told was about a FBI agent named Robert Hanssen who had led a double life as a Russian spy for fifteen years, and how the poly exam helped bring him to justice.

Gregory spoke for twenty minutes, then asked if there were questions.

Bart raised his hand and asked, "How can a polygraph machine tell if a person is lying?"

Gregory replied, "The machine records the body's involuntary responses to my questions, and it measures changes in blood pressure, breath rate, and respiration rate. When a person lies, it's assumed that these changes occur in such a way that a trained expert can tell if the person is lying."

Marianna raised her hand. "Do polygraph examiners have to be licensed?"

"Absolutely," Gregory replied. "Most states insist that examiners must qualify for a license to conduct exams."

Rhonda asked, "I've heard that polygraph tests are inadmissible as evidence in court. Is that true?"

"Many people believe that, but the truth is that polygraph results are admissible in most courts. The Supreme Court has not yet ruled on the issue of admissibility, so it's been up to individual jurisdictions to allow or disallow them. Both the plaintiff and the defendant have to agree for the results to be used in court."

"Have you had pretty good luck with your examinations?" John asked.

"I've had 92% success rate," Gregory replied.

"That tells me you're very good."

Gregory grinned. "Thank you. If I do say so myself, I'm an expert in my field."

When there weren't any other questions, Jamie raised her hand. "Would you like to give me a lie detector test, so the crowd can see how it's done?"

"I think that's a great idea. Come on up."

Gregory proceeded to give Jamie a professional polygraph examination, which interested everyone, and when he'd finished, he announced that she'd passed the test.

After his talk was finished, Rick, Rhonda, Patricia and Gregory piled into Rick's van. Suddenly, Rhonda groaned, "Oh, no, I left my purse inside. I'll run in and get it. Be right back."

Rhonda opened the car door and hopped out. She dashed back into the house and went to the room where the talk was held. Her purse was not there. She thought that Jamie had probably found it and had taken it upstairs to her office, so she ran up the stairs to ask her about it.

She was surprised that nobody was in the office. She glanced around the room, but didn't see her purse. She decided to go downstairs and check the kitchen. Perhaps somebody was in there who knew where her purse was. Just as she walked through the master bedroom to the hallway between the outside balcony and the staircase, she felt strong hands against her back. Somebody was trying to push her over the banister.

Rhonda screamed and fought back. As she struggled with her assailant, she turned around and got a quick glance of someone with a ski mask pulled over their face. The person then fled down the stairs and out the back doorway.

Rhonda was not brave. She didn't follow the assailant. Instead, she ran down the stairs and out the front door. She raced to their van and yelled, "Somebody tried to kill me. She tried to push me over the upstairs railing!"

Gregory didn't question her. He yanked open the door, jumped out, and ran back into the house. Rick and Pat followed him. Rhonda wasn't going to sit in the car all alone, so she ran behind them. Gregory was a homicide detective as well as a polygraph examiner, and Rhonda felt safe with him around. He and the others were met at the front door by Jamie.

Gregory said, "I'm going to search the rooms," and without further ado, he and Rick ran upstairs together.

Jamie asked, "What happened? I thought I heard somebody scream."

"I'm the one who screamed," Rhonda said. "I came back to the house to get my purse and somebody attacked me. I think it was a woman. She tried to push me over the banister from the top of the stairs." She pointed up the stairs to the place where she'd nearly met her Waterloo.

"Oh, no! Are you okay?" Jamie asked.

"I'm fine."

"I put your purse in a closet that locks."

"That was thoughtful. Thank you."

"Did you see who attacked you?"

"Not really. When I screamed and struggled with the assailant, he or she turned loose of me and ran down the stairs. The person was about my height and had a ski cap over her head."

"I'm going to call Detective Preston," Jamie said. "He should know about this attack."

Now that she was surrounded by people, Rhonda was feeling braver. "Oh, let's don't bother Preston. I'm okay. All's well that ends well."

"No. I'm going to call him. If you'd been pushed over that railing, you could've broken your back or been killed."

Jamie phoned Detective Preston and explained what had happened. "He wants to talk to you, Rhonda." Jamie handed the phone to her.

"Hello, this is Rhonda. I'm okay, but I can't imagine why anyone would want to kill me."

Preston said, "It was probably the same person who killed Bob. Maybe the assailant was angry with you because you were responsible for bringing Gregory here tonight. He might've tried to pitch you over the banister because you asked Gregory to give lie detector tests to the six suspects."

"That must be the reason. Gregory and Rick are searching the house, but I imagine she was wearing gloves, so why don't we just forget this? I'll write up and sign a statement tonight while things are fresh in my mind, and I'll give it to you tomorrow for your records. No, you don't need to come to my house tonight. That's not necessary, but thanks for offering. You're tired, and Gregory and Rick will be there."

After they ended their conversation, Rhonda returned Jamie's phone to her.

"Thanks. I think I hear Gregory coming."

When Gregory came into the foyer he said, "We've searched all of the rooms in the house, but didn't find anyone. I imagine he or she's long gone."

Jamie said, "Yes, I think so, too. Before I forget it, I'll go to the closet and get your purse." She went after it, then returned and gave the purse to Rhonda.

"Thank you. I'm sorry I left it here and caused all this trouble. That creep scared the daylights out of me!"

"I would've been scared, too. Is Preston coming here tonight?"

"No," Rhonda said. "He said he'll stop by my house in the morning, so you can go ahead and lock up. I hope I'm not next on the killer's list."

CHAPTER EIGHTEEN

THE NEXT MORNING, DETECTIVES JOHN Preston and Kirk Woods stopped by Rhonda's home and talked to her about the attempt on her life. Woods warned her not to go out alone. Preston picked up her signed statement about the villain who tried to push her over the railing at the Wornall House, then took it to his car and put it in his attaché case.

Preston then called Marianna. "Hello, Mrs. Kelly. This is Detective John Preston. Could Detective Kirk Woods and I stop by your house for a short talk?"

"Yes. When would you like to come? This is my day off, so I'm going to be home most of the day."

"I'm just leaving Rhonda Winters's house. Could I come right over?" John asked.

"Yes. That would be fine."

When the two detectives arrived and were seated at the kitchen table with a cup of coffee in front of each of them, John asked, "Do you know the names of the women who Bob Lane dated before you met him?"

"I think he dated two women after his divorce before I met him, but he didn't tell me their names."

"Do you remember where they worked?"

"Once he mentioned that he'd dated a chef, but I don't know the name of the restaurant where she worked."

"Could it have been Mandy Todd, the volunteer cook at the Wornall House?"

"I don't know. I didn't know she'd dated him."

"Can you think of anything about Mr. Lane that could help with our investigation?"

"Just as you asked that question, a memory popped into my mind. One night we were in Bob's car and we were on our way to a movie theatre when he got a call on his cell phone. Since I was sitting next to him, it was easy for me to hear some of the conversation. The call was from a woman who sounded angry. At one point, she was almost screaming at him. He finally just hung up on her."

"Was it his ex-wife?"

"No. He apologized for taking the call and said she was a woman he'd dated after his divorce was final. I heard her say something about coke."

"Do you think she was talking about a Coca Cola or some cocaine?" Kirk asked, grinning.

Marianna laughed. "I don't think it was Coca Cola since she said she was bringing a hundred pounds of it back to Kansas City!"

"Oh? What else did she say?" John asked, interested.

"He asked her if she was in Laredo, Texas. She told him she was in Nuevo Laredo, which is over the border in Mexico."

Kirk let her know he knew where that city was located when he said, "Nuevo Laredo's a dangerous city. There's lots of drugs, murders, and kidnappings there."

"What was she screaming at Mr. Lane?"John asked.

"She yelled, 'I can't believe how you've treated me after all I've done for you! I'll make you sorry for dropping me like a hot potato'!"

"Interesting," Woods nodded.

"I guess her call made Bob angry because he hung up on her."

"He probably hung up because he was afraid you'd heard enough of the conversation to put two and two together," John said, bluntly.

Marianna nodded. "Apparently Bob wasn't the nice man I thought he was."

John shook his head. "Don't waste time grieving for him."

Marianna replied, "I won't anymore."

Kirk asked, "Do you know the names of the docents who volunteered the night Bob died?"

"I know their faces, but not their names. Jamie and Anna would know. I hope you're going to check them out. So far, your attention seems to have been focused on us diners, though the docents and the cooks had the best chance of slipping peanuts into the cider."

"We're focusing our attention on everyone who was in the Wornall House that night," John assured her. "If you think of anything else, please call me. Here's my card."

"I will," Marianna said, and put his card in her pocket.

They thanked her for her time and left.

A few minutes later, Marianna called Rhonda. "Hello! This is Marianna. Can you and Rick come to dinner on Saturday evening?"

Rhonda checked the calendar and said, "We'd love to come. What shall I bring?"

"How about a cheesecake?"

"Okay, and I'll bring strawberries for the topping."

Sounds great. I'll invite Bart and Sally, too. See you Saturday at seven."

"We'll be there, and when I see you, I'll tell you about a scare I had last night."

CHAPTER NINETEEN

RHONDA WENT INTO THE FAMILY room where Gregory and Patricia were watching the news with Rick. When a commercial came on, she asked, "Gregory, how was your visit with the chief?"

"He's a nice man. As it turned out, the chief was in the audience at the Wornall House last night when I made the talk. I had no idea he'd be there. He said he was impressed with what I had to say and that he wants John and Kirk to offer the poly exams to all of the suspects and the witnesses. They'll all be contacted today and I'll give the tests tonight and tomorrow. Some people won't be too happy about taking the tests on Saturday."

"What do you mean by 'offering the tests'?" Rhonda asked.

"We can't force anyone to take the test, but we can offer it to all of them."

"I'd think that if a person refused to take the test, he'd be a prime suspect," Rhonda said.

"Not necessarily. The test can make people nervous and they might refuse for that reason."

"I see your point. I wouldn't want to take it, either," she admitted. "I haven't been contacted. When do you want Rick and me to take the exam?"

"John said you two don't have to take it, because you guys aren't suspects."

"Thanks. I was dreading to take it, but I'm willing."

"No. I have too much to do already. Just forget it. If anyone asks how you did on the test, tell them that Gregory said you passed it!"

"Marianna is giving a dinner party for the dining room suspects, which includes Rick and me. I'm sure she would be happy to have you two come for dinner. I'll call her and tell her I have guests."

"No, thanks. I'll be involved with the poly exams all day and possibly even as late as nine o'clock, so I can't go," Gregory said.

"What about you, Patricia?"

"Thanks, anyway, but I think I'll go to Winsteads for a hamburger and a chocolate malt tomorrow evening. Ever since you mentioned that place I've been hungry for a burger. I'll pick one up for Gregory, too, and take it to him."

"That sounds good to me," Gregory said.

Well, that takes care of dinner for tomorrow night, Rhonda thought to herself. But what shall we have tonight?

Rhonda asked Gregory, "What time do you start giving polygraph exams tonight?"

"In one hour."

"Who's taking the tests tonight?"

"I have a list. He took a note out of his shirt pocket. "The ones who wanted the test tonight are Marianna, Sally, and Bart. I guess the rest are on for tomorrow."

"I haven't started cooking dinner. Is it okay if we just have ham and cheese sandwiches with a salad and brownies a la mode? I can have that ready in fifteen minutes."

Patricia said, "That's fine with us. By the way, we have to leave on Sunday."

"Then we'll have to catch the killer today or tomorrow!"

CHAPTER TWENTY

When Marianna's four guests arrived at her home, she invited them into her blue and white living room. They sat on the blue sofas and white chairs surrounding the large coffee table and chatted for awhile.

Marianna asked, "We're having Mexican food tonight. I have a casserole in the oven. Would you like to come and sit at the kitchen table and have some nachos and chips and dip?"

They moved to the large round table and Marianna asked, "What would you like to drink? I have Pepsi, cranberry juice, and ice tea." The guests gave her their order.

After Marianna had served the drinks, she said, "Since I don't serve wine and beer, I guess you can see I'm a teetotaler! Once when I was at a restaurant and the waiter asked if I'd like to order a before dinner drink, I said 'No, thanks. I'm a teetotaler.' So he brought me a cup of tea!"

Everyone laughed.

Sally said, "I guess he hadn't heard that expression."

"I was looking forward to meeting your children. Aren't they home?" Rhonda asked.

"No. Their grandmother invited them for dinner tonight. You'll meet them next time."

Bart said, "Since all of us are volunteers at the Wornall House, I thought you might be interested in hearing a story about John and Eliza Wornall's grandson, Kearney Wornall."

Rick said, "I'd like to hear it. I met Kearney about a year before he died. He was a true gentleman."

Bart began, "Not long after Kearney got a law degree from the University of Missouri, he worked as a cashier at the Army Bank in Camp Funston, Kansas. On January 11, 1918, while he and four other men were working at the bank, it was held up. The robber walked in the door holding a revolver and an ax. He ordered Wornall to tie up the other four men. Wornall did as he was told, then the robber grabbed the hand ax and used it to beat Wornall on the head until he fell unconscious to the floor. The robber hacked the other four men to death, and stole over sixty two thousand dollars before he left the bank.

When Wornall was found, he was still alive, and was taken to the hospital. He was the only survivor of the bank robbery.

It was soon discovered that the killer was an army officer, Captain Lewis Whisler, of Company E, 354th Infantry. The following day, his body and the bank's money were found in his office. He'd left a note admitting what he'd done, then presumably he had committed suicide.

The military police threw Whisler's body onto a stretcher and took his corpse to Wornall's hospital bedside. They asked Wornall if this was the man who robbed the bank and killed his co-workers. Though Wornall was weak and could hardly talk, he feebly nodded, identifing him.

People who knew Whisler had long believed he was mentally ill. His ex-wife said she couldn't imagine why the army had promoted him to captain.

Kearney Wornall was in the hospital for five months, but he survived. After he moved back to Kansas City, he became Chairman of the Board of the Wornall Bank, which he helped organize in 1920. He also helped organize the Broadway Bank, which merged with City National Bank. He served as vice president until he retired. He was a civic leader and president of several organizations. He died in 1975 at the age of eighty three."

"That was an interesting story, Bart," Marianna said. "Thank you for sharing it."

Sally changed the subject. "Detectives Preston and Woods interrogated us at our home one day this week."

"They were at my house, too," Marianna said.

"They were at our home yesterday," Rick said.

Marianna said, "I don't like being a suspect. I took the polygraph exam today."

"We took it, too," Bart said.

"We haven't had it yet," Rick said.

"I'm sure all of us will pass it," Marianna said. "I certainly don't think any of us killed him."

"Sally, why don't we invite the docents and the cooks to our house for dinner?" Bart asked. "Maybe we can learn something from them when they have their guard down."

Sally said, "Good idea. It's our turn to have the next dinner."

Marianna said, "I'm sorry to interrupt, but dinner is going to be cold if we don't eat now. I hope everyone likes Mexican food."

"I love it! Sally exclaimed.

"I'm glad. Let's sit down at the dining table now."

When everyone was seated, Marianna said, "We're having beef enchiladas, tacos, salad, guacamole, and cheesecake. Oops! I nearly forgot to play the Mariachi CD that Bob brought back from Mexico." She got up and turned on the CD player.

The Mariachis began playing and singing such rousing Mexican favorites as "Cielito Lindo" and "Guadalajara."

"I love Mariachi music. This is a treat," Rhonda said.

Marianna turned to Rhonda and asked, "Tell us what you and Rick do in Mexico."

"We're involved with a Mexican Baptist church. The Emmanuel Baptist Church in Overland Park, Kansas, has sent three medical mission groups to the Guanajuato Baptist Church. Another time they bought the building materials for a new Sunday school classroom and a bathroom while we were there. Emmanuel also collected about fifty bed sheets which we took to the orphanage.

"The orphans live mostly on beans, rice, and tortillas. I belong to the Arco Iris Club which helps the poor. They gave a picnic for the orphans, and we served them ham and cheese sandwiches, chips, and cookies, while some men painted one of the buildings. The club also bought about fifty blankets and collected clean used sheets to give to them."

Rhonda continued, "The director of the orphanage is called the Padre. He said the children were his family. He has a unique way of making money to pay the expenses of the orphanage. All of the kids join the choir, the orchestra, or the mariachi band. He takes the most talented musicians on concerts tours all over Mexico."

Marianna said, "That's a great idea."

Rick added, "The director said they have about three hundred children and the orphanage is financed by faith. It isn't sponsored either by the state of Guanajuato or by the Catholic Church. The director believes God will provide for their needs. And He has."

Marianna asked, "Do the children attend church?"

"Yes. A former governor of the state of Guanajuato has an American wife who built a large beautiful church on their property."

"How wonderful!" Marianna said. "Thanks for telling us about the orphanage and the church."

"I'm sorry I talked so long," Rhonda apologized. "Let me help clear the table and serve dessert."

After they'd finished the strawberry topped cheesecake, Sally said, "There's a Victorian Tea and Fashion Show tomorrow at the Wornall House. It starts at two in the afternoon. It might be an opportunity to find out a few things about the suspects!"

"In that case, I'm going!" Rhonda exclaimed. She reached in her pocket and turned on her tape recorder.

"So am I," Sally said. "Do you want to go with me, Rhonda?"

"Sure. We'll go sleuthing!" Rhonda said, laughing.

"That will be fun! Oh, I just remembered something I want to tell all of you," Sally said. "One day when I was volunteering, I overheard Bob talking to someone. You know Bob had a loud voice and his voice carried. I don't know who he was talking to, but he asked if he was supposed to take the COKE OUT OF THE COOKIES AND PUT IT IN THE SHOEBOXES. Does that make any sense to anyone? Do any of you know what he was talking about?"

CHAPTER TWENTY-ONE

When Rick and Rhonda returned home from Marianna's dinner, they joined Pat and Greg in the family room.

Rick said he was going to take the dogs for a walk. When he took out their leashes and halters, the poodles were so excitedly jumping up and down that Rhonda had to help him put their halters on. They loved to go for walks.

After they left, Pat said, "Caesar has the most beautiful brown eyes."

"Yes, he does," Rhonda said. "He's a lover. He'd sit in my lap all day long if I had time to hold him."

"Did you have a good time at the dinner?"Pat asked.

"Yes. The food was delicious."

"Do you suspect either Sally or Marianna?" Gregory asked curiously.

Rhonda said, "I have some suspicions. Marianna's a RN. Don't you think she should've known what was wrong with Bob that night he died? And if she did, why didn't she grab his epi pen out of his pocket and give him an injection? She could've saved his life."

"So you think Marianna is a suspect?" Pat asked.

"I don't know. Maybe. I like her and she seems to be a good woman, but I think she should've been able to help Bob. It bothers me that a RN didn't recognize his symptoms and fish that epi pen out of his pocket."

"Not every nurse knows about the seriousness of peanut allergies. She probably didn't have much training in allergic reactions. Isn't she a surgical nurse? What do you think about Sally?" Greg asked.

"Sally seems to have it in for Bob. I don't think she liked him, but I don't know why. There must've been something that happened between the two of them that we aren't aware of. She keeps hinting that he was involved in drugs."

"Well, he was, wasn't he?"Gregory asked.

"Yes, he was. Even though I have some misgivings about Marianna and Sally, I still think they're the least likely of all the suspects to have killed Bob."

Pat said, "Remember the killer is often the last person you'd expect."

"That's what I've heard."

"Oh, by the way, Greg, before I forget it, I want to ask you about the Voice Stress Analyzer Test. What do you know about that?"

"Every person's voice is as distinctive as their fingerprints or handwriting. The test measures the amount of stress in one's voice."

"Do you give those tests?"Rhonda asked.

"No. I only specialize in polygraph examinations."

"Can you tell us if all the suspects and witnesses took the poly exam?" Rhonda asked.

"Yes, they all took it."

"Did they all pass it? I'm asking because I want to find out who pushed me."

"Two flunked it, but I can't give you their names," Gregory said.

"Will you tell me if I guess correctly?" Rhonda asked, grinning impishly.

"No. I'm sorry. I can't."

Pat said, "I nearly forgot to tell you that Jason Valores called you from Guanajuato. He said he'd call back."

"Thank you. He must have some information for us. I'm sorry I missed him. I'll call him back since we have SKYPE. Skype can be used to call anywhere in the world for two cents a minute!"

"We use Skype for long distance calls, too. Is Jason going to help you with the Mexican drug connection?"

"I'm sure he will. He said he'd call when he learned something."

Rick returned home then from taking the two dogs for a walk. He took off their leashes and he and the dogs joined them in the family room. Caesar jumped into Rhonda's lap and put his head on her shoulder. Cleopatra sat beside Rick, who scratched her ears.

Changing the subject, Pat asked, "Are you going to the Victorian Tea and Fashion Show at the Wornall House tomorrow?"

"Yes, I'm planning to go. Would you two like to go with me?"

"Not me!" Gregory exclaimed. "That's a girly show!"

Rhonda giggled. "Pat, do you want to go to the girly show with me?"

"With pleasure." Pat joked, "I'm going to make sure nobody pushes you over the banister!"

Before Rhonda could reply, the phone rang. It was Sally. She called to tell Rhonda she'd pick her up at one thirty for the tea and fashion show."

"Thanks. Can my friend, Patricia, go with us?"

"Of course," Sally said.

The next day the three of them arrived at the Wornall House at two o'clock for tea. After everyone was seated at the dining room table and at small tables set up in the family room and the parlor, Earl Grey tea was served with tiny chicken salad sandwiches, cucumber sandwiches, scones with strawberry jam, tea cakes, and cookies.

While they ate, the moderator told them, "The custom of afternoon tea began in the mid 1800's. Lunch was usually served around noon, but the upper classes didn't eat dinner until nine o'clock in the evening. Anna, the seventh Duchess of Bedford, was too hungry to wait for dinner, and she asked her maid to serve hot tea with bread and butter to her in her boudoir every afternoon about four o'clock. Before long she expanded the menu and began to indulge in a mid-afternoon feast of tea, sandwiches, crumpets, muffins, and scones with jam and Devonshire cream.

The custom soon caught on, and the duchess began inviting her friends for Afternoon Tea. It became a fashionable past time for ladies of nineteenth century English society.

The moderator added, "Afternoon tea is not the same as High Tea, which is a full meal served at six o'clock in the evening."

Next, an eighteenth century tea etiquette lesson was presented, and also the ladies were taught how to flirt with their fans.

Tea cups were refilled and the Victorian fashion show began while the guests sipped their tea. The elegant models featured outfits from the early Victorian period. The women modeled everything from work clothes to ball gowns, to the proper attire for a widow.

Volunteers refilled tea cups and passed around platters of sandwiches, cookies, and tiny decorated cakes several times, so that everyone had all the tea and food they could eat. After the tea and the fashion show were over, guests were invited to tour the Wornall House.

After the tour, Rhonda suggested to Sally and Pat, "Let's take another look at that beautiful piano in the parlor. We rushed past it and I'd like to see it again."

Sally, who often led tours through the house, took them back to the parlor and said, "There's a well-known musician, Dr. Prince-Joseph, who's played several concerts of Civil War songs and Stephen Foster melodies here on this restored 1859 square Steinway piano. He also keeps the piano tuned for the Wornall House."

"I'm sorry I missed his concerts. I love those songs," Rhonda said.

"He's wonderful. You would enjoy his concerts very much."

While Sally and Pat stood in the parlor, talking, Rhonda went out on the front porch for a breath of fresh air. While she was out there, she called John on her cell and said, "I talked to Jason last night and he said he has some information for you. He wants to know the names of Bob's two truck drivers. He hinted that he'd come to Kansas City on his vacation if you think he could help you with the drug trafficking case."

John replied, "I'll get that information to him. Thanks, Mom."

"You're welcome. Bye."

Rhonda noticed it was starting to snow harder. She phoned Nikki and asked, "Can Rick and I take the kids sledding about four, then out for dinner?"

"Sure. They'd like that."

"How are they enjoying the snow? I know they didn't see much snow in San Antonio."

"They're outside building a snowman right now," Nikki said.

"I'm glad they're having fun. We'll be there at four. Bye, honey."

Rhonda went back inside and said, "The snow is really coming down."

"Maybe we'd better go," Sally said. "I'm not the world's best driver in snow."

As Sally, Pat and Rhonda walked to the car, Rhonda said, "Well, we didn't do any sleuthing."

"No. We were too busy drinking tea and eating that delicious food," Sally said.

"I overheard a conversation that might be of interest," Patricia said. "Unfortunately, I don't know the people's names, but a lady wearing a purple pant suit and an amethyst necklace and ring, said she'd heard that Bob's ex-wife, Karen, was the prime suspect in his murder and that she had flunked the lie detector test."

The next day, after a breakfast of cheese and bacon omelets, hash browns, and fresh fruit, Gregory and Patricia went to Wornall Road Baptist Church with Rick and Rhonda. Doctor John Mark Clifton preached an interesting sermon, as always.

Gregory insisted on taking Rick and Rhonda to a restaurant for lunch, so they went to Mimi's near the Oak Park Mall. They ordered roast turkey, which was served with dressing, cranberries, mashed potatoes, gravy, broccoli, rolls, and carrot cake.

When Gregory and Patricia returned to the house for their luggage, they thanked Rick and Rhonda for an enjoyable visit. They hugged them good bye, and warned Rhonda to be careful and not to go out alone. They promised to keep in touch by e-mail and Skype.

Rhonda said, "We appreciated your speech and the poly tests. I hope you'll come back soon. We'll have fun next time. You won't need to work."

"We had a great time," Pat assured her.

Gregory added, "I'm happiest when I'm working. John told me he thinks the poly exams have helped break the case. One of the persons who flunked the test is his prime suspect."

"Is it Karen?"

"Sorry, but I can't answer that question."

CHAPTER TWENTY-TWO

JASON PHONED RHONDA ON MONDAY morning and asked, "How's my favorite sleuth?"

"Feeling good!" she exclaimed.

"I have some news for you. The police raided a church service here in Guanajuato and arrested a drug smuggler who moves at least one thousand pounds of cocaine each month into the United States!"

"They raided a church service?" Rhonda gasped. "I'm amazed the police did that on Sunday."

"Sometimes you have to strike when the iron is hot, as you're fond of saying. The authorities arrested him and one of his cohorts right there during the mass, and they took thirty others in for questioning!"

Rhonda laughed. "I hope the police waited to make the arrest until after the collection plate was passed!"

"I hope they did, too!" Jason exclaimed. "Isn't it amazing how drug smugglers can sell drugs all week that ruin people's lives, then piously dress up in suits and go to church on Sunday?"

"Well, at least they went to church. I hope the sermon was about the Ten Commandments!"

"How's John doing with his peanut murder case?"Jason asked.

"He's been working on it for a week now. He's done background checks, reviewed the autopsy and lab reports, interviewed people, searched houses, and found cocaine packed with cookies in Bob's basement. The DEA was called and they did a search and seizure. Greg and Pat were here, but they've left. Greg gave lie detector tests to all of the suspects and witnesses to Bob's murder. Everybody took the test, but two flunked."

"Sounds like John's been busy."

"Yes, he has. Has your snitch given you any new information?"

"Yes, he has, and I need to call John about it. I've misplaced John's cell phone number. Can you give it to me again? I hope he and I can bust this Mexico-to-Kansas City drug smuggling ring wide open."

"Do you have paper and pen? Here's his number."

Rhonda gave him the number, then asked, "What info do you have?"

"John e-mailed the names of the two truck drivers to me and they are my two Guanajuato drug dealers. I need to talk to John about them."

"I wish you were here so you and John could catch these crooks and keep them out of Kansas City."

"I'll fly in if John wants me to come. I'm sure he's aware that tons of cocaine have already hit the streets of KC this year."

"I wasn't aware of that. Let us know when you're coming and we'll pick you up at the airport. I guess you know I'm going to be very upset if you don't stay with us."

"I'd like to stay with you and Rick. I love your good old fashioned country cooking."

"Like fried chicken, mashed potatoes, biscuits and gravy?"

"You're making me hungry. Does John have any idea yet who killed Bob?"

"He has a prime suspect. It's hard to believe any of the diners or docents killed him. They're all too respectable. Still you never know."

"It's unbelievable what can be learned about people when you dig into their past."

Rhonda told him about the attempt on her life at the Wornall House. "I could've been killed."

"That really upsets me. Please be careful and don't go anywhere by yourself."

"I won't. I have some funny drug stories for you, if you have time to hear them."

"Tell me. I'm not busy right now, and I could use a laugh."

"These are true stories. I read about them and cut them out of the newspapers. The first article stated that jars of peanut butter have been banned from state prisons in Tennessee because the inmates were concealing drugs in the peanut butter jars."

Jason chuckled.

"A second article said customs agents at the Port of New Orleans found about a thousand pounds of cocaine hidden in a shipment of Colombian coffee."

"Not surprising."

"The third one happened in Kansas City. A guy driving an ice cream truck was selling cocaine on the side. After he offered the drug to a parent buying ice cream for his son, the dad tipped off the police. The cops arrested the drug peddler for possession of a controlled substance. When they checked his records, they saw he had carefully kept separate accounts for the ice cream and the cocaine."

Jason laughed. "Those are good stories."

Rhonda said, "Isn't it unbelievable what smugglers will do to sell their drugs? I hope you come to K.C. soon."

"I'd love to come. Be careful. I'm worried about you. The killer must think you know something about him. Don't go out alone."

"I'll be careful."

"It was fun talking to you. Bye, Rhonda."

CHAPTER TWENTY-THREE

RHONDA SUDDENLY REMEMBERED HER PROMISE to Marianna. She'd promised to introduce her to a pediatrician at her church. She'd bragged about her talent as a matchmaker and she wanted to keep her word. If she hadn't been 98% positive that Marianna was innocent in Bob's death, she wouldn't have called him. She took out the church directory and looked up his name and phone number.

He answered the phone on the second ring. She greeted him and identified herself. "Do you have five minutes, or did I call at a bad time?"

"I have plenty of time, Rhonda. What's up?"

"I'd like to introduce you to a pretty nurse. Are you interested in a blind date? Before you answer, let me tell you she's a Christian, smart, friendly, pretty, and nice!"

"How can I pass that up?"

"I hope you won't."

"Has she been married before?"

"Yes. Her husband was killed in a car wreck. She has two children."

"I like children, so that's no problem. Sure, I'd like to meet her."

"If you have a pen, I'll give you her name and phone number." She gave him the information and he wrote it down, then read it back to her.

"I'll call her tonight. Thank you for thinking of me. I don't have children, and since my wife died, I've been rather lonely."

"Marianna's probably lonely, too. I think you'll like her. My five minutes are up, so I'm going to say good night."

"Thanks again, Rhonda. Goodnight."

About thirty minutes later, the phone rang, and it was Marianna. "I just wanted to thank you for matchmaking. Jack seems very nice. He's taking me to dinner tomorrow night, and he offered to take the kids with us."

"He is nice. I hope you'll have a good time."

"I'll send you an e-mail tomorrow night after I get home, and give you a report!"

"Okay! Don't forget."

After Marianna said goodnight, Rhonda called John. When he answered she said, "Jason called today. He said he has some information for you. He wanted your cell phone number. If you invite him to come to Kansas City, he can stay with us."

"I'd like for him to come. I'll call him and invite him. Thanks, Mom."

Rhonda had just hung up the phone when it rang again. It was her grandson Jeffrey. He said, "Nana, I don't know how to do my math homework. Could Papa Rick help me?"

"Sure. He'll pick you up, and after you finish your homework, we'll go out for dinner."

"Oh, good!" Jeffrey exclaimed. "Can we go to Waids? I like their home cooking!"

"I know you like their grilled chicken with mashed potatoes and gravy."

"Yes, I do. After dinner can we go to your house and make peanut Butter cookies?"

She agreed, and after dinner, Jeffrey made and baked a batch of peanut butter cookies.

"These are so easy, Nana," Jeffrey said as he took a bowl and mixed together one cup of peanut butter, one cup of sugar, and one egg. He shaped the dough into balls and arranged them on a greased cookie sheet. He used a fork to flatten them and make a criss-cross design. He baked them at 375 degrees for ten minutes.

As Jeffrey ate one, he said, "I can't believe these cookies only have three ingredients!"

CHAPTER TWENTY-FOUR

A few weeks ago, Rhonda's six year old grandson, Jeremy, had asked her if she would go on a school field trip with him to the Wornall House Museum on the tenth of December , and she had agreed to go. Today was the big day. Rhonda arrived early at the school so she could help the teacher load the kids onto the bus.

Jeremy sat beside Rhonda on the bus. He tucked his hand into hers. "I'm glad you came with us, Nana."

They stopped talking when Jeremy's teacher, Mrs. Carroll, stood at the front of the bus and spoke into a microphone. "Today, we're going to see a house that was built about one hundred and fifty years ago by John Bristow Wornall, the man whom Wornall Road is named for. When we arrive at the Wornall House, we'll go on a tour with a tour guide who's called a docent. I think you'll especially enjoy the open-hearth cooking demonstration in the kitchen.

One of the children named Kenny raised his hand. "What's an open hearth?"

"When this house was built, there were no electric or gas cooking stoves. Eliza and Roma Wornall had to cook in the fireplace when they lived there. I was told that the cook will be baking cookies in the fireplace. If you're good, she'll probably give one to each of you."

After the bus parked beside the Wornall House, the children climbed out and walked single file up to the front door. The docent saw them coming and opened the door for them. They were ushered into the foyer, and she introduced herself as Mrs. Davis.

Mrs. Davis said, "Before we tour the house, I'm going to tell you some stories about Mr. John Bristow Wornall, the man who built this house. Many years ago, Mr. Wornall's family came from England to Virginia. Later, they moved to Kentucky, where they lived on a large farm. John Wornall was born there. His parents were Richard and Judith Ann Glover Wornall. They had bad luck in Kentucky. There'd been a severe drought and they lost their crops, so they decided to move west to Missouri. Who knows what a severe drought is?"

Jeremy raised his hand and said, "Severe means very bad, and a drought means there was no rain for a long time."

"That was a good answer, young man."

"Thank you. I'm very smart."

Mrs. Davis's lips twitched as she tried not to grin. She continued, John Wornall was only twenty-one years old in 1843 when he and his family moved to Missouri. Richard Wornall bought five hundred acres and a four room cabin from John McCoy.

It wasn't long before the Wornall family had more bad luck. Both Richard Wornall's wife and his son died. He was so sad he gave his farm to his only living son, John, and he returned to Kentucky.

John was married three times. Matilda Polk, his first wife, died one year later. Next he married Eliza Johnson and five of their seven children died when they were very young. Then Eliza died when she was only twenty nine years old. The next year, John married his third wife, Roma Johnson. Roma was a good mother to John and Eliza's two sons, and she and John had two more sons.

John was a very religious man. He climbed out of bed every morning singing hymns. He took his family to the Baptist church in Westport every Sunday. God blessed him and he became president of a bank and a Missouri state senator."

"Now we'll go on a tour of Mr. Wornall's home. The first room we'll see is the parlor."

"What's a parlor?" Ruby asked.

"A parlor is like the living room in your home. Now, I want you to look at the three portraits on this lovely antique table," Mrs. Davis said, pointing. "These are pictures of John Wornall, Eliza Wornall, and Roma Wornall. The originals were painted by the most famous

Missouri artist of his time, George Caleb Bingham, who was John Wornall's friend.

"Mr. Wornall was married to Eliza when the Civil War started. Colonel Jennison of the Union Army and his two hundred soldiers took over the Wornall House and farm for eight days. The soldiers killed livestock and destroyed the crops. The colonel used this parlor as his office, he slept upstairs in the Wornall's bedroom, and Eliza had to cook for him and his men.

"During the Battle of Westport, this house was turned into a hospital, and many soldiers died here.

Glenna raised her hand. "I heard if people die in a house, they come back as a ghost. Do you think there are ghosts in the Wornall House?"

Mrs. Davis replied, "I don't believe in ghosts. Let's walk across the hall to the family room. All of the furniture in this room dates back to the time of the Civil War. I want to tell you a story about what happened to Mr. Wornall one Sunday morning. His family was in a carriage on their way to church when some bad men called Bushwhackers stopped him. They told him to go home and unlock his door. He did as he was told, and they robbed him. Hans, who was one of Mr. Wornall's hired men, sneaked out of the house and ran for help. Fortunately, the Bushwhackers didn't see him leave. They told Mr. Wornall they'd heard he'd buried money in his garden, and if he didn't get it for them they'd kill him. When he said he'd never buried money anywhere, they put a rope around his neck and threatened to hang him. Just as the Bushwhackers started to tie the other end of the rope around the balcony and hang him, Hans and some soldiers rode up. They had loaded guns and they threatened to shoot the Bushwhackers, so the Bushwhackers jumped on their horses and galloped away. Hans saved Mr. Wornall's life!"

The children applauded.

Jimmy asked "Did any of Mr. Wornall's sons fight in the Civil War?"

Mrs. Davis said, "No, they were too young. Let's walk upstairs and I'll show you the boys' bedroom." After they climbed the stairs, she pointed to the balcony. "The Bushwhackers had planned to hang Mr. Wornall from this balcony."

"This balcony is also the place where Frank, Mr. Wornall's oldest son, was standing when he got his dad into trouble. Frank was only about seven years old at that time. When some Union soldiers were riding past their house, Frank was dared by a girl, named Mittie Pigg, who was staying at their home, to yell, "Hurrah for Jefferson Davis!" Frank took the dare, and he yelled as loudly as he could, "Hurrah for Jefferson Davis!" The soldiers stopped and glared at Frank, but then rode on. However, later that day, those soldiers returned to the house and marched Mr. Wornall away at gun point. They threatened to shoot him over the incident. When he was gone, Frank and Eliza prayed that God would take care of Mr. Wornall, and God answered their prayers. The soldiers turned Mr. Wornall loose, and about an hour later, he returned home."

Janice exclaimed, "I'll bet Frank got a spanking!"

Mrs. Davis grinned, "He probably did! Now let's go into the children's bedroom so you can see where Frank slept."

From there, she showed them John and Eliza's bedroom and told them this is where Colonel Jennison slept when he and his soldiers took over the house.

"Let's go back downstairs and see the rest of the house." The children followed her into the dining room. "This is where the Wornall family ate their meals."

Next, Mrs. Davis brought the children to the restored kitchen at the back of the house. A volunteer cook, who was dressed in a long dress, an apron, and a gingham bonnet of the style worn in the 1860's, had been waiting for them.

She smiled, greeted them, and introduced herself. "Hi, everyone! My name is Mrs. Todd. You guys are lucky that you came today because this is the day I give an open-hearth cooking demonstration. I'll show you how Eliza and Roma Wornall cooked in this very fireplace. Notice that the fireplace is fitted with a crane for cooking." She pointed to the crane. "See this iron kettle hanging over the hot coals. Both Eliza and Roma used one like this to steam a Christmas Plum Pudding. Look at this pot. It's called a Dutch oven. Mrs. Wornall baked pies and cookies in it. Now, I'm going to mix up some cookie dough and bake Quaker cookies for you."

Regina asked, "Do they have chocolate chips in them? I love chocolate chip cookies!"

Mrs. Todd shook her head. "There weren't any chocolate chips in the 1800's. The recipe I'm making is about one hundred and fifty years old. It's similar to Oatmeal-Raisin cookies. I'll show you how to make them."

She demonstrated by taking a mixing bowl and combining brown sugar and shortening together. She stirred in beaten eggs, molasses, and vanilla. Then she mixed in flour, soda, salt, and cinnamon. Last of all, she stirred in the oatmeal and raisins.

Mrs. Todd said, "Pecans or walnuts could be added, but sometimes people are allergic to nuts, so we don't use them in this kitchen."

She shaped the dough into balls, rolled each in sugar, placed them on a greased Dutch oven, and flattened them with her fingers. The cookies were baked over hot coals in the fireplace.

Mrs. Todd said, "The Wornall House is the only historic home in the Kansas City area with an open hearth cooking program. Family cooking in 1858 was nearly a full time job. Since there's no running water in the house, water had to be carried into the kitchen. The fire had to be started hours before the food could be cooked so the coals would be just the right heat. It was in this fireplace that Eliza Wornall prepared breakfast for both the wounded Union and the Confederate soldiers while the Battle of Westport was fought. Also, it was here that Eliza prepared meals for Colonel Jennison and his troops. Eliza was said to be a very good cook."

Billy raised his hand and asked, "Why is there a door lying on the floor in this kitchen?"

Mrs. Todd explained, "There's a root cellar underneath the kitchen floor. Notice the metal ring on the door. Watch while I grasp that metal ring and pull the door up and back and lay it flat on the floor. There were steps leading downstairs to the floor of the cellar. The floors and walls are made of concrete."

"Can we go down there?" Ernie asked.

"No, there's a furnace down there now, but in 1858, when the house was built, it was heated only by the three fireplaces. When the Wornalls lived in this house, the cellar served a dual purpose. It was both a storm cellar and storage for canned foods, potatoes, apples, and dried fruit. Eliza and her son, Frank, hid in this cellar while the Battle of Westport was raging nearby.

Betty Jean pointed to an unusual looking table and asked, "What's that used for?"

"That's a sugar safe. Sugar was very expensive back then and hard to get, so it was locked up in the sugar safe. Only the lady of the house had the key to it, and she probably kept it hidden."

"What's the other little table?" Mary Sue asked, pointing.

"That's the beaten biscuit machine. Without that machine, it would take strong arms to beat the biscuits. The Wornalls loved to eat biscuits for breakfast and for dinner with fried chicken and mashed potatoes. Oh! I'd better check the Quaker Cookies! We don't want to eat burnt cookies, do we?"

The children shouted in unison, "No!"

Mrs. Todd checked the cookies. "They're ready," she said, "and they're just perfect!" She used a spatula to lift the cookies onto a platter. She handed the platter to Jeremy. "Will you pass these cookies around and let each person take one?"

"Yes, Ma'am!" he exclaimed, pleased that she had asked him. He gave one to each of the students.

Janice said, "These are so good. I wish we could have another one."

"I'm glad you like them, but there's only one to a customer!" Mrs. Todd said with a smile.

The children thanked her for the cookies.

"You're welcome. You were a wonderful audience. Thank you for coming."

The docent walked into the room and told the children, "We're glad you came today."

Mrs. Carroll smiled. "Thank you for having us. Mrs. Todd, thank you for an interesting cooking demonstration and for the cookies. Goodbye." Then she turned to the students, "Follow me out the kitchen door onto the veranda, and walk single file back to the school bus."

The children waved to the docent and to Mrs. Todd as they exited.

Rhonda rode the school bus back to the school with Jeremy and the other children. When they climbed off the bus, Jeremy hugged

Rhonda goodbye, and said, "Thanks for going with us, Nana. I love you."

Rhonda smiled at him. "I love you, too, Jeremy, and I enjoyed going on the school tour with you."

CHAPTER TWENTY-FIVE
COOKIES FROM THE 1860'S

LISTED BELOW ARE THREE COOKIE recipes, baked in the 1860's over hot coals in an open-hearth fireplace, that the Wornall family and their friends enjoyed.

During this time, according to etiquette, ladies paid visits or social calls in the afternoon to each other. Victorian society had strict rules about these visits. Calls were made between three o'clock and five o'clock in the afternoon. Calling at any other time was considered rude and improper. When the ladies went calling, they dressed in nice dresses, wore hats and gloves, and carried a parasol. At each home, the visit lasted for only fifteen to thirty minutes. Sometimes they made several calls to various friends in one afternoon. This is how the ladies kept in touch since there were no telephones or computers. Ladies who didn't call on friends in the afternoon and adhere to the strict rules of etiquette were considered ill bred.

Calling cards, which were introduced in the 1850's, were an important part of the calling ritual. If a lady called on a friend who was not at home, she left her calling card and two of her husband's cards. There were also a variety of rules about the size, type of engraving, and script written on the calling cards.

When Eliza and Roma's lady friends came to call, they entertained them in the parlor, and they might have served tea or coffee with one of these three cookie recipes that date back to the1860's.

GINGERSNAPS

¾ cup butter

2 cups sugar

2 beaten eggs

½ cup molasses

2 tsp. vinegar

3 ¾ cups flour

2 to 3 tsp. ginger

1 ½ tsp. baking soda

½ tsp. cinnamon

¼ tsp. cloves

In a large mixing bowl, cream together butter and sugar. Stir in beaten eggs, molasses, and vinegar. In a separate bowl, sift together flour, ginger, soda, cinnamon, and cloves, and stir into the creamed mixture. Mix well, then shape into balls. Bake on greased cookie sheets at 350 degrees for twelve minutes.

JUMBLES

½ cup butter

½ cup shortening

1 cup sugar

1 beaten egg

½ tsp. vanilla extract

2 Tbsp. milk

1 tsp. cinnamon2 ½ cups flour

In a mixing bowl, cream together butter, shortening, and sugar. Stir in beaten egg, vanilla, and milk. In a separate bowl, sift together cinnamon and flour and add it to the creamed mixture. Shape dough into balls, roll balls in additional sugar, and press cookies flat. Place on greased cookie sheets and bake at 350 degrees for about twelve minutes or until browned.

QUAKER COOKIES

2 cups brown sugar

1 cup shortening

2 beaten eggs

1/ cup molasses

2 tsp. vanilla extract

2 cups flour

1 ½ tsp. baking soda

1 tsp. salt

½ tsp. cinnamon

3 cups old-fashioned oatmeal

½ cup raisins

Additional sugar

In a mixing bowl, cream brown sugar and shortening together. Stir in beaten eggs, molasses, and vanilla, and mix until blended. In a separate bowl, sift together flour, soda, salt, and cinnamon and gradually stir into the creamed mixture. Add oatmeal and raisins and mix well. Shape into balls and roll balls in additional sugar. Place on a greased cookie sheet and flatten balls with your fingers. Bake at 350 degrees for about twelve minutes, or until brown.

CHAPTER TWENTY-SIX

RICK AND RHONDA WENT TO the Kansas City International Airport to pick up their friend, Jason Valores, the Mexican Director of Police Security. He and Rhonda had worked together in the past, and they had high hopes that he'd help them crack the smuggling ring.

Not long ago, Jason had phoned Rhonda and told her he'd had contact with a snitch in Guanajuato. The informant had said there were two Mexican drug dealers from Guanajuato who were now living in Nuevo Laredo, and they were running drugs to Kansas City.

Jason had put two and two together after Rhonda told him about Bob Lane's death, and that the police thought Lane was involved in smuggling cocaine from Mexico to Kansas City before he was killed. He felt there was a connection.

When Jason came through the gate and saw Rhonda and Rick waiting for him, his face broke into a big smile. He grabbed Rhonda and gave her a bear hug, then he shook hands with Rick.

"I've sure missed you two," he told them.

"We've missed you, too," Rhonda assured him. "I'm so glad you're going to stay with us."

Rick steered them over to pick up Jason's luggage. He said, "I'll get the car and pick you up." He pointed at some seats beside two large windows. "Why don't you wait there? You'll be able to see me pull up."

Rhonda settled into a chair, then Jason reached into his carry-on bag and pulled out a beautifully wrapped gift box. He handed it to Rhonda. "This is for you. I think you'll like it."

Rhonda opened the box and took out a pendant. The large onyx stone, surrounded with decorative sterling silver, hung on a heavy sterling chain.

"Thank you, Jason. It's beautiful. I love it."

"You'll like it better when I show you what it can do." He took it from her and turned it over. "It has a hidden microphone in the back. Wear it whenever you want to hear what someone is saying, but you aren't close enough to hear clearly, turn it on and it will magnify and tape their conversation. When you get home, you can hit replay and listen to every word they said."

Rhonda was excited. "Thanks! It's a perfect gift! You know how I love sleuthing gadgets."

Just as she put the necklace around her neck and tucked the gift box into her purse, Rick pulled up outside. Jason picked up his suitcase and overnight bag, and they headed for the door. He put his luggage in the trunk of the car. Rhonda climbed into the front seat and Jason sat in the back with the two poodles, Caesar and Cleopatra. They remembered him and they were jumping up and down with excitement. He petted them until they calmed down.

Rick and Jason were talking non-stop. Rhonda snapped on the microphone and picked up their conversation. She'd play it when she got home so she'd know it was working.

After they arrived home and showed Jason his room, Rhonda served them a luncheon of barbecued brisket sandwiches, cole slaw, baked beans, and strawberry shortcake.

"Lunch was delicious. Thanks," Jason said.

"I'm glad you liked it. Kansas City is famous for barbecue, you know. Let's go into the living room and sit and talk about what's been going on in Guanajuato."

They chatted a few minutes then Jason said, "Rick, I have something for you. I left it on the table in the foyer. I'll get it." He went to the foyer for it, and gave the small box to Rick.

As Rick opened it, Jason said, "It's called a Stealth 1 DVR Camera. It looks like an ordinary motion sensor, but it's a wireless surveillance camera. It records up to forty-five days worth of high-quality digital on its card, which is included in the camera."

"Hey, Jason! What a great gift! Rhonda will try to take it away from me."

He grinned. "Don't let her. She has a gift, too. Hers is a pendant that magnifies and tapes conversations. Show it to him, Rhonda."

Rhonda pointed to the necklace hanging around her neck. "Isn't it pretty, Rick? And it's just what every sleuth needs!"

"It's very pretty." Rick turned to Jason. "Tell us more about this DVR camera."

"It's easy to operate. Just mount it on the wall and set it to record. There are three modes. It can record continuously, at scheduled times, or when motion is detected."

"How do you view what you've filmed?"

"You just connect the included cable to a TV or a VCR, or you can remove the SD card and put it in your computer for archiving. It runs on the included AC adapter or up to twelve hours on four AA batteries."

Rhonda said, "Rick, that's a great gift."

"It sure is. Jason, you've given us too much," Rick said. "Let's hook the camera up in the kitchen. Knowing all the predicaments Rhonda can get herself into, you never know when it might come in handy."

"I'm glad you like it," Jason said. "It's small, just five inches high, three inches wide, and almost three inches deep. Let me hook it up for you." Jason picked it up and proceeded to mount it on the wall and set it to record.

"Did you say it will record for forty-five days?"

"Yes, it will."

"Thanks for mounting it on the wall for us."

"You're welcome."

"If you aren't tired after your trip, I'll take you to John's office. He wants to introduce you to his chief."

"I'm not tired. I slept on the plane, but I want to clean up a bit before we go."

When they arrived at the Brookside Police Station, Rick introduced Jason to John and left him at John's office.

"You don't need to pick Jason up. I'll take him back to your house," John offered.

While they were gone, Rhonda went into her office and turned her necklace over. She hit re-play and listened to enough of their conversation to know that the microphone was working.

Marianna called, "Hi, Rhonda. I want to thank you again for introducing me to that charming pediatrician. He's taken me to dinner twice already."

"I'm delighted you've hit it off," Rhonda replied.

"The kids like him almost as much as I do. I just wanted to tell you that your reputation as a matchmaker is well deserved. I'm cooking dinner for him tonight, so I have to get busy. Thanks again. You're a real friend!"

That evening, Rick and Rhonda took Jason on a tour of Kansas City at night. They ate dinner at the Italian Gardens. After they returned home, they watched the ten o'clock news together in the family room, and then they turned in early.

The next morning after a breakfast of bacon, eggs, cheese grits, biscuits and gravy, Jason said, "That was a delicious breakfast. I haven't had grits and biscuits and gravy since I was at my parents' ranch in Texas."

"In what part of Texas do they live?" Rick asked.

"The hill country. They love it there, and I do, too. I usually spend my vacations with them. Why don't you and Rhonda come there for a visit sometime when I'm going to be with them? Mom and Dad love to have company, and they have plenty of room."

"Thanks for the invitation," Rick replied. "Maybe we can."

"How many acres do they have?" Rhonda asked.

"Twenty thousand. They raise cattle and horses and need a lot of grazing land."

"That's a huge ranch," Rhonda said. "You'd told me they lived on a ranch, but I had no idea it was so large."

After breakfast, Jason went with Rick and Rhonda to the Wornall House. Kirk and John had arranged with Jamie to meet them there. John had told Rhonda there was something in the kitchen he wanted to double check and to show her.

Rick parked the van and said, "Jason, while we're waiting on the guys to get here, let's go upstairs. I want to introduce you to Jamie and Anna."

They walked up the side stairs and went into the office. Rick introduced them. Jamie said, "I'm so glad to meet you, Jason. I heard that you and Rhonda caught some crooks in Guanajuato. I'm hoping you'll catch Bob Lane's killer here in Kansas City."

Jason grinned, "There's not much I'd rather do than catch crooks!"

"That's good. Your English is just perfect. No accent."

"That's because my mother is English. Her maiden name is Wellington. My dad is Spanish and he was born in Spain, but I was born in Texas and we always spoke English at home."

Just then the two detectives arrived. They greeted and shook hands with everyone.

John asked Jamie, "Is it all right if we walk through the downstairs rooms? I'm especially interested in checking something in the kitchen."

"Of course. Make yourselves at home," Jamie replied with a smile.

"Sure. Do whatever you need to do," Anna, her attractive blonde assistant, agreed.

"Thanks. Let's get started," John said.

"Don't bump into the ghost soldier on the staircase," Anna reminded John. "He guards the front door, you know!"

"I've heard about him, but I don't know if Jason has ever been in a haunted house before."

"No, this is my first one," Jason said.

John led them down the staircase and took them straight back to the kitchen.

"What are you looking for?" Rhonda asked.

"When we were searching this room the night Bob died, I saw something that interested me, and I want to check it out."

Jason jokingly asked Rhonda, "Have you thought of any tricks yet to catch the killer?"

"No, but I've just had an idea. Perhaps John could tell his prime suspect that he'd found a hidden camera in the Wornall House kitchen, and that when the film was developed, he saw a clear picture of her stirring peanuts into the cider. I'll bet he'd get a confession!"

Jason laughed. "Now, you're cooking! You're sounding like the Rhonda I know! Maybe that would work." Jason turned to John, "What do you think?"

"I think Rhonda stole my thunder! That's exactly what I'm looking for. The night this house was searched, I saw an odd looking object in the kitchen ceiling. It looked like a smoke detector, but I thought it might have a hidden camera tucked inside it. That's what I came to check out." John pointed, "Do you see it? It's right there." He used a step ladder to reach up and take hold of the smoke detector and pull it down.

John looked it over carefully, then he removed a tiny covert camera and showed it to them.

Then he took out his cell phone and dialed Jamie's number. When she answered, he said,

"Hi, this is John Preston, downstairs in the kitchen. It's easier to call you than to walk back up the stairs past your ghost!"

Jamie laughed.

John said, "I think there's a hidden camera in the kitchen. If so, and if there is a clear picture of the suspect stirring peanuts into the punch, this case may be solved. What do you know about this camera?"

"I don't know much about it because the camera was installed before I became the director. Why don't you ask Anna what she knows about it? Here she is." Presumably, Jamie handed the phone to Anna.

"Anna, this is John Preston. I'm downstairs in the kitchen. What do you know about a hidden camera being installed here?"

"About this time last year, a man who owned a security company came and offered to install hidden cameras free of charge. He called them pin hole cameras. Since it was free, we gave him permission. Our security system is supposed to monitor the batteries in the hidden cameras as well as the ones in the alarms. He said he used lithium batteries, which should be good for years, so the camera should still be working."

"Why did the man want to donate the cameras?" John asked, curiously.

"He thought it would take pictures of our ghosts! He put one in the parlor, also, to try to get a picture of the ghost we call the 'Lady in Blue' who plays the piano."

"With your permission, I'll take both of the cameras to the station. We'll get a specialist to check them out and develop the film. Let's hope we have a picture of Bob's killer doctoring the cider. I'll write a receipt for the two cameras and film and give it to you before we leave. We'll return the cameras to you as soon as possible."

"Of course you can take them. Let us know what you find out."

John said, "We will, and I'll let you know if there's a picture of the Lady in Blue!"

While John worked on the peanut case, Rick and Rhonda took Jason to lunch at Jalapenos Mexican Restaurant and then they went to a movie.

Later that day, John called Rhonda. "I don't have any news about the film yet. Maybe we'll know tomorrow."

While Rick, Rhonda, and Jason were eating a roast pork dinner and having chocolate meringue pie for dessert, Rhonda said, "John told me when he and Woods searched Bob Lane's home, they took Bob's computer, cell phone, answering machine, and business records to the police station for experts to check out. Do you know what he learned?"

"No. John hasn't mentioned that to me. I'll ask him about it and tell you. I think you should know, because if you hadn't e-mailed the story of the peanut murder to me, we wouldn't be close to cracking this case. When I read your email, I knew I'd heard Bob's name before. I'd given my snitch a cell phone so he'd be easy to contact when I needed him. I phoned him and asked if he knew anything about a man named Bob Lane. He said that's the guy the Guanajuato smugglers were working for. The snitch said they were driving two trucks to Kansas City, stuffed with cocaine, for Bob Lane."

"Interesting. Have you and John been collaborating?" Rhonda asked.

"Yes. I knew about the drug smuggling ring, and I gave what evidence I had to John, and he gave me what he had. We've been working together since you e-mailed me about Lane. Hopefully, we're getting ready to draw in the net. I'm here to tie up some loose ends on the case pertaining to the two truckers. But to catch the killer, we still might have to use your idea about the hidden cameras!"

CHAPTER TWENTY-SEVEN

DETECTIVE JOHN PRESTON WAS HAPPY that Jason Valores had come to Kansas City. They worked well together. John asked Jason if he'd like to go with him to interview Mandy Todd. "Feel free to ask her any questions you might have."

John had phoned Mrs. Todd and had asked if he could come to her home for a chat. He explained to her that he hadn't had much time to talk to everyone on the night of Bob's death, and now that he had more time, he wanted to finish all of the interviews he'd started.

She asked if she could stop by his office at two on her way home from the Wornall House.

John told her that would be fine.

Mandy arrived at the Brookside Police Station on time, and she was ushered down the hall to John's office.

"Good afternoon, Mrs. Todd." John shook her hand. He introduced her to Jason Valores, then asked her, "Can I get you a Coca Cola or some coffee?"

"A coke, please."

John took a can out of the refrigerator and handed it and a napkin to her.

"Thank you." She opened the can and took a drink. "I was thirsty. This hits the spot!"

John smiled. "I hear you're a real asset to the Wornall House, and that they're happy to have you."

"That's nice to hear. I enjoy volunteering there."

"Where were you born, Mrs. Todd?"Jason asked.

"In Louisiana. I attended a culinary school in New Orleans. I always liked to cook, and I wanted to be a chef. My first job was as a chef's helper at an upscale restaurant in New Orleans, and I married the chef."

"Are you still married to him?" Jason asked.

"No. We were divorced three years ago."

"How long were you married?"

"Twenty years."

"Do you have children?"John asked.

"One son. He's at the University of Texas."

"Why were you divorced?"John asked.

"He started running around with his helper. History repeats itself, they say."

John grinned. "Did he marry her?"

"Yes."

"I'm sorry."

"Don't be. He always had a roving eye. I was glad to be rid of him!"

John chuckled

"Who introduced you to Jamie, the director of the museum?"

Mandy hesitated for a minute before replying, "Mr. Lane."

"Was it the same Mr. Lane who died during the Christmas Candlelight Tour?"

"Yes, sir."

"How did you meet him?"

"We met at a restaurant," Mandy replied. She took another sip of her coke.

"In New Orleans?" John asked.

"No. I didn't know him there. After my divorce, I moved to Texas. That's where I met him."

"What city in Texas?"Jason asked. "My parents live in Texas."

"Laredo. Bob came into the restaurant where I worked. I was on break and I was eating lunch. He sat at a table next to mine, and he struck up a conversation with me."

"Did you begin to see him socially?"John asked.

"Yes. He said he was in Laredo once or twice each month, and he didn't know anyone there. He asked me if I'd go to some movies with him. The first one we went to see was 'Julie and Julia,' about Chef Julia Childs. I'd been wanting to see it."

"Did you ever go out to dinner with him?"John asked.

"Yes, occasionally."

"Did he tell you about his peanut allergy?"

"No. He always ordered a steak, a baked potato, and a salad."

The detective scratched his head. "I don't know much about cooking, but I do know that peanuts are sometimes sprinkled over salads and some foods are cooked in peanut oil. Since Bob Lane's death, I've read up on peanut allergy. Another thing I learned is that when a person has an extremely dangerous peanut allergy like Bob had, he could not eat in a restaurant where peanuts, peanut oil, peanut butter, or any kind of nuts were served."

"Nuts were not served in the restaurant where I worked. Usually, if peanut oil is used, there's a warning written on the menu or on a small sign on each table. Bob probably had phoned ahead and talked to the chef or to the restaurant manager about that before he made a reservation."

"That's possible, "John conceded.

"What's the name of the restaurant where you worked in Laredo?" John asked.

"Margarita's Steak House."

"Thank you." Detective Preston wrote that information in his notebook.

"How many times would you estimate you'd been out with Mr. Lane?"

Mrs. Todd thought for a minute then replied, "About a dozen times."

"Do you mean to tell me that after a dozen dates with him, he never told you about his peanut allergy?"John asked, surprised.

"Well, one night he asked me if I had any food allergies and I said I didn't. He said he had to be careful what he ate because he had allergies, but he didn't say what he was allergic to and I didn't ask."

"Weren't you curious about his allergies?"John asked.

"Not really. We were just friends. I wasn't interested in him romantically. If I had been, I'd probably have been more interested in the subject."

"Well, I guess that makes sense," John said. "But if you weren't interested in him, why did you move to Kansas City, where he lived?"

"He was a pilot, and he invited me to fly to Kansas City with him one weekend. While we were here, he took me on a tour of the city, and I thought it would be a pretty place to live. I told him I was tired of living in Laredo, on the Mexican border, because it's so dangerous. He said if I wanted to move to Kansas City, he'd help me get a job. I thought about it that night, and the next day, I told him I'd decided to move here."

"Did Bob offer you a job in his business?"Jason asked.

"Yes, but I told him I wanted to be a chef, not a sales lady. I'd brought a copy of my resume with me, and he helped me get a job as a chef."

"That was nice of him," John said.

"Bob was a nice man. I remember once when a guy lit up a joint and began to smoke, Bob told him to throw it away, that it would mess up his head."

"Good advice. Did you continue to see Mr. Lane socially after you moved to Kansas City?"

"Occasionally. Actually he'd been dating another woman here, and he continued to see her. It didn't bother me since we were just friends."

"Do you live in an apartment?"Jason asked.

"No. I've rented a house here in the Brookside area for my son and myself. My son spends his vacations here with me."

"What's your son's name?"

"Nathan. I call him Nate."

"What's his major?"

"Business."

She finished drinking her cola and set it down on a nearby table.

"Who are you renting your home from?"John asked.

"Bob Lane rented it to me. My rent is nearly due and I'm not sure whom I should pay. I hope I don't have to move."

"What's your monthly rent?"John asked.

"One thousand dollars. I guess I should pay his beneficiary. Do you know who it is?"

"Why don't you call his ex-wife, Karen Lane, and ask her if she knows who you should pay?"

"Good idea. Thank you. I'll do that."

"Mrs. Todd, I've enjoyed talking to you, and I'd like to visit with you longer, but I have another appointment. I'll call you soon so we can finish our chat."

"If you wish." Mandy Todd stood. "Thanks for the coke."

"You're welcome. Would you like for an officer to drive you home?"

"No, thanks. I drove my own car. Goodbye." She shook hands with the two men.

"Thank you for your time. Goodbye."

He opened the door for her and she left.

Detective John Preston began detecting as soon as she was out of the building. He grabbed his notebook and pen and followed her at a discreet distance to check her license plate. He jotted down the number and the kind of car she drove in his notebook, then returned to his office. He pulled on Latex gloves, and picked up the empty coke can and put it in a plastic bag.

John said, "Jason, excuse me while I do some checking on Mandy Todd."

Jason said, "Go right ahead."

John sat down behind his desk and phoned one of the officers in the building. He asked him to pick up a sample and take it to the police lab for him.

When the officer came to John's office, John handed him the plastic bag. "This can should have a full set of Mrs. Todd's fingerprints on it. Also, I want her DNA. The tech should be able to get it from the saliva she left on the can as she drank the coke."

The officer said, "I'll take it to the lab right now."

"Thanks," Preston said. Then he ran Mandy's license plates through the DMV.

John told Jason, "I'm pleased that I'm getting information about Mrs. Mandy Todd. The night Bob died, I got prints and DNA from each of the suspects, but it won't hurt to re-check it."

After running her plates he found out her car was registered to Amanda Marie Todd. He had her address and quite a bit of other information. He was anxious to get the lab report on her prints and DNA. He believed Bob had told Mandy about his peanut allergy and he was curious why she wouldn't admit it. He thought she might've been afraid he'd believe she'd killed Bob if she admitted she knew about it.

"Is there anything I can do to help you?" Jason asked.

"Do you want to ride with me while I stalk a suspect?" John asked with a grin.

"Why not? It might be exciting."

As it turned out, the suspect only went to the grocery store. Sitting in the car waiting for her to come out was as exciting as watching paint dry. Finally, she came out of the store with a cart of groceries and they followed her home. After John and Jason returned to the station, Jason caught a taxi and went back to Rick and Rhonda's home.

John sat at his desk and looked through his notes about Bob, notes from the things he'd confiscated from his home. Bob's computer had been quite informative. John had read several e-mails on it from two different women. One signed her name with the letters 'A.T'. The other one hadn't signed her name at all. He assumed A.T. was Amanda Todd. The unsigned e-mails were from a mystery woman who'd squabbled with him about some cookies. He assumed that was the cookie packages that had been stuffed with cocaine. This woman was probably the one who had made jealous comments about someone who Bob was seeing. John assumed Marianna was the other woman. There were also several discussions about trips to Laredo or to N.L., which he guessed was Nuevo Laredo, Mexico. He made a note to re-read these e-mails more carefully when he had time.

John had listened to Bob's messages on his Caller ID, both on the land phone and on his cell. There were calls from Bob's brother and sister, from a man named Mario, from Mandy, Jean, Marianna, Jamie, Bart, and from some other men who had Spanish accents.

John had also checked Bob's calendar and noted the people he'd had appointments with and those he'd made future appointments to see. John thumbed through Bob's address book. There were phone numbers for several suspects whom John had already talked to, such as Mandy, Marianna, Karen, Rhonda, Rick, Bart, Sally, Bob's brother and his sister.

In some of Bob's papers that John had borrowed, he read info about an unnamed woman's involvement in the drug trade. John also found records in a notebook of Bob's monthly runs from Laredo to Kansas City and the total number of cookie packages 'imported' on each trip.

There were several names and phone numbers of people he didn't know. John decided to ask Kirk to call each of these people, talk to them about Bob, and see what he could find out. He'd also asked Kirk to phone people who'd left messages on Bob's answering machine, and people he'd made appointments with on his calendar.

John phoned Kirk, asked him to come into his office. When Kirk walked in, John said, "Concerning the Bob Lane case, I've made a list of things I want to do and a list of people I want to talk to. I simply can't get all the work done that I want to do. There are only twenty four hours in a day. Can I delegate some of these calls to you?"

Kirk was agreeable. "Sure. Just give me a list of what you want done, and I'll get right on it."

"Thank you. Here's the list. I sure appreciate your help."

"What do you think about pulling Bob Lane's bank records and checking his finances, to find out what checks he's received and what bills he's paid?"Woods asked.

"Yes, that should be done. Can you do that, too?"

"No problem. This case is our priority. I know it will take both of us to do everything we need to do to solve it." Woods took the list to his office and started making calls.

John made a list of people in his notebook whom he'd already interviewed and a list of people he wanted to interview in the next day or so. He made lists of questions he wanted to ask each person.

Next, John wrote notes on his 'TO DO LIST' to remind himself to get copies of fingerprints, the DNA result of various suspects, and to personally search any other security lockers Bob might've had. When he finished that, he jotted down his plan to review reports from all of the experts and specialists who'd examined Bob's computer, his faxes, phone calls, answering machines, billfold, and so on.

John leaned back in his chair and yawned. Just thinking about all he had to do exhausted him. He needed to relax and enjoy himself for a change. He'd been so busy on this case he hadn't had time for his wife or his kids. He picked up the phone and called Nikki. When she answered he said, "Hi, honey. Do you want to go out for dinner tonight?"

"I'd love to," she replied.

"Great! Call your mom and ask her to keep the kids. I'm feeling romantic!"

CHAPTER TWENTY-EIGHT

Before John left the office, he decided to call Jean Murphy and make an appointment with her. When she answered, he said, "Mrs. Murphy, this is Detective John Preston. How are you today?"

"Fine, thank you."

"On the night of Bob Lane's death, I talked for a short time to all of the witnesses and told them when I have more time I'd call so we can finish our talk. I'd like to make an appointment to see you."

"I'm home right now. Can you be here in thirty minutes?"

"Sure. I'll be there."

"I live in Brookside, near the police station. 6239 Market Street."

John hadn't planned to interview Jean today, but he decided he'd better strike while the iron was hot, as Rhonda was fond of saying. He stopped by Kirk's desk and asked him to go with him.

John called Nikki. "Something has come up, and I'll be about an hour late. Sorry, hon. I'll be there as soon as I can."

Jean lived in an attractive two-story brick home with dark green shutters. She had taken good care of her home. It was located on a corner lot, surrounded with trees and shrubs.

They parked on the driveway in an unmarked car, walked to the front door, and rang the door bell. John was wearing a dark blue suit and a red tie. Kirk was more casual in a navy jacket and khaki slacks.

Jean opened the door and invited them to come into the living room and sit down."

They sat on the brown sofa and she sat in a gold wing back chair. "I thought there was just going to be one of you," she said.

"Kirk wanted to come with me," John fibbed. "He likes to talk to people."

"Would you like a glass of ice tea?"Jean asked, politely.

"Yes, thank you, no sugar," John said.

"Nothing for me. Thank you," Kirk said.

Jean brought in a glass of ice tea for John and one for herself and a plate of sugar cookies on a tray and placed it on the coffee table in front of them. "I made these Amish Sugar Cookies today. I hope you'll like them."

"Thank you," John said. He picked up a cookie and ate all of it. "These are delicious, just like my mother used to make." He picked up another cookie. "It's hard to stop eating them."

"I have plenty. Eat all you want."

"Thanks." John took a sip of tea. "Do you mind if I tape our conversation? My memory isn't as good as it used to be."

"No, I don't mind," Jean replied. She took a sip of her tea.

When she wasn't paying attention to him, Kirk took her picture with his Blackberry.

Jean was about forty five, and she was average height and weight. Her brown hair was neatly styled and she had gray eyes. Her only makeup was pink lipstick. If she'd worn eye make-up, she would've been more attractive. Without it, her eyes looked like two burnt holes in a blanket. She was wearing gray slacks, a pink sweater, and gray loafers.

John began, "You have a nice home."

"Thank you. It's comfortable."

"Where were you born?"

"In Fredericksburg, Texas."

"That's in the hill country, isn't it?"

"Yes."

"Were you raised on a ranch?"

"Yes. My father was a rancher and my mother was a school teacher."

"You came from a good family."

"Yes, except Dad was terribly strict."

"So was mine," John said, then he got down to business. "Are you married?"

"Divorced."

"Where do you work?"

"I work out of my home. I design web sites."

"How long have you known Bob Lane?"

"We met about a year ago."

"Were you and his wife friends?"

"No. I met Bob about the time he was getting a divorce. We were drawn together since we're both divorced."

"Where did you meet him?"

"At a church singles group. I invited him to a social at the Wornall House Museum and I introduced him to Jamie. He told her he'd like to volunteer there. Since he was a friend of mine, she was pleased. She said she needed more volunteers."

"That's a lovely old place, isn't it?"

"Yes, it is. I've been both a docent and a kitchen worker there."

"Weren't you working in the kitchen the night Bob died?"

"Yes. Mandy, the volunteer cook, knows I'm a good cook, so she asked me to help her prepare the Christmas dinner the night of the Candlelight Tour."

"Did you know that Bob had a serious peanut allergy?"

"No, I had no idea. After I found out about it, I wondered why he hadn't told us."

"I'm curious about that, too," John said. "Have you ever socialized with Bob?"

"I saw him at events and parties at the Wornall House, and we sometimes sat together and talked. He was a nice man. I think he was lonely after his divorce, so I invited him to attend my church. He thanked me, but said he was Catholic and he preferred to attend his own church."

"Did you ever have dinner with him?"

"No, but he phoned me one night and asked if he could come over and watch a movie with me. He said his TV was on the blink. He came, and I offered him some refreshments, but all he would accept was a Pepsi. He refused a glass and drank it out of the bottle. I thought that was odd at the time, but now that I know about his peanut allergy, I guess he was just being careful."

John said, "He wasn't being too careful the night he drank spiced cider out of a glass."

"I guess it never occurred to him that there would be peanuts in spiced cider," Jean replied.

"What do you know about Bob's occupation?"

"He said he was an engineer, but he lost that job, so he started his own import company."

"What things did he import?"

"Products made in Mexico, I presume."

Kirk said bluntly, "Somebody told me Bob was smuggling drugs over the border."

"I don't believe that for a minute."

"Sometimes people will surprise you," Kirk told her.

"That's true, but Bob was a good man."

John glanced at his wrist watch. "Jean, I want to thank you for allowing us to come on such short notice. I've enjoyed talking to you, and I'd like to get to know you better. But I have another appointment in twenty minutes. May I visit you again someday?"

"Of course. Just call first. I'm in and out of the house a lot."

John picked up another cookie and took a bite. "My, these are delicious. Do you mind if I take a couple with me?"

"Not at all. Here's a napkin to wrap them in."

John took the napkin and wrapped up two cookies. "Would you give me your recipe for these cookies so my wife could make them?"

"Certainly. It will just take me a minute." She went into her office and made a copy for him.

While she was gone, Kirk took two Q-tips wrapped in a piece of foil from his pocket, and used them to swab the saliva off of her glass so the lab could get her DNA. He put foil around them and placed them in a bag. He stuck it in his pocket just seconds before Jean returned.

Jean handed John the recipe. "I'm pleased you liked the cookies."

"They were delicious." Thanks for being willing to see us today, and also for both the cookies and the recipe." He put the recipe in his case and drank the last of the tea. He set the glass back on the tray.

She showed them to the door, shook hands with them, and said, "Goodbye."

When they got in the car, John said, "You did a good job of playing bad cop to my good cop."

"Thanks. What do you think about her?"Kirk asked.

"She appears to be a nice lady, but as we know, things aren't always what they seem," John replied.

"That's just it with this case. All of the people seem nice."

John said, "I think this killer is the kind of person you meet, shake hands, and enjoy talking with. Until forensics match the DNA and the prints, you'd think he was just an ordinary Joe."

With a twinkle in his eye, Kirk added, "Or that she was just an ordinary Joanne!"

JEAN MURPHY'S SUGAR COOKIES

1 cup sugar

1 cup powdered sugar

1 cup butter, softened,

1 cup oil

2 eggs, beaten

1 1/2 tsp. vanilla

4 ½ cups flour

1 tsp. baking soda

1 tsp. cream of tartar

Cream together the two sugars, butter, oil, eggs, and vanilla. Combine flour, soda, and cream of tartar in a separate bowl and combine the two mixtures. Mix until blended, cover, and chill for 3 to 4 hours. Shape into balls and place on a greased cookie sheet. Flatten balls and bake in a preheated 375 degree oven for 10 to 15 minutes.

CHAPTER TWENTY-NINE

Rick, Jason, and Rhonda were watching the morning news on TV when Rick said, "I'm looking forward to Bart and Sally's dinner tonight."

"So am I, and that reminds me, I'm taking a Tiramisu dessert, so I'd better jump up and start preparing it. I'm glad Sally invited the docents and the cooks."

"Do you think one of tonight's guests is the killer?"

"Your guess is as good as mine."

"Jason, don't you want to go to Sally's dinner with us tonight?" Rhonda asked.

"No, thank you. John and I discussed that, and we decided it might be better if they don't meet me in case I should need to do some undercover work. Nikki invited me to their home for dinner tonight."

That evening, the guests sat in Sally's living room and were served drinks with some cheese, crackers, mini sausage balls, and grapes. Sally had invited the two cooks, Mandy Todd and Jean Murphy, and the three docents who were still inside the Wornall House when Bob died. Their names were Luanne Myers, Marlena Jennings, and Tracy Jones. Karen Lane was the surprise guest. Rhonda had not known she'd been invited, but she was glad Karen came.

Rhonda greeted Karen. "Hello, I'm happy to see you. How are you enjoying your new job?"

"I like it, but it keeps me busy."

Marlena walked over to Rhonda's side just then and said, "I'm planning a trip to Mexico in the summer. I was told to ask you for suggestions of places to visit."

Rhonda said she had especially enjoyed Guanajuato, San Miguel, Cuernavaca, and the Yucatan. "I'm not crazy about the beach, though. Too hot."

Marlena opened her purse and took out pen and paper. She wrote down the names of the cities.

Rhonda added, "I loved Mexico City and seeing the pyramids and the Floating Gardens, but the city is not safe. It's full of thieves."

Sally said, "Marlena, I heard you're a doctor."

"An endocrinologist," Marlena replied.

"What type of illnesses do you treat?"

"I specialize in thyroid disorders and diabetes."

"Are you married?"Sally asked,

"No, but I've been dating a guy for six months who proposed to me last week."

"Is he a doctor, too?"

"Yes, he's an oncologist."

"How long have you volunteered at the Wornall House?"Marianna asked.

"For over a year."

Sally sat beside Tracy, "Tell me all about yourself. I'd like to get better acquainted with you."

"What do you want to know?"

"Start with your birth," Sally replied, laughing.

"You asked for it. Here goes a boring recitation. I was born in Ohio and lived there until I graduated from college, then I moved to Kansas City to work as an artist at Hallmark Cards. I'm married and we have two teenagers. I'm a substitute Sunday school teacher. I've been volunteering at the Wornall House for nearly two years, taking people on tours as well as working in the herb garden. That's about it!"

"That wasn't boring," Sally said, smiling.

Marianna popped a mini sausage ball in her mouth and ate it. "Your sausage balls are delicious," she complimented Sally.

"Thanks. It's from Rhonda's cookbook. It's just sausage, baking mix, and cheese."

Mandy said, "Rhonda, I didn't know you write cookbooks."

Sally said, "Sure, she does. The recipes are all fast and easy. They're for sale in the Wornall House gift shop."

"That's what I need. After cooking all day, I want quick and easy recipes to fix at home."

Rhonda smiled. "Even gourmet cooks need fast and easy recipes."

"Absolutely," Mandy agreed. "I'll buy one tomorrow."

"Thank you. By the way, I've been planning to tell you that I went with my grandson on a school trip to the Wornall Home. He said his favorite part of the tour was when you baked cookies in the fireplace. Now, he wants me to cook in our fireplace!"

Mandy laughed. "I learned to do that when I cooked in an antebellum home in New Orleans. I thought I might as well use that knowledge in the Wornall House."

Sally said, "The director is thrilled that you know how to cook in the fireplace."

"I'm enjoying it." Mandy put her arm around Jean's shoulder and said, "Jean is my right hand. She's a great cook. I'm so glad she's volunteering in the kitchen."

Rhonda asked, "What is your specialty, Jean?"

"I love to bake."

"I'll bet you make scrumptious chocolate meringue pies!" Rhonda exclaimed.

"Actually, pies are my number one specialty. My mother taught me to bake."

"My grandma made the best chocolate meringue pies I've ever eaten," Rhonda said. "Why don't you open a bakery? I'll be over to buy your pies."

"I've thought about it," Jean admitted.

Luanne said, "Mandy, the food you cooked for the Patron's party was fabulous. I'll bet you helped her, didn't you, Jean?"

"I made the hors'douvres, the dinner rolls, and the desserts."

"I remember eating some of each! Everything was delicious."

Jean smiled. "Thank you, my dear."

Rhonda turned to Luanne and asked, "Are you a teacher?"

"Yes, I teach history. I'm not married, so I have plenty of time to volunteer at the Wornall House."

"Do you lead tour groups through the Wornall House?" Jean asked.

"Yes, I do."

"Your tour is very interesting. I was in a group once that you took through the house," Sally said.

"Thank you. I enjoy it."

Sally said, "Dinner is ready. I'm serving it buffet style. Some of you can sit in the dining room and some at the kitchen table. Sit wherever you wish."

Rhonda said, "Sally is an excellent cook, too. I know we'll enjoy her Italian feast."

Everyone loaded their plates with lasagna, spaghetti and meatballs, romaine- strawberry salad, and crusty garlic bread.

Later, Sally passed around the leftovers and they had second helpings. For dessert, she served Rhonda's Tiramisu with cups of coffee.

Jean said, "I'd love to have your recipe for Tiramisu, Rhonda."

"The recipe's in my purse. I'll give it to you after dinner."

Marianna leaned over toward Rhonda and said in a low voice. "Jack and I have another date tomorrow night."

Rhonda smiled. "Good! I was sure you'd like him."

After dessert, they moved into the family room. Before long, the conversation turned to the murder at the John Wornall House Museum.

Marianna asked Luanne if she'd known Bob very well.

Luanne replied, "We were merely acquaintances. He was a nice man, and I hope the police soon find out who killed him."

Mandy said, "I'll always believe peanuts were dropped into the punch by accident. Everyone liked Bob. Nobody would've killed him on purpose."

Marianna added, "I'd hoped that there would be a memorial service for Bob at the Wornall House, but I haven't heard a thing about it."

Bart, in his usual blunt way, said, "That's probably because there's talk that Bob was mixed up in drugs. I doubt there will be a service unless his name is cleared."

"I don't believe Bob would sell drugs," Tracy said.

"Neither do I," Marlena said. "He was a kind man."

"Who do you think killed Bob?" Tracy asked the group.

Sally said, "If he was a member of a drug smuggling ring, one of his cronies might've done it."

"That must've been what happened," Karen said.

"I think we're all suspects, but I don't believe any of us would've killed Bob," Jean said.

"It's lucky that none of us were allergic to peanuts," Rick said. "If we were, we'd be dead."

"Oh, my, I hadn't thought of that," Marianna groaned.

"I'm thankful I don't have any food allergies," Tracy said.

"So am I," Luanne agreed.

"Let's change the subject and talk about happy things," Sally suggested.

Rhonda said, "Since we're all volunteers at the Wornall House, I thought you might be interested in hearing a story about John Bristow Wornall Junior, the son of John and Roma Wornall. He married a pretty woman named Louise Woodbridge. They had three sons and one daughter. His wife died when she was sixty three, but he never re-married. Two of his sons moved into the Wornall House at different times and lived there with him until he died in 1962 of a heart attack when he was eighty nine."

"Yes, I'd like to know more about him. Tell us your story," Luanne said.

"Years ago, there was an elderly lady named Ruth Bradfield in my DAR group. She told me she'd worked for John Bristow Wornall Jr. at the Westport Bank where he was vice-president. She was a young lady when she began working for him. She was very smart and had wanted to go to college, but her family couldn't afford to send her. Mr. Wornall was a kind- hearted man who was a member of the Board of Directors at the William Jewell College in Liberty, Missouri. In the past, he had obtained scholarships for some well-deserving students. When it came to his attention that Ruth wanted to go to college, he obtained a scholarship at William Jewell College for her. After Ruth graduated from the college with high grades, she continued to work for him. She never forgot his kindness, and said he was a wonderful man."

Rhonda added, "Ruth Bradfield died in the early 1980's. After her death, a small park, located in Waldo on the east side of Wornall Road and 77th Street, was dedicated to her memory and named for her."

"What a nice story about Mr. Wornall," Sally said. "I'd heard he had a heart of gold. Thank you for telling us this story."

"Who else has a happy story to tell?" Sally asked.

Several people told interesting stories and a few jokes before the evening was over.

Bart said, "I have a story to tell. It isn't happy, but I think it's interesting. I read it in the newspaper. It said scientists had analyzed a sample of two hundred and fifty bank notes from seventeen cities and they discovered that ninety percent of the bills had traces of cocaine on them. The articles said some of the bills were tainted because addicts had rolled them up and used them to snort cocaine or because the bills had been involved in drug deals. The scientist said cocaine is such a fine powder it could be easily spread from those polluted bills to many other ordinary bills."

"It doesn't seem possible that ninety percent of the bills could have traces of cocaine on them," Rick said.

"Remember that was ninety percent of a sample of only two hundred and fifty bank notes, not of all the bills in circulation," Bart reminded them. "I thought it was an interesting story, though."

"Yes, it was," Rick agreed.

Rhonda remembered that Jean wanted the Tiramisu recipe so she took it out of her purse and gave it to her.

Jean said, "Thank you. It was delicious."

"How do you stay slim and eat desserts?" Sally asked.

"I'm getting fatter every day," Rhonda said. "We go out to restaurants too often. Rick's taking me to Ruby Tuesday's tomorrow for their salad bar."Rhonda suddenly remembered she had not turned on the recorder in her pendant, so she turned it on.

Luanne asked, "Does anyone know if the police are close to finding Bob's killer?"

Rhonda decided to try a new strategy. She hadn't thought this out, but she'd turned on the pendant and wanted to record whatever comments were made about the murder. If she had thought it out, she probably would've kept her mouth shut. She said, "I know who killed Bob, but I can't tell you until after I talk to the police."

There was shocked silence in the room for a minute, then Jean asked, "Why haven't you told the police?"

"I've tried to get hold of that detective, but everytime I call the station, he's out."

Sally said, "Rhonda, you've got to tell us. You can't throw out a bombshell like that and not tell us. Come on, who was it?"

"On the night of the Candlelight dinner, before we sat down at the table, I walked by the kitchen and looked in. I saw someone put peanuts in the cider."

Marlena asked, "Who was it?"

"I can't tell you yet."

Sally asked, "Why didn't you tell the police you saw who put peanuts in the cider?"

"At that time, I didn't realize the significance of what I saw."

"Is the suspect in this room?" Marianna asked.

"I'm taking the Fifth Amendment on that one!" Rhonda exclaimed.

"Does Preston know who killed Bob?" Mandy asked.

"I heard he has a prime suspect, but I don't know who it is."

The guests saw that Rhonda was not going to tell them. Before long, they started to leave.

Rhonda waited for most of the people to leave then she asked, "Sally, may I use your bathroom?"

"Yes, of course."

Bart walked over to Rhonda and said in a low voice, "Be careful, Rhonda. There's a killer on the loose. You've put yourself in danger."

"Thanks. I shouldn't have said that," she admitted before walking down the hall to the bathroom.

After Rhonda closed and locked the bathroom door, she took out her cell phone and called her son-in-law, Detective Preston. When he answered, she said, "I shot off my mouth and told the eleven people at Sally's dinner that I knew who killed Bob."

"Oh, Mom, why did you do that?"

"I was trying to flush out the killer."

"Now the killer will be after you again."

"Maybe we can catch her this time."

"I'm worried about you. Are you at Sally's house now?"

"Yes, but we're getting ready to leave."

"Who's at the party?"

Rhonda told him the names of the guests.

"Don't leave until I get there. I'm afraid your life is in danger. I'm going to follow you home and make sure your house is secure," John said. "I was going to drive Jason back to your home, anyway, so we'll be at Sally's in ten minutes. I'm going to turn on my siren so we can get there faster, but I'll turn it off a couple of blocks before I get to Sally's. See you soon."

Rhonda went back into the living room and visited with the three people still left in the room. They were talking about the economy. After the others left, Rhonda peeked out the window and saw that John was there. She thanked Sally for the delicious dinner, and reminded her that she would have the next dinner party. I'll call you about the time."

As Rick and Rhonda drove away from Sally and Bart's house, Rhonda saw John pull in behind them.

Rick asked her, "Why would you tell the group you know the killer's identity? I think the killer was there tonight."

Rhonda shivered. "So do I. I called John, and he and Jason are following us home."

When they arrived home, John and Jason climbed out of their car and scanned the area. John said, "We're going to search your house. Just sit in the living room until we're finished. I'm glad Jason is staying with you and Rick."

After a quick search, John said, "Everything looks okay. Keep your doors locked and don't go out alone until this case is solved." He kissed Rhonda's cheek and left.

The next day, while Jason was at the police station working with John, Rick asked Rhonda if she still wanted to have lunch at Ruby Tuesdays. He said, "I know you like their salad bar."

"I certainly do," she smiled.

Rhonda and Rick's two poodles loved to ride in the car, so Rick put sweaters on them and took them along. Rick usually parked in a place where the dogs could watch the traffic while they waited in the car.

Rick said, "I'm going to park over there across the street from the restaurant." He turned into the parking lot and parked. "While I put the dogs out on that grassy area, why don't you go on to the restaurant and get a table for us?"

Rhonda grabbed her purse and hopped out. Just as she started to cross the street, a car pulled out of nowhere and headed straight for her. She jumped back in time and the car missed her. Before the suspect could turn the car around and make another lunge at her, she ran as fast as she could into the restaurant. She was shaking so hard, she went into the ladies room and stood there until she'd calmed down. When she returned to the dining room, the hostess seated her.

When Rick joined her, she said, "Someone tried to hit me with their car when I crossed the street. I think it was Bob's killer. Did you see that?"

"I'm glad you're okay. No, I didn't see it. I don't guess you got the license number, did you?"

"Are you kidding? I was too busy dodging the car's right bumper," she replied irritably.

"I don't understand why you'd tell those volunteers you know who the killer is."

"Why would you bring me here when you heard me say in front of everyone that we were eating at Ruby Tuesday's today?"

"I'd forgotten about that, but since you remembered, why did you come?"

"I'm trying to help catch the killer."

"By putting yourself in danger? Sometimes I wonder about you and your harebrained schemes," Rick said, lowering his voice. "Are you trying to get yourself killed?"

"Be quiet. People can hear you."

"I'm just worried about you," he said.

Her eyes flashed with anger. "Well, you have a strange way of showing it."

SAUSAGE BALLS

2 cups biscuit mix

1 (1 pound) pkg. hot pork sausage

1 cup shredded cheddar cheese

Combine all ingredients in a bowl and mix with a wooden spoon or our hands. Shape into balls. Place on a jelly-roll pan and bake at 350 degrees for twenty minutes. These freeze well.

CHAPTER THIRTY

THE NEXT DAY, RHONDA PUT the pendant recorder around her neck, and wore it to a cousin's wedding reception that was held at the Wornall House. She loved it because it magnified conversations and taped them so she could listen to them when she returned home.

At home, as she listened, Rhonda heard some guy say that the police weren't doing a very good job of solving Bob Lane's killer. Whomever he was talking to replied, "See that dark-haired woman over there in the burgundy dress. Her name is Rhonda Winters. I heard she told some people at a dinner last night that she knew who the killer was."

That was all Rhonda heard on the subject because somebody stopped by the table whose conversation she was listening to and greeted them, and they began to chat about their children. Jason had attended the wedding with Rhonda and Rick, and on their way home she'd asked, "Jason, are you going to church with us in the morning?"

"Of course. Didn't I go to church with you in Guanajuato? Remember me, I'm Jason the Baptist!"

Rhonda grinned. "Yes, Jason the Baptist, you did go to church with us!"

"What's the name of the church you attend here?"Jason asked.

"Wornall Road Baptist Church. It's located on the corner of Wornall Road and Meyer Boulevard. Rick has been a member there since he was twelve years old. I joined a few months before we were married, thirty five years ago. It's a beautiful brick church with a tall white steeple. I think you'll enjoy the pastor's sermon. Doctor John

Mark Clifton is an excellent speaker. Also, Desiree Wornall will be singing a solo and I wanted you to hear her."

Jason said, "I'll be looking forward to attending the church service and hearing her sing."

The next day at church, after Desiree sang "He's My All in All," the pastor, Dr. Clifton, told the congregation, "Desiree Wornall is the great, great grand daughter of John and Roma Wornall. Roma Wornall donated the land for this church. In October, 1929, when Roma was in her eighties, she attended the first worship service held at the new Wornall Road Baptist Church and she became a charter member. I think it's interesting that Roma's descendant is singing here in the church that she helped start eighty years ago."

The pastor also pointed out that the brass pulpit which Desiree stood behind when she sang, was given in memory of Roma to Wornall Road Baptist Church by her two sons.

After the service, the pastor asked Desiree if the Wornall family had been musically inclined.

Desiree replied, "Granddad was an excellent pianist. Grandmother often talked about how he played the piano at parties. She said the guests would gather around the piano and sing along. He played by ear, and could play any song they requested. My dad has a good baritone voice, and my brother and I both play piano and violin. In college, my brother, John, played guitar in a band."

The pastor asked, "Let's see, wasn't John Wornall III your grandfather?"

"Yes. He died in 1978 when I was two years old. I have a picture of us sitting at his piano together. Mom took that picture of us. It was the last picture ever made of him. He died about two months later from a brain tumor. Since Uncle John, who was John Bristow Wornall IV, had two daughters, Granddad Wornall told Mom if she and dad had a baby boy he wanted her to name him John Bristow Wornall V, and she promised she would. Mom kept that promise to Granddad in 1980 when my brother was born."

CHAPTER THIRTY-ONE

THE NEXT AFTERNOON, WHILE RICK was playing golf, Jason and Rhonda were sitting in the living room talking about drugs being brought from the Mexican border to Kansas City. "There's a Mexican cartel that smuggles cocaine into Kansas City, and there are numerous dealers who sell it here."

Rhonda said, "John is working so hard to catch the ringleader and put a stop to the drug trafficking here."

"I'm wondering if Bart uses drugs," Jason said. "He seems to know quite a bit about them."

"No, I'm sure he doesn't use them. Since he's a doctor, he knows what coke can do to a person."

"Have you ever tried cocaine?" Jason asked.

Rhonda was shocked he would ask her such a question. "No! I certainly have NOT! I've never even seen any. The only things I know about cocaine are what I read in the newspaper and on internet. The only time I ever saw what cocaine looked like or saw how people snort coke was when I saw the movie titled "Cocaine", starring Dennis Weaver."

"I didn't think you had. I haven't seen that movie. What was it about?"

"The guy who Dennis Weaver was playing started out as a nice man, but when he started having problems at work, somebody talked him into snorting coke. Before long, he became an addict, and he lied, cheated, and spent all of his family's savings to buy it. He began having mood swings that threatened his job, his family life went to pot, and finally he overdosed on coke, and was hospitalized. The police found a Ziploc bag of cocaine in his pocket and he ended up before a judge who gave him two years probation, sent him to rehab, and fined him five thousand dollars. The movie showed how drugs can ruin a person's life."

They discussed the drug situation awhile longer, then Jason said, "I see you're wearing the pendant I gave you."

"Yes, I wear it nearly every day. I'm fascinated with its tiny recording device. I've used it to record several conversations."

"I bought it for you because I'd hoped it would be helpful in this investigation. By the way, John asked me to go on a stakeout with him this morning and we saw a woman exchange a hollowed-out book filled with cash for a package the size of a shoe box. We don't know the man's identity, but I think John knows who the woman is. We only saw their backs so we don't know how much money was paid for whatever was in the shoebox."

"What was the woman's name?"

"John didn't say, but I think she's the suspect he followed to the cemetery."

"How did you know the book was hollowed out?"Rhonda asked.

"We were using high powered binoculars that had a special device from an electrical store that amplified sound, but the two conspirators didn't talk much. When I couldn't see anything but their backs, I zoomed the binoculars in on the book and saw the stack of bills. There was a hundred dollar bill on the top, so I presume it was stacked with hundred dollar bills."

"What else did you see?"

"I saw the dealer count the money before he turned over the box to the buyer. When he gave her the box, she opened it and dug through it. Because of the way she was turned, I couldn't see her face or what was inside it. I snapped some pictures of the exchange with my Blackberry."

"How did Bob know this exchange was going to take place?"

"Kirk has worked at the Brookside station for several years and he deals with several snitches. One of them called and told him when and where this transaction was going to take place."

"Thanks for telling me about the stakeout. I wish there was some way we could find out who the woman was. Can you tell me anything about her, the color of her hair, her size, or what she was wearing?"

Jason said, "She was about average height and weight. Her hair was brown and fairly short. It didn't reach her shoulders. She was wearing sunglasses, jeans, and a black sweat shirt. Does that sound like anyone you know?"

"It sounds like about a dozen women I know," Rhonda laughed. "Did John take pictures of them, too?"

"Yes, he did."

"Talking about pictures reminds me of the film in the hidden cameras at the Wornall House. Did it show who stirred peanuts into the cider?"

"There were pictures of various people in the kitchen, but none that showed the face of anyone actually stirring peanuts into the cider," Jason told her.

"Oh, no. I had hoped there would be proof."

"So had I. John was disappointed, too."

Rhonda said, "This case has been difficult because there's two crimes wrapped up in one, murder and drug smuggling. If John had used an undercover agent in that exchange today, he could've cracked the case."

"I talked to John about that this morning, and I offered to go undercover on the next drug deal he hears about. I could do it since I speak fluent Spanish and I know the drug jargon."

"Isn't that dangerous?"

"I'm tough! I can take care of myself. John said he'd think about it."

"I wish I had access to the background checks on all the women suspects. It might help me figure out which woman you saw today."

"Your wish is my command. Guess what I brought to Kansas City with me? My sophisticated police computer! Let's do profiles on your suspects."

"You've made my day!" Rhonda exclaimed excitedly. "John ran background checks on all the suspects, but he wouldn't tell me much."

"You and I have worked together on three cases and we're used to sharing information. This is the first one you've worked on with John. He'll probably be more forthcoming next time."

Jason dashed upstairs to his bedroom and grabbed his computer. He and Rhonda went into her office and he booted it up. He asked, "What name shall I run first?"

She gave him a name and he punched it into the computer. A few minutes later, he had six pages of information.

"People sure leave a paper trail, don't they?" Rhonda asked after she'd finished reading it.

"Yes, they do. They say to follow the money, too. Was there anything in the report that points to her as the perpetrator?" Jason asked.

"Oh, yeah! She's the killer! She's the one who could afford trucks and a plane, too."

"Shall we do some more profiles?"

"Absolutely!" Rhonda exclaimed. "Let's check out all of the suspects."

They were still doing background checks at five when Rick called to tell Rhonda he was on his way home for dinner.

Rhonda was so caught up in reading the profiles, she forgot to start dinner. She said, "Jason, thanks for doing the background checks. Now, I'm positive I know who the killer is."

"Is it the same person you've suspected all along, or have you changed your mind?"

"It's the same one," she said. "Do you want me to tell you her name?"

"Of course!"

She told him.

He laughed. "I think that's John's suspect, too."

"Well, I hope we're right."

Rhonda glanced at the clock. "Oh, my, it's too late to start dinner. Rick will be home any minute. Shall I order pizza or Chinese? Which do you prefer?"

"I have a good recipe for egg salad sandwiches, so I'll cook our supper."

"I love egg salad. What's your recipe?"

"I'll boil some eggs, chop them and mix them with sliced green olives, then add enough mayonnaise to moisten. Do you want yours on wheat or pumpernickel bread?'

"Pumpernickle. Are you sure eggs, olives, and mayo make a good sandwich?" she asked.

"This recipe's delicious with the olives that are stuffed with pimento. It's to die for! Will you make a green salad and some fresh fruit to go with it? Aren't there brownies for dessert?"

CHAPTER THIRTY-TWO

DETECTIVES JOHN PRESTON AND KIRK Woods were at Mandy's home. They sat on her black leather sofa. She was sitting on a black and white striped chair across from them.

"Oops! I'm a lousy hostess," Mandy said. "Can I get you some coffee or a Pepsi?"

They both thanked her, but said they didn't care for anything.

Mandy looked comfortable in a blue jogging suit and white tennis shoes. Her blonde hair had been trimmed in an easy-to-style cut. She was wearing dark eye liner, mascara, and pink lipstick.

Preston took out a tape recorder and asked, "Do you mind if I tape our conversation?"

"Not at all."

Preston said, "I want to ask you some questions about the volunteers at the Wornall House. Did you attend Sally's dinner party?"

"Yes, I had a good time. The food was excellent.

"Who was there besides you?" Woods asked.

"Just the volunteers from the Wornall House—Marianna, Jean, Rhonda, Rick, Bart, and three docents named Tracy, Marlena, and Leanne. I don't remember their last names. Oh, also Bob's ex-wife, Karen, was there."

"Did you talk about Bob Lane's death?"

"Yes, that was one of the topics. Somebody mentioned that they thought Bob was involved in drugs."

"Do you think he was?" Preston asked.

"I think it's a possibility. One time he asked me if I'd drive a van back from the border for him for two thousand dollars. I was dubious about that, so I told him I had to work that weekend. Two thousand was awfully good pay to haul pottery and silver platters."

"Did you ever drive anything back from the border for Bob?"

"No. I never did."

"Who do you think 'doctored' the spiced cider at the Candlelight dinner?"

"If I was a betting woman, I'd bet on either Sally or Karen."

"Why would you bet on Sally?"

"She's from a town in Arizona that's very close to the Mexican border, so it would've been easy for them to be involved in drugs."

"True, but you were from Laredo, which is just across the border from Mexico."

She ignored his comment. "I heard Sally and Bart's son was arrested for possession of drugs."

Woods asked, "Are there other reasons why you suspect her?"

"Her husband is a dentist. He'd have access to drugs."

"Those are good reasons. Now, tell me why you'd suspect Karen?"

"Isn't the wife always a suspect?"she replied.

"What about Jean?" Preston asked.

"Now that you mention it, Jean might've killed him. I think she used to date Bob. If he'd dumped her for Marianna, she'd be jealous, and jealousy is a motive for murder."

"Do you know for sure that Jean used to date Bob?"Woods asked.

"I don't know for sure. That's just what I heard."

"Didn't you date Bob occasionally?"Woods asked.

"Well, yes, but that was mostly when I lived in Texas, and we went out when he was in town. We were just friends."

"You followed him to Kansas City, didn't you?"Preston asked.

"No. I'd been thinking about moving for some time. When he invited me to fly up for the weekend, I came and I liked it here."

"What cargo did Mr. Lane carry in the plane?"Preston asked.

"I have no idea. He had several suitcases in the plane. I remember thinking that he must've brought his entire wardrobe to Texas."

"Were you surprised when Rhonda said she knew the killer's identity?"

"No. Frankly, I didn't believe her. I can't imagine why she'd say that."

"Why didn't you believe her?"

"I don't think Rhonda could know who killed him when nobody else does?"

Woods said, "Mrs. Todd, while we're here, we'd like to search your house."

"You're kidding!"

He pulled a search warrant out of his case and gave it to her. He said, "No, we're serious. Since Bob Lane owned this house, he might've stored something here that *would* interest us. May we begin now?"

"I guess so. I don't have any choice in the matter, do I?"

"No," Woods replied, curtly.

The two detectives gave the house a thorough search, but didn't find any drugs or records.

"Thank you for your time and for permitting the search," Woods said.

Preston said, "Before we go, I'd like to know if you ever told Lane to get his drugs out of your house?"

"No, I never said that, but I overheard that conversation. I know who said it!" Mandy exclaimed.

"Who?"

Mandy told him.

CHAPTER THIRTY THREE

THE NEXT MORNING, RHONDA CALLED John. "I hope you aren't angry at me for telling Sally's dinner guests that I know who the killer is? I know who it is. When I see you, I'll tell you."

"You think it's either Karen or Sally, don't you?"

"We need to discuss this in your office. Can I stop by?"

"Well, I just got back here after searching Mandy's house, and I'm way behind on writing my reports. Can't we discuss it on the phone?"

"I'd rather come to your office. I have an idea about how to catch Bob's killer, and I want to discuss it with you."

"Well, how soon can you get here?" he asked with a sigh.

"I can be there in fifteen minutes."

"Okay. See you then."

Rhonda hung up the phone, grabbed her purse and car keys, and hopped in the car. She headed down Ward Parkway, on her way to Brookside.

She and John had both forgotten he'd told her not to go out alone. She could've asked Jason to go with her, but he was in her office sending emails and faxes to authorities in Mexico, and she didn't want to disturb him.

A few minutes later, Rhonda pulled into a parking lot behind the police station. She dashed into the building and made her way back to John's office.

John was waiting for her. "Come in, Mom, and have a seat. What bee do you have in your bonnet today?"

"I want to discuss some ideas with you. I'm suspicious about a certain suspect."

"Suspicion is not sufficient. A case has to be made that will stand up in court."

"I'm working on that. Did I tell you about the pendant Jason gave me?"

"No. Why would he give you a pendant?"

"A hostess gift, I suppose. Anyway, it's unique. It contains a tiny recording device and it also magnifies voices. I've been recording a lot of conversations and listening to the playback, though I haven't heard anything of real importance so far. I'm wearing it most of the time since I never know when it might come in handy."

"Let me know if you hear anything helpful to the case. I trust your sixth sense."

"I certainly will. Today when Jason and I were talking, I said I wished you had an undercover agent in the Kansas City drug smuggling ring who could help catch the ringleader, and Jason said he had offered to go undercover."

"Kirk's working on it. So who do you think killed Bob?"

Rhonda told him.

He whistled, "She's my prime suspect, too! Now we have to prove it."

"Since I made a guinea pig out of myself at Sally's dinner, and the suspect knows that I'm aware she killed Bob, she might be waiting for me near my home. If a patrolman could follow me home, he could arrest her if she tries to attack me when I get out of the car. I'll have the pendant on in case I can get a confession."

"What if she's already in your house when you get there?"John asked.

"I think Jason is in the house now. Why don't I call him and see if he's still there?"

"Go ahead."

Rhonda punched in his number, and Jason answered.

"Hi. Where are you?" Rhonda asked.

"I'm in your office on my computer communicating with the Nuevo Laredo Police Department."

"Good. Will you be there for awhile?"

"Yes, for at least two hours," Jason said. "Where are you? You weren't supposed to go out alone. Why did you run off without telling me?"

"I didn't want to disturb you. I had to talk to John, but I'll be back in about twenty minutes. Please stay in the house in case our suspect decides to visit me."

"I wish you hadn't gone out. She might try to ram your car on your way home."

"I'm hoping John will ask a cop to follow me home."

"If he doesn't, call me back and I'll come and get you."

"Okay, thanks. Bye."

After she put the cell back into her purse John said, "I'll be the cop who follows you home."

"What about all of those reports you have to write?" Rhonda reminded him.

"They can wait. Nikki would divorce me if I let you get hurt."

"While I'm here, there are a couple things I want to talk about," Rhonda said. "Who showed up on the film in the Wornall House kitchen?"

"We only saw the killer's back. She was shown stirring peanuts into the cider. The picture wasn't too clear. We didn't see her face."

"How do you know it was peanuts they were stirring into the cider? Maybe the cook was just stirring the spices and the cider together to mix it before serving it."

"We made close ups of a whole peanut and what we think were crushed peanuts in the brew."

Rhonda suggested, "Well, the suspect doesn't know about the hidden cameras, so why don't you tell her the police have clear pictures of her stirring peanuts into the cider?"

"I've been thinking about that idea of yours. I think it might work."

"I think the suspect will be so surprised when she thinks she's caught red handed, you'll get a confession."

"If that doesn't work, I'm sure you can think up another wild idea," John laughed.

"I haven't told you this, but someone tried to hit me with their car when Rick and I went to Ruby Tuesdays. With God's help, I was able to jump out of the way in time."

"Do NOT leave your house again unless Jason and Rick are both with you," John ordered.

John picked up his phone and called Jason. He told him to keep his gun handy. "There's already been two attempts on Rhonda's life. I'm following her home, and leaving now."

"I'll be ready," Jason said. "See you soon."

Rhonda stood. "Well, let's go."

Just then Rhonda's cell phone rang. It was her granddaughter, Jacquelyn.

"Hello, sweetheart, I'm so glad to hear from you. Sure, we'll take you to the Wornall House to see Father Christmas. Yes, you can have your picture made with him. Ask your mom and dad when you can go and call me back tonight."

John said, "I don't want you to take the kids out until this case is solved. I have to think of their safety."

"Then you've got to solve it soon! They want to visit Father Christmas!"

"One step at a time. First, we've got to get you home. I'll be following you."

"Sorry to be a nuisance."

"I don't consider you a nuisance."

"Thanks."

"Well, Mom, since I don't have any other trick up my sleeve, I've decided to try yours. I'm going to tell the suspect we have her on camera. I hope it works!"

"I think it will."

"As you're fond of saying, 'Nothing ventured, nothing gained'."

CHAPTER THIRTY-FOUR

RHONDA DROVE HOME AND PARKED in her driveway. She turned on the recorder in her pendant, threw her purse over her shoulder, and punched in the code to open the garage door. She walked inside, but before she could close the garage door and unlock the kitchen door, Rhonda suddenly felt the hard prod of metal shoved against her back. Shocked, she turned around and saw someone standing behind her wearing a ski mask. When she saw the ski mask, she knew it was the same person who had tried to push her over the banister at the Wornall House the other night.

The suspect pushed the metal object harder into Rhonda's back and said in a falsetto voice, "Move it! Walk inside with your arms raised."

Rhonda was terribly tensed up and nervous. When she walked into the house, the dogs greeted her, yapping excitedly, leaping up and down, their tails wagging. When she didn't reach down and pet them or pick them up and hug them like she always did when she came home, they looked at her with puzzled expressions on their faces.

"What's this about?" Rhonda asked the intruder.

"Do as I say or I'll squeeze the trigger," the suspect ordered, pointing a forty-five automatic at her. "Put your purse on the floor."

Rhonda did what she was told to do. Shaking, she knew this was the person who had cold-heartedly killed Bob by stirring peanuts into the cider.

She wondered why Jason hadn't come to her rescue.

The suspect stood a few feet away from Rhonda, gun pointed at her, and growled, "Do as I say! I'd as soon shoot you as look at you!"

"Please put the gun down and let's talk," Rhonda pleaded. "What do you want? Money and jewelry?"

The dogs carefully watched the suspect. They understood this person was threatening their owner. Suddenly, both dogs turned toward the suspect, snarled, and began barking ferociously at her.

The suspect ordered gruffly, "Make those stupid mutts shut up!"

When the suspect kicked at them as hard as she could, both dogs simultaneously attacked her, which caught her off guard and caused her to drop the gun onto the floor.

Rhonda scrambled to grab the gun. She picked it up and pointed it at the suspect, slowly moving backwards. She screamed, "Get out of my house right now before I blow your head off, and don't think I can't do it. I'm an expert marksman! Get out! NOW!"

The suspect turned and raced out the door.

Rhonda locked the door behind her and yelled, "Jason, where are you?"

Jason stepped from behind the dining room door, his gun in his hand.

"Why didn't you confront her?" Rhonda asked angrily. "She could've killed me!"

"I was watching. If she'd started to shoot you, I was ready for her, but you and the dogs handled the situation just fine. If I'd come out when she was holding the gun, she could've grabbed you as a hostage and threatened to shoot you unless I threw down my gun. Then we'd both have been unarmed. It worked out for the best this way. She didn't see me and I didn't blow my cover. Now, I can still go undercover tomorrow."

Rhonda was upset with Jason. "All you cared about was not blowing your cover. She could've killed me while you hid behind that door."

Jason decided not to argue the point. He said, "I'll go outside and see if John needs help."

Just as Jason opened the door, John sailed through it and complained, "I ran a red light trying to stay up with you, and a cop stopped me. I flashed my badge and he let me go, but that slowed me down. I got here as the suspect started to drive away. She didn't see me, and I didn't want to arrest her because first I wanted to make sure you were all right. We know who she is. There's plenty of time to nab her. I saw her face after she yanked off her ski mask."

"I guess you realize she was the one who tried to push me over the railing and tried to run me down. "Not only did I get the entire episode on my pendant tape recorder, but I also filmed the entire scene on the hidden video camera that Jason installed in the kitchen!"

"What camera are you talking about?" John asked. "I didn't know you had a camera in here."

"Jason gave it to Rick and he installed it for us. It's called a Stealth 1 DVR Camera."

"That's good news! I'll look at it later. Just tell me the gist now of what happened."

"In a nutshell, she stuck her gun to my back, the dogs barked at her, she kicked them, they attacked her, she dropped her gun, and I picked it up. Then I aimed her own gun at her and told her if she didn't get out of my house, I'd shoot her head off! I told her that I'm an EXPERT marksman! She believed me, and got the heck out of Dodge!"

John said, surprised, "I didn't know you were an expert marksman."

Rhonda laughed. "I've never shot a gun in my life!"

CHAPTER THIRTY FIVE

Before John left Rhonda's home, she gave him the suspect's gun and said, "I hope it's registered in her name."

John took it. "Thanks, I'll check it out."

"Let's take a quick look at that film before you take off," Rhonda suggested. "You might want to take it with you."

Jason connected the unit from the Stealth camera to the TV and they watched the entire episode. As they heard the dogs barking on film, Rhonda put her arms around both of the poodles at the same time, and gave them a hug. She took turns holding each dog on her lap, petting them, and whispering, "Good puppies. You saved my neck!"

After they finished watching the film, John said, "Jason, what a fantastic gift you brought to them! That film will help convict our suspect. I've got to run. Kirk and I have an appointment in an hour to interview Jean Murphy.

"I thought your appointment was with Mandy," Jason said.

John shook his head. "I searched her house this morning."

Jason said, "The suspect didn't see me, so I'm available if you want to use me as an undercover agent."

"When we first talked about you going undercover, I was against it, but something has happened since then to change my mind, so I've reconsidered. I'll call you about it later."

After John left, Rhonda turned to Jason, "Your Stealth1 camera saved the day. I guess I'll forgive you for letting me stew in the suspect's clutches."

"I'm sorry you were scared, but I think I did what was best. I was watching her carefully, and if she'd started to shoot you, I'd have shot her before she could've pulled the trigger! I really am an expert marksman!"

Detectives John Preston and Kirk Woods arrived on time at Jean Murphy's home. Jean invited them into the living room. She was friendly and kind as always when they'd been there. She offered them tea and gingerbread.

"Nothing for me, thank you," Woods replied.

Preston smiled and accepted. "Thank you." He ate a couple bites of the gingerbread and said, "This is delicious."

"Here's the recipe. I thought you might want it, so I made you a copy."

"Thank you, Mrs. Murphy. You're so thoughtful and your gingerbread is the best I've ever eaten. You're a wonderful cook."

She smiled. "There's plenty. I know you like sweets."

After he finished eating the gingerbread, he put the recipe in his attaché case.

While Preston was eating, Woods asked, "Mrs. Murphy, how is your web site design business coming along?"

"Very well, thank you," she replied.

Preston then turned to her. "Mrs. Murphy, we appreciate the tea, the gingerbread, and the recipe. You've been so nice to us that I hate to bring up such an unpleasant subject as drugs."

"Drugs?" she asked, surprised. "What are you talking about?"

"We want to talk to you about Bob Lane's import-export business."

She said, "I don't know anything about Bob's business."

"It's come to our attention that when Bob's trucks went to the border to pick up a load, sometimes packages of cocaine were tucked into some of the imports. What can you tell us about that?" Preston asked.

"Well, that's news to me, gentlemen. I don't know anything about it."

When they saw they weren't going to learn anything from Jean about Bob's extra-curricular activities, Kirk handed her a paper and said, "Mrs. Murphy, this is your copy of a search warrant. We'd like to search your house now."

"Why?" she asked warily.

"We've been conducting searches in the homes of some witnesses. It's standard procedure in such cases."

"Have you searched Mandy's house?" she asked.

"Yes, we did."

"What did you find?" she asked.

"We can't give out that information."

"You said you wanted to come over here for a chat," Jean grumbled.

"We've chatted. Now, we'd like to search your house."

Jean became angry. "You've pulled a fast one on me. You're a wolf in sheep's clothing, pretending to be so nice, then after you finish eating my gingerbread and drinking my tea, you want to search my house and make a big mess of everything I own."

"I promise you, we'll be very careful and put everything back where it belongs. We won't make a mess, if that's what's worrying you."

"I don't understand why you'd want to search my home simply because you think Bob was mixed up in drug trafficking."

Preston said, "I know you and Bob were friends. We thought he might've stored something at your home that he hadn't been able to retrieve before he died."

"Well, you thought wrong. If you're interested in Bob's business, why don't you go search his house instead of mine and leave me along? I'm busy. I have web sites to design."

"Mrs. Murphy, we've searched the homes of several people. None of them have liked it, but all of them have allowed us to do it. We're going to start our search now," Woods said.

They put on latex gloves. "We'll start in this room where you're sitting so you can see that we're being careful with your things and that everything is put back just the way you had it," Woods told her.

Preston removed the cushions, unzipped them, and edged his hand inside to check all around it. He did the same with the loveseat and chairs. Kirk opened the drawers in the end tables and coffee tables, removed every item and carefully looked through them. The men methodically searched everything in the first and second floors, and in the attic. They took one shoe from her bedroom and bagged it. As agreed, they replaced everything else just as it had been before they started their search.

Last of all, they went downstairs to the basement, which had been divided into an office, a work room, and a storage room. They carefully looked through Jean Murphy's office, the desk, the file cabinets, and the bookcases. At one end of the room, there was a place for customers to sit. A green sofa set on an Oriental rug. There were lamp tables on either side of the sofa, and a small coffee table in front of it. The men moved the furniture and pulled up the rug. Beneath the rug, they discovered a narrow door. They pulled it back and found a cellar had been dug into the basement floor. They looked inside the cellar and were surprised to see that it was filled with shoeboxes. They opened the boxes and took pictures of the contents in each.

From there, they searched the work room and the storage room, but found nothing of significance. At the back of the storage room, there were two locked closets. Woods used a special key to open the locks, and John searched the first closet. The second closet contained a huge locked safe. Woods had a talent for opening safes. He fiddled with the combination until he cracked open the safe. It was filled with hollowed out books. They opened them and took a picture of each one.

They carefully replaced the shoeboxes, closed the door, placed the rug over it, and arranged the furniture just as it had been when they came downstairs. Woods closed the safe door, and locked both closet doors.

The men went back upstairs and saw Jean sitting in her living room, reading a book.

"Well, are you satisfied?" she asked.

Woods explained, "Mrs. Murphy, we just got a call from the dispatcher and there's an emergency at the station we have to take care of. We haven't had time to finish searching the basement, so we'll need to come back tomorrow about three o'clock to finish."

"Three o'clock tomorrow will be fine," she agreed.

"Thanks." Preston handed her a receipt. "This is for one shoe. You'll get it back ASAP."

"Why are you taking my shoe?"

"It's no big deal. We just want to check something on it. It won't be damaged. We have to go. Thanks for allowing us to search your home, for the delicious gingerbread, and the recipe. Goodbye until tomorrow."

The two men hurriedly left.

That night the two detectives, Preston and Woods staked out a house in the Brookside section of Kansas City. Though they were exhausted from a very busy day, they sat patiently in an unmarked car in the dark and waited.

Before two hours passed, their patience was rewarded when they saw a van pull into the driveway of the house they were watching. Two men got out of the van and went around to the back of the house and began carrying boxes and suitcases from the basement of the house to the car. It only took about twenty minutes for them to fill the van.

After finishing their work, the men climbed into the vehicle and drove away. The detectives followed them at a discreet distance until they turned onto the interstate.

Once they were on I-435, Preston notified the Missouri State Police to stop the van and search it. He and Woods stayed behind the men until they saw two state patrol cars pull in behind them and turn on their sirens. The van driver pulled over and stopped. Preston and Woods stopped also, in case the state patrol needed back-up. After a patrolmen opened one box and found cocaine, they cuffed the two men and put them in the back of one of the state police cars.

The police searched the van and found one hundred and twenty hollowed-out books filled with cash and fifty shoeboxes of neatly packed cocaine packages. The authorities confiscated the cash and the cocaine.

The next morning, a few hours after the coke and cash seizure on the interstate, Detective Kirk Woods was involved in another cocaine confiscation.

On the previous day, Woods had been contacted by an informant who occasionally called with information. Woods always used the slush fund to pay the snitch for his help. The snitch, named Tomas Gomez, had told Woods he'd been asked to take the place of a courier and meet with a lady drug smuggler the next morning at ten to exchange a shoebox of cocaine for cash. He said the exchange was to take place at Loose Park, located on Wornall Road.

Detective Woods asked the snitch if he'd be willing to allow an undercover agent to take his place. The snitch agreed, and Woods was excited about it. He talked to Preston, who told him to set it up. The details were worked out in Woods' unmarked car, which was parked in an underground parking garage at the Plaza. The snitch briefed the undercover agent about what to do and exactly where he was to meet the woman.

Before the informant courier, Jason Valores, arrived at Loose Park, Woods wired him for audio and video surveillance so the police could listen in on his conversation. If necessary, they could also come to his rescue.

When Valores arrived at the park to make the exchange, the woman was waiting for him. She was sitting at a picnic table with a large white wicker picnic basket. Before she gave him the money, she waited to hear the agreed upon code word.

The courier said, "I should have brought you some roses."

'Roses' was the code word. When it was spoken, the woman stood and handed the man a hollowed-out book filled with hundred dollar bills in exchange for the shoebox he was carrying. He opened the book and counted hundred dollars bills, as she opened the shoebox and counted to make sure it was filled with all of the cocaine packages she'd paid for.

The courier said, "I'm a little hesitant to accept hundred dollar bills because they're often counterfeit."

The dealer said, "Let me assure you there's nothing to worry about. All of these hundreds are the Real McCoy!"

"I hope so. I'll be in hot water if they aren't. And we'd both have the feds after us. As you know, the feds are interested in phony money."

"I'd never do something to attract the feds," she said. She touched the coke with her finger, put her finger to her mouth, and tasted it. She nodded. "Good quality."

Satisfied with the trade, she placed the box inside her picnic basket, thanked him, put the basket on her arm, and headed for her car.

While the transaction was taking place, four police officers were quietly surrounding them. Just as the dealer started to put the basket into the trunk of her car, the officers closed in, with guns drawn.

The dealer was shocked. A narcotics agent seized her picnic basket while an officer took the cash-filled book from the courier.

When the narcotics agent started to arrest Valores, he showed him his badge and ID. He said in a low voice, "I'm sure you'll check the hundred dollar bills for counterfeits."

The agent nodded. "We always check the hundreds, and we've found a lot of phonies."

Valores represented Mexico in the war on drugs when he joined forces with Preston and Woods while he was in Kansas City. He'd been willing to assist them in anything they needed him to do. He was thankful the two Mexican truck drivers from Guanajuato, Mexico, had been arrested by the Highway Patrol.

It was also exciting news to Valores that the female drug trafficker was caught red handed in Loose Park. She was arrested there and taken to the Brookside Police Station.

JEAN MURPHY'S GINGERBREAD

COMBINE IN A BOWL:

1 cup sugar

1 tsp. ginger

½ tsp. cloves

½ tsp. cinnamon

STIR IN AND MIX WELL:

1 cup Canola oil

1 cup molasses

A mixture of 1 ½ tsp. baking soda and 1 cup boiling water

STIR IN AND MIX WELL:

2 ½ cups flour

3 beaten eggs

Mix well. Beat until blended. Pour into a greased 9 x13-inch pan and bake in a pre-heated 350 degree oven for 40 to 45 minutes.

CHAPTER THIRTY-SIX

After John's suspect was apprehended at Loose Park, she was brought to the Brookside police station for questioning. She was taken into the interrogation room that had two-way mirrors. Jason and Rhonda were invited to sit in the adjoining room on the other side of the mirrors. They couldn't be seen, but they could see and hear everything that was said. Detectives John Preston and Kirk Woods interrogated her.

Detective Preston said, "Before I ask you any questions, I want to tell you what we've been doing since we saw you yesterday. When we searched your house and left early, it was because we saw and photographed the hollowed-out books stuffed with hundred dollar bills. We also looked inside your cellar and counted the fifty shoeboxes packed with cocaine. We wanted to give you, figuratively speaking, enough rope to hang yourself.

"We assumed if we left early you'd think we had not seen the cash or the cocaine. We believed you planned to have it hauled off sometime through the night so we wouldn't find it if we returned to continue our search. Woods and I staked out your house that night, and sure enough we saw two men park a van in your driveway about midnight. We watched them fill the van with the cash and coke.

We followed the van as it left your house. When it turned onto I-435, we called the State Patrol and asked them to stop the van and search it. The state troopers arrested the two men, who turned out to be your two truckers, and they seized the contents.

"Before you tell us the cash and cocaine weren't yours, we want you to know that we have two DVD's of you paying two couriers with cash in exchange for cocaine. In fact, the most recent transaction took place at Loose Park this morning where you were arrested. We took a close-up of your face. The courier was an undercover agent who will testify against you in court. Do you have anything to say?"

"Yes, I do. I want to hear my Miranda rights, and I want an attorney."

John read her rights to her, then let her call a lawyer.

After she hung up the phone, she said, "My attorney said he'll be here in thirty minutes."

"That's fine. We won't ask you any questions until he's here," Woods said, "but instead of sitting here and twiddling our thumbs while we wait for him, I'll tell you what else we know about you. We've arrested the two truck drivers and the pilot who work for you. Believe me, they sang like canaries! They told us you're the master mind of the smuggling operation that brought cocaine from Mexico to Kansas City."

Kirk continued, "You've been followed for several days by police officers. We know what you've been doing. You were seen driving into the Forest Hills Cemetery and digging a hole by John Wornall's tombstone where you buried a box with a key inside it."

She sat quietly, her hands folded, her head bowed, her eyes closed.

Kirk continued, "You'd instructed your pilot to dig up the key, take it to a storage area, unlock it, and take the cocaine hidden there, and distribute it. We have a DVD of both you and the pilot. The pilot was arrested and the narcotics agents seized your coke.

"If that's not enough proof of your guilt, you shoved Rhonda, trying to push her over the railing to her death two floors below. When that failed you tried to hit her with your car. Next, you pushed your way into Rhonda's kitchen, armed with a forty-five automatic and threatened to shoot her, and you might have if her dogs hadn't attacked you, causing you to drop your gun.

Here are two things you didn't know that will help convict you. Rhonda was given a pendant that tapes everything that is said in a room.

Rick had also been given a hidden video camera which was installed in his kitchen by an undercover agent. This small DVR Camera looks like an ordinary motion sensor, but the wireless surveillance camera silently records up to forty five days of high-quality digital video of anything that happens in her kitchen. As you probably have guessed by now, it has pictures of you in your ski mask. Even though you were wearing a mask, we have ways of identifying you, and even though you spoke in a high falsetto voice, we can still identify the voice as yours. We are very high tech here in Kansas City!"

"I drove up about the time you came running out of Rhonda's house. I saw you jump in your car, pull off the ski mask you'd worn inside, and I saw your face. I can identify you. So, don't waste time denying your involvement."

"By the way, the narcotics agents are checking those hundred dollar bills to find out if you were passing counterfeit."

She spoke before they could stop her. "I don't pass phonies."

Her attorney arrived at this time. He introduced himself as Roger Barnes. He asked the detectives, "Have you been interrogating my client?"

"No. We've only been explaining the charges against her."

Barnes turned to her and asked, "Do you wish to answer questions at this time?"

"Yes, we might as well get it over and done with."

Detective Preston asked, "Why were you at Rhonda's home trying to kill her?"

She glanced at her attorney and asked the detective, "What are you talking about?"

"There were three witnesses who saw you at Rhonda's home threatening her with your gun. When you dropped the gun and Rhonda grabbed it and pointed it at you, you ran away, leaving it. The serial number was not scratched off. We traced the gun to you since it was registered in your name."

Preston added, "I saw you run out of Rhonda's house, jump into your car, and yank off your ski mask."

"Don't say anything," the lawyer warned her.

Preston continued, "The reason you were at Rhonda's house with a gun was because you planned to kill her! You heard her say that she saw

Bob Lane's killer stirring peanuts into the spiced cider. Incidentally, we have you on film doing just that. There was a hidden camera in the kitchen of the Wornall House."

The attorney asked, "What's this all about?"

"Murder and drug trafficking!" Preston exclaimed.

"I didn't mean to kill Bob," she said. "I only wanted to punish him for dumping me for Marianna. I couldn't believe how he treated me after all I'd done for him. He was threatening to turn me into the police, which would've been stupid since he was also involved."

"How many years have you been a drug smuggler?" Woods asked.

Barnes shouted, "She doesn't have to answer that!" He turned to her and asked, "Why do you need me? You've been confessing to these detectives in spite of my objections."

"I want you to make a deal with them. I did not mean to kill Bob. He never told me he had a life threatening allergy. It boggles my mind that two or three little peanuts could've killed him."

"Who's the ringleader of this smuggling operation?" Preston asked.

"Don't answer that!" the lawyer shouted.

"I'm the ring leader," she admitted, proudly, her head high.

"Which drug did you distribute?"

"Cocaine," she replied, ignoring him.

Woods said, "The DA will charge you with Murder One and drug trafficking."

When her attorney realized the seriousness of the charges against her, he tried to cut a deal. He suggested that if she confessed to charges of drug trafficking and murder, the charge should be reduced from first degree murder to manslaughter.

Woods said, "We'll talk it over." Then he turned to her. Before we call it a day, tell me why you got involved in drug trafficking."

"My ex-husband got me involved in it, then he left me for another woman. By this time, I was in too deep to get out. I wish I'd never met that man."

"Where is he now?" Kirk asked.

"He's married to the other woman and they're both involved in the drug trade."

"If you want to get even with them, give us their names and addresses," Woods said. "We'll get them for you!"

That thought cheered her up. Her face broke into a big grin. "What a wonderful suggestion! His name is Gary Murphy. I can't give you his exact address, but he lives in Savannah, Georgia. I know his birth date and his social security number. That should help you catch him!"

"Yes, it will," Detective Woods said, a big grin on his face. "Yes, it sure will!"

Showing them that she still had a sense of humor, she said, "Just don't put them in the same prison I'll be in. That would be double jeopardy!"

CHAPTER THIRTY-SEVEN

As soon as Rhonda got home from the police station, she called Jamie and Anna. Jamie answered and Rhonda said, "I have news about Bob's death! I know this is a last minute invitation, but if you two are free tonight at six, and you want to find out WHO killed Bob, could you come to a short meeting at my house? Afterwards, we'll have pizza, ice cream, and cokes."

"I'll be there. Let me ask Anna if she can come."

A minute later, Jamie returned to the phone and said, "Anna said wild horses couldn't keep her away!"

"Great. I'll see you two at six."

Rhonda then talked to Sally and Marianna in a three-way telephone conversation. "As you know, it's my turn to have the meeting and the dinner. I have some exciting news for all of you about who killed Bob and why he was killed. Can you come here at six tonight?"

They both said they'd be there.

Sally added, "I'm sure Bart will come, too. Shall I call Karen?"

"Yes, please call her," Rhonda said. "It's four o'clock now. I don't have time to cook a delicious dinner like you two served to Rick and me. I'll have to order pizza, and serve it with a green salad, colas, and Spumoni ice cream for dessert."

"That's fine. Pizza sounds like manna from heaven!" Marianna exclaimed. "I can't wait to find out who killed Bob and why."

The group arrived promptly. At six o'clock, they were all seated in the family room. Rhonda had set out a snack of cheese, crackers, and a bowl of fresh strawberries with a fruit dip made with a mixture of a jar of marshmallow crème and one cup of softened cream cheese.

As soon as they were seated, Marianna said, "Rhonda, we've been worried about you. When you told us you knew who the killer was, we were afraid she might attack you."

"I nearly met my Waterloo! The suspect tried to shove me over a banister and mow me down with her car. When I jumped out of the way, she came to my house with a loaded gun. She threatened to shoot me, but before she could pull the trigger, my dogs attacked her. They caused her to drop the gun, so I grabbed it and threatened to shoot her! She ran out the door. Crime doesn't pay! I'm still alive and she's a jailbird!"

Jamie laughed, "What an adventure! We're all thankful you're safe."

"Thank you."

Marianna said, "We learned one thing about the suspect from your terror story. The suspect is a woman."

Sally said, "Oh, come on, Rhonda, tell us who killed Bob."

""You'll find out in a few minutes," Rhonda said. She couldn't wait to see the expressions on their faces when they learned the identity of the killer and the drug peddling ringleader. Also, two surprise guests were coming.

When the doorbell rang and John and Jason walked in, Rhonda went to the front of the room and stood behind the podium. She said, "Our guest speaker will tell you who killed Bob and why he was killed. You'll also learn how Bob got mixed up in a drug trafficking operation. Our guest speaker brought a friend with him."

Rhonda motioned for them to join her at the podium. They came and stood beside her, and she said, "I'd like to introduce you to our son-in-law, Homicide Detective John Preston and to one of our best friends, Jason Valores, the Director of Police Security in Guanajuato, Mexico."

"Rhonda, you can sure keep a secret!" Sally exclaimed. "We had no idea that Detective Preston was your son-in-law or that your friend was a Mexican police director."

They all laughed.

Marianna said, "Jason, it's nice to meet you. Have you been sleuthing with Rhonda?"

"A little," Jason replied smiling.

Rhonda said, "Jason will testify in court against the suspect. There's no need to introduce John since you've all met him. He'll talk to you about murder and the drug peddling ringleader's secret life."

Rhonda sat down.

John began with a bang. "Jean Murphy killed Bob. She's been the ringleader of a drug trafficking operation here in Brookside for ten years!"

He paused to let that sink in.

There was stunned silence.

Finally, Jamie exclaimed, "Jean? I can't believe she was a killer and a drug smuggler!"

"Believe it! She's tried to kill me three times in the past few days," Rhonda said.

Marianna said, "What a shock! Jean seemed like a nice woman."

"People can sure surprise you, can't they?" Anna asked.

John said, "if you have any questions, just ask."

Karen asked, "Detective Preston, how did you find out that Jean killed Bob?"

"When I told Jean about the hidden camera in the Wornall House kitchen, and said there were clear pictures of her popping peanuts into the punch, she confessed."

Preston added, "That was Rhonda's idea, and it worked!"

Rhonda said, "It was actually a lie, and I feel guilty about it. The film showed a back view of someone stirring the brew, but that's all."

Preston said, "The police are allowed to stretch the truth if that's what it takes to solve a crime."

"That makes me feel better," Rhonda admitted.

Marianna asked, "Do you mean there weren't any pictures of a woman putting peanuts in the cider?"

"No. Just a picture of someone's back. We tricked Jean, but she fell for it, hook, line, and sinker," John said.

Jamie asked, "Did any ghosts show up on the film?"

"Not a one!" John exclaimed with a grin. "Not even the Lady in Blue. Jean was an evil woman who involved Bob in the drug trade and ruined his life. She killed him out of jealousy and fear. Bob wanted to get out of the drug smuggling business and he threatened to tell the police about Jean's involvement if she didn't let him out. Jean couldn't let that happen, so she retaliated. She knew about Bob's drug allergy, so she stirred crushed peanuts into the spiced cider."

"Did she know the peanuts would kill him?" Marianna asked.

"Jean swore she didn't mean to kill him. She said she just wanted to punish him. I don't know if that's true or not. She knew Bob could turn her in if he lived. She might've said that in the hope of a lighter sentence. We all make choices, and she chose a life of crime. Now she has to pay the piper."

"How did Jean involve Bob in the drug trade?" Marianna asked.

"She set him up in the import-export business. She bought two trucks and a plane to haul his imports to KC. Bob ran an honest business at first, but soon the trucks began hauling cocaine."

"How did you find out that Jean was the ringleader of the drug trafficking operation?" Bart asked.

"She confessed it to us. She seemed proud of it. The police followed her for three days and caught her in several illegal drug deals. We told her the truckers and the pilot, who had also been arrested, ratted on her. When she realized we knew everything about her drug trafficking operation, she admitted she'd been the ringleader for ten years."

John said, "I'll tell you a secret. Jean had me fooled for awhile. She was a great cook and she fed me tea and cookies like my mom used to make. She was a good actress. She would have done well in Hollywood!"

Mandy asked, "What did Jean say when she realized she was caught and was on her way to the pokey?"

She hung her head, closed her eyes, and muttered, "MY GOOSE IS COOKED!"

EPILOGUE

JEAN MURPHY'S COURT DATE HAD come and gone. The web site designer and volunteer assistant cook at the Wornall House Museum, was found guilty of the murder of her former lover and co-volunteer, Bob Lane.

Jean Murphy also pled guilty to charges of conspiracy to possess and distribute cocaine and for being the ringleader of a drug trafficking operation for ten years. She received a combined sentence of thirty years in prison for manslaughter in the death of Bob Lane, for the attempted murder of Rhonda Winters, and for her drug trafficking operation.

The investigation also involved agents and officers from ICE, Immigration and Customs Enforcement, the DEA, Drug Enforcement Administration, and the IRS Criminals Investigations.

The federal investigators cracked a huge cocaine smuggling ring in Kansas City and thwarted the drug dealers. In just the past six months, the drug traffickers allegedly had imported over two tons of cocaine to Kansas City, with a street value of several million dollars.

"Four co-defendants in the case were two Mexican truck drivers from Guanajuato, Mexico, Joaquin Melendez, and Luis Villagrande, a pilot from Kansas City named Ray Carter, and Mark Martin, from Mission Hills. These men received sentences ranging from two years for Martin to twenty years in prison for the truckers.

The police chief stated, "This successful operation has dealt a blow to cocaine trafficking in Kansas City, Missouri."

Detective Preston gave credit to four people: Detective Kirk Woods; Director of Police Security, Jason Valores, of Guanajuato, Mexico; Gregory Garson, an expert polygraph examiner; and to an amateur sleuth who wished to remain anonymous.

Preston added, "Without their help we wouldn't have had a GHOST of a chance of solving THE MURDER AT THE JOHN WORNALL HOUSE MUSEUM in ten days!"

CHRISTMAS RECIPES FROM THE 1860'S

BOTH ELIZA AND ROMA WORNALL may have used these recipes when they prepared Christmas dinner for their families in the 1860's.

These recipes were prepared this year for the volunteers in the dining room scene who participated in the Christmas Candlelight Tour. They were cooked in the same open hearth fireplace where Eliza and Roma once cooked.

Copies of these recipes are available for those tour members who desire them.

ROAST DUCKLING

1 (4 -5 lb.) duck, cleaned and left whole, giblets removed

¾ tsp. black pepper, plus an additional 1/2 tsp. black pepper

¾ tsp. salt, plus an additional 1 ½ tsp. salt

¼ tsp. cayenne pepper, plus an additional ¼ tsp. cayenne

½ tsp. dried thyme leaves

Wash duckling and dry it inside and out. Season the inside or cavity of the duck with ¾ tsp. black pepper, ¾ tsp. salt, ¼ tsp. cayenne, and all of the thyme leaves. Sprinkle the additional pepper, salt, and cayenne on the outside of the duck and rub it in. Place duck in a greased roasting pan and roast at 475 degrees for twenty minutes. Reduce heat to 350 and bake it for one hour and twenty minutes, basting frequently with pan drippings. Increase heat to 475 degrees and roast duck for twenty minutes longer to make the outside crisp. Remove duck from pan, and drain off excess fat. Cool fifteen minutes before carving.

CONCORD GRAPE PIE

4 cups Concord grapes

½ cup sugar

¼ cup flour

2 Tbsp. butter

Pastry for 9-inch double crust pie

Stem grapes and slip pulp out of the skins. Reserve skins. Cook pulp until seeds loosen. Press through colander or sieve to remove seeds. Combine pulp and skins with sugar and flour. Blend filling and pour into a crust-lined pie plate. Dot with butter. Cover with top crust and cut slashes in crust. Crimp edges together. Bake in a 400 degree oven for ten minutes. Reduce heat to 350 and bake for 25 to 30 minutes longer.

CHRISTMAS PLUM PUDDING

2 eggs

Small blade of mace

Pinch of nutmeg

Pinch of cinnamon

½ tsp. salt

1 cup milk

½ cup sugar

¾ cup suet, chopped fine

¾ cup raisins

1 cup currants

2 Tbsp. candied lemon peel, sliced

2 Tbsp. citron, sliced

1/3 cup bread crumbs

1/3 cup flour

In a large bowl, beat together the eggs, mace, nutmeg, cinnamon, and salt. Add milk slowly, mixing after each addition. Stir in sugar, suet, raisins, currants, lemon peel, citron, bread crumbs, and flour. Mix well. Pour batter into a greased and sugar-dusted two quart mold. Place mold on a trivet in a steamer over one-inch of boiling water. Cover the steamer or kettle tightly. Place over high heat until steam begins to escape, then lower heat to medium low and steam for six hours. Serve with sauce. Recipe follows.

SAUCE FOR PLUM PUDDING

4 Tbsp. brown sugar

1 Tbsp. flour

1 cup water

2 Tbsp. butter

Mix brown sugar and flour in a medium saucepan. Add water and stir as it cooks, uncovered, over low heat until sauce thickens. Add butter and mix until blended. Spoon sauce over slices of steamed pudding.

PARTIAL GENEALOGY OF THE WORNALL FAMILY

1. ROBY WORNALL-- born in England, married Edith, and had five children: Ann, Drucilla, Elizabeth, James, and Thomas. He died in August, 1784 in Loudoun County, Virginia.

2. COLONEL THOMAS WORNALL-- born December 13, 1775, married Sarah Ryan, daughter of John and Susannah Ryan in 1797. Their 10 children were: John Ryan; Richard; Keturah; Thomas; Eliza Ann; Alfred; James Ryan; Nancy Tucker; Oliver Perry (1819-1889); and Susan Ryan. Col. Thomas Wornall died Nov. 3, 1838 at the age of 62. Sarah died in 1854 at the age of 77.

3. OLIVER PERRY WORNALL, born October 12, 1819 in Clark County, Kentucky. He was a farmer in Paris, Ky. He was the son of Colonel Thomas Wornall and Sarah Ryan. He moved to Bourbon County in 1845. On Feb. 25, 1815, he married Elizabeth Ewalt. They had two sons: Samuel, born March 27, 1845 and Thomas, born December 13, 1847. He died on January 28, 1889, at the age of 69.

4. Ben Woodford Wornall was born June 13, 1909, and he married Katherine Hardin on May 31, 1947. They had one son, Dr. Perry Woodford Wornall, who lives in Kentucky with his family.

5. RICHARD WORNALL—BORN September 9, 1799, married Judith Ann Glover on September 23, 1820. Their children were: John Bristow Wornall and George Thomas Wornall. His second wife was Polly Williams. Richard died on June 10, 1864, at the age of 64.

6. JOHN BRISTOW WORNALL—born October 12, 1822 in Kentucky, married Matilda Polk in 1850, Sarah Eliza Johnson, on September 20, 1854, and Roma Johnson in Sept, 25, 1866. John and Eliza had seven children, but five died by the age of three. Their two living sons were Francis Clay (1855-1954), and Thomas Johnson,(1865-1923). John and Roma had two sons, John Bristow Wornall Junior, (1872-1962) and Charles Hardin Wornall, (1876-1938). John Wornall Senior died in 1892.

7. FRANCIS CLAY WORNALL (FRANK), born Sept. 28, 1855 and died in 1954. He married Kate Chrisman on Dec. 8, 1886, and they had one son, John Chrisman, who died as an infant. On Feb. 14, 1888, he married Julia Kearney. Their children were: Kearney, who married Bernice Edna Fowler; and Francis ("Brick"),who married Mona Belle McDonald. Neither Kearney nor Brick had children. Frank's third son was Julian. He married Eula Penn Wheat, and they had one daughter, Charlotte Wornall, who married Steve Kirk and had two daughters, Julia and Louise. Both are married and Julia has two daughters, Meredith and Katie, and Louise has one daughter.

8. THOMAS JOHNSON WORNALL was born June 28, 1865. He married Emma Petty on May 17,1886, and they had three children: Thomas Wornall, who married Pearl Van Sheets; and his second wife was Floy Crews; Richard Wornall, who married Kate Gilmer, and he had a daughter named Lucy Wornall.

9. JOHN BRISTOW WORNALL JUNIOR—born March 13, 1872 and died February 4, 1962. He was the son of John and Roma Wornall. He married Louise Woodbridge, daughter of Jahleel and Virginia Woodbridge, on October 2, 1902. Their children were John Bristow Wornall III, who married Lucy Thorning; Roma Wornall, who married Charles Elnore Cropley; Jahleel Woodbridge, who married Virginia Wilson;

and William Dobyns, who married Sybil Shufflebotham. Roma Cropley Powell had one daughter, named Louise, who is married to Bill Eaton. Jahleel Woodbridge married Virginia Wilson and their children are: Virginia, Robert, Henry Tomlin, and Woodbridge. Virginia is married to Harold Hulen and they have three children: Sarah, Julie, and Clay. Sarah is married to Dr. Ward Brown and they have a daughter named Elizabeth and twin daughters, Jennifer and Katherine. Clay is married and has two daughters. Robert Wornall has three children: Jessica, Hunt, and Benjamin. They are married. Hunt has two sons, and Ben and Kelly have two sons. Woody is married and has two daughters. William Wornall had three children, William, Roma, and Al. They live in North Carolina.

10. CHARLES HARDIN WORNALL, was born August 26, 1876 to John and Roma Wornall. He married Jennie Barnett and had two children: John Wallace, who married Jeanette Davis; and Charles Hardin Jr.

11. JOHN BRISTOW WORNALL III, born October 2, 1903 in Kansas City, Missouri, married Lucy Thorning, born December 14, 1908, on November 28, 1931. They had two sons: John Bristow Wornall IV, born October 13, 1934, and James Frederick Wornall, born January 16, 1938. John Wornall died May 3, 1978. Lucy died in November, 2006.

12. JOHN BRISTOW WORNALL IV—born October 13, 1931, married and divorced Nancy Arnold. They have two daughters, Leslie Ann and Robyn Bristow. Both are married. Leslie has two daughters and one son and Robyn has one son.

13. LT. COL. JAMES FREDERICK WORNALL, born January 16, 1938, married Ruthie Davis on November 23, 1974. They have 2 children, Desiree Blythe, born February 21, 1976 and John Bristow Wornall V, born September 9, 1980. Both are married and Desiree has three children, John Oscar, born January 15, 2000, and twins, Jasmine Velora and Derek Anthony, born July 6, 2002. James Wornall Jr. is in the Air Force in Hawaii, is divorced, and has no children.

14. REV. JOHN BRISTOW WORNALL V—born September 9, 1980, to Jim and Ruthie Wornall. He married Gwendolyn

Ann Culpepper on August 6, 2005. Gwen was born Nov. 29, 1980. John is an ordained Baptist minister and is a hospital chaplain in Texas.

NOTE: This is a partial genealogy, since I didn't have access to a complete one. I apologize for any mistakes and for names that were inadvertently omitted.

Portrait of John Bristow Wornall Sr.

Portrait of Eliza Johnson Wornall

Portrait of Roma Johnson Wornall
(1866)

John and Roma Wornall's wedding-1866

Photograph of John Bristow Wornall Jr.

Photo of Louise Woodbridge Wornall

Picture of Wornall Family Picnic--1909

John B. Wornall III & his granddaughter,
Desiree Wornall, age 2, March, 1978

REV. JOHN BRISTOW WORNALL V

MURDER AT THE WORNALL HOUSE

A THREE-ACT PLAY

BY

RUTHIE WORNALL

CAST OF CHARACTERS

Bob Lane	Owner of an import-export Co.
John Preston	Homicide detective
Rhonda Winters	Sleuth, teacher, writer
Rick Winters	Retired vice-president of a corporation
Karen Lane	Bob's ex-wife; legal secretary
Marianna Kelly	Registered nurse
Sally Ashley	Real estate agent
Doctor Bart Ashley	Dentist
Mandy Todd	Chef; and volunteer cook at Wornall House
Jean Murphy	Web site designer; cook
Jamie Jackson	Director of the Wornall House
Anna Martin	Jamie's assistant at the Wornall House
John Bristow Wornall Senior	Builder of the Wornall House; banker, senator

Eliza Wornall	Second wife of John Wornall; daughter of Rev. Thomas Johnson
Frank Wornall	John and Eliza Wornall's son
Colonel "Doc" Jennison	Civil War general who commandeered John Wornall's home
Bushwhacker	Civil War soldier who tried to hang John Wornall
Hans	German hired hand who worked for John Wornall and saved his life during the war

ACT ONE

SCENE I

Scene One takes place in the dining room and in the parlor of the Wornall House.

NARRATOR #1.--(Standing in the doorway of the dining room)

John Wornall built the Wornall House in 1858 for his wife, Eliza. They lived there during the Civil War through many hardships. During the Battle of Westport, the house was used as a military hospital for wounded soldiers. Because numerous people died there, some people believe the house is haunted. Ghost tours through the house are quite popular, as are school tours.

NARRATOR #2.--On December 4, 2009, the annual Christmas Candlelight Tour was in full swing. The docents led people through the various rooms of the John Wornall House Museum and described how the Wornall family had celebrated Christmas from 1858 until 1932. Christmas dinner in the dining room was reenacted each year by six volunteers, dressed in period costumes. This year, there are six diners seated at the dining table. They are: BobLane, owner of an import-export business; Marianna Kelly, a registered nurse and Bob's date for the evening; Sally Ashley, a realtor, who sold Bob his house; Bart Ashley, a dentist at the Plaza; Rhonda Winters, an amateur sleuth, teacher, and writer; and Rick Winters, a retired businessman. The two volunteers who cooked the Christmas dinner are Mandy Todd, a restaurant chef and Jean Murphy, a web site designer. (Stand when named).

The two cooks carried out the platters and bowls of food and set them on the dining table.

MANDY—(Stands and talks to the diners) All of the foods served are from recipes that Eliza and Roma Wornall might've cooked in the kitchen's open-hearth fireplace. I'll also be serving two desserts that the Wornall ladies used to prepare Concord Grape Pie and Christmas Plum Pudding.

NARRATOR #1.—While Mandy spoke to the diners, Jean returned to the kitchen to get the pitcher of spiced cider. She came in and poured cider into each of the six glasses, then the two cooks returned to the kitchen, BART raised his glass and asked

BART--Shall we make a Christmas toast?

BOB—Absolutely!

BART--Merry Christmas and Happy New Year! May you have peace and plenty!

NARRATOR #2.--The six of them raised their glass and drank. Bob must've been thirsty. He drank down his glass of cider in one gulp. Just as Rhonda looked over at Bob to wish him a Merry Christmas, the words stuck in her mouth when she saw his empty glass tumble to the floor. Bob's face had contorted as if he was having a convulsion. His face was flushed, his eyes were bulging, and he clutched his throat with both hands as he gasped for breath. Then using one hand, he frantically began to dig at his jacket pocket, but wasn't able to find what he needed. (Bob acts out every symptom the narrator mentions as it is said).

BOB--(gasping for breath) Epi. Help! Pen.

SALLY—I can't understand you.

BOB—(Choking) Epi.

RHONDA—Does anyone know what an epi is?

BART—Bob, do you want me to get something out of your pocket?

BOB—Epi.

NARRATOR #1.—Just as Bart started to reach into Bob's pocket, Bob clutched at his throat again, then suddenly crumpled to the floor, shuddered, and lay still. Both Marianna and Bart dropped to their knees, one on either side of him, and tried to help him. Just as Marianna began to take his pulse, a doctor from the audience raced to Bob's side. Marianna returned to her seat to make room for the doctor. The doctor took his pulse, then shouted…

DOCTOR—Someone call 911. He isn't breathing. Tell them to bring a defibrillator.

NARRATOR-#2.-The doctor began CPR on Bob while Sally called 911.

SALLY--(Excitedly yelling into her cell phone) Emergency! Man not breathing! Send an ambulance to the Wornall House ASAP! Bring a defibrillator!

MARIANNA--(Asks doctor) Shall I start mouth-to-mouth resuscitation? I'm a nurse.

DOCTOR—Yes, right now!

NARRATOR #2.—Marianna knelt beside Bob again and began mouth-to-mouth. The ambulance arrived within five minutes. Two paramedics rushed through the door, carrying oxygen and other gear. Marianna and the doctor moved away so the paramedics could work on Bob. They gave him oxygen and used the defibrillator on him, but after several tries, one of them shook his head and muttered…

PARAMEDIC--He's gone.

NARRATOR #1.--Somebody called the police. The dispatcher sent two officers from the patrol division and the medical examiner.

POLICE OFFICER—(Entering) We're going to treat this as a crime scene. Don't touch anything!

NARRATOR #1--The Medical examiner, often called ME for short, examined Bob, but there was no response. He pronounced Bob dead at the scene.

DOCTOR—(Talking to the ME) Mr. Lane apparently couldn't breathe. He was clutching his throat and gasping for breath. I think he suffocated. I checked his pulse and did CPR. At the same time, a nurse did mouth-to-mouth, the paramedics used the defibrillator—all to no avail. I think Bob was dead by the time he hit the floor.

MEDICAL EXAMINER--His symptoms sound like a life threatening food allergy reaction.

DOCTOR--I think you're right, and if so, he should've had an epipherine auto injector and some antihistamine pills in his pocket. (He reached in Bob's pocket and pulled out an item about the size of a magic marker and a bottle of pills.) Here they are! His epi pen and his pills!

MEDICAL EXAMINER--I wonder what food he was allergic to?

SALLY—How could spiced cider kill Bob? One minute he was sitting at the table, laughing and talking. Then after he drank the cider, he started choking and fell over dead!

RHONDA—It had to be an allergy. We all drank cider from the same pitcher, and we're okay.

RICK--Bob had convulsions and his speech was so garbled we couldn't understand him. Maybe he had a massive stroke.

MARIANNA--He might've had a heart attack.

BART--(Shakes his head) He died so fast, I think he was poisoned! Someone must've spiked his cider with cyanide!

POLICE OFFICER—Don't touch the glasses, the plates, or the pitcher. We're going to send them to the lab for analysis. The homicide detective and the crime lab techs have arrived.

DETECTIVE—Hello, I'm Detective Preston. Mr. Lane's death is suspicious, and we're going to treat it as a homicide unless that can be ruled out. This is a crime scene. First of all, I want the lab techs to get fingerprints and DNA swabs from the remaining five diners and from the two cooks. Bag the glasses and the pitcher and take them to the lab and run tests for poison or on any residue not normally in spiced cider. More officers will be arriving, and each person here, including the tour members and the docents, will be interviewed. All of you are witnesses. Do not leave until you have written a statement and signed it.

The first responding officers have done a fine job of treating this as a crime scene. They've made sketches, taken photos, careful notes, and warned the witnesses not to touch anything. Good work, guys! Now, please isolate all of the witnesses.

MEDICAL EXAMINER--I've pronounced the victim dead at the scene. I'm almost sure he died from an anaphylactic shock due to a food allergy.

DETECTIVE—We have to find out what food or spice Mr. Lane was allergic to and how it got into his cider. We also must find out WHO put it in his cider. Mr. Lane's death could be an accident, but we won't know for sure what killed him until we get the autopsy report.

MEDICAL EXAMINER--I'll have the autopsy report for you tomorrow, if possible. Now, I need your permission to take the body to the morgue.

DETECTIVE--You may remove the body from the scene.

MEDICAL EXAMINER—Paramedics, please load Mr. Lane onto a gurney and carry him out to the ambulance. (They put him in a body bag and carry him out).

DETECTIVE--Officers, I'll interview the diners and the cooks. Will the rest of you interview the members of the tour and the docents? I'll talk to each person, one at a time, in the parlor. I'll start with Bob Lane's date for this evening. Please send her in. (He walked out of the room, went to the parlor, and sat down in one of the antique chairs flanking the fireplace).

MARIANNA (entering the parlor) Detective Preston, my name is Marianna Kelly.

DETECTIVE--I'm glad to meet you. Have a seat, please. (She sat). Why were you chosen to be one of the diners at the Candlelight Tour?

MARIANNA--Bob Lane invited me as his guest.

DETECTIVE--How long have you known him?

MARIANNA—For just one month. Tonight was our fourth date.

DETECTIVE--Did Mr. Lane tell you about his food allergy?

MARIANNA--No, he didn't. This is the first time we'd been out to dinner. He must've been allergic to one of the spices in the cider. His ex-wife would know about his allergy. I have her phone number. (She reached in her purse, pulled out her billfold and extracted a card from it.) Her name is Karen Lane. Bob gave me her card and said I should call her if anything ever happened to him.

DETECTIVE—I'll call her right now, if you don't mind.

MARIANNA--Please call her. I want to know about Bob's allergy.

DETECTIVE—(Takes out his cell phone to call). Hello, Mrs. Lane. This is Detective Preston of the Kansas City police at the Brookside station. I'm sorry to inform you that your ex-husband died tonight, apparently from an anaphylactic shock.

KAREN—Oh, no! I'm so sorry to hear that. Poor Bob, he had a life threatening peanut allergy. Eating just one peanut could've killed him. He always carried his epi pen with him. I wonder why he didn't give himself an injection?

DETECTIVE—I think his breathing difficulty and the pain came on too suddenly. His speech was so garbled the people couldn't understand him when he asked for his epi pen. He was probably gone within five minutes.

KAREN—Oh, that's so sad. His allergy was deadly. His symptoms would start within a couple of minutes if he ate a peanut. He's had several close calls in the past.

DETECTIVE—The odd thing here is that, to our knowledge, Mr. Lane did NOT eat a peanut. He merely drank a glass of spiced cider.

KAREN LANE—Then someone must've dropped a peanut in his cider. The only way he could've had that reaction is if he ate a peanut or something cooked in peanut oil. I wonder if peanut oil could've been stirred into his drink?

DETECTIVE—The lab will analyze the cider. Thanks for your help. If you think of anything else that could help us solve this case, call me at the Brookside Station. Please accept my condolences. Goodbye, Mrs. Lane.

MARIANNA—I'm a nurse. I should've recognized Bob's symptoms. If he'd told me about his allergy, I could've given him an injection and saved his life. He was a nice guy and I'll miss him.

DETECTIVE—What else can you tell me about Mr. Lane?

MARIANNA—He's been divorced for a year. He didn't have any children. He owned an import-export business and he made frequent trips to Texas and Mexico. He was a volunteer at the Wornall House.

DETECTIVE- Did he have any enemies?

MARIANNA—I don't know of any. People seemed to like him.

DETECTIVE—I'll want to talk to you again. I'll call you for an appointment. Thank you for your time. Would you ask Mrs. Ashley to come in next?

MARIANNA—Of course. Goodbye. (She exits).

SALLY—(Enters) I'm Sally Ashley. I liked Bob, but I think he was mixed up in the drug trade.

DETECTIVE—Why would you think that?

SALLY—He owned an import-export business, and I suspect he was bringing drugs back from the Mexican border with the pottery, copper pans, and silver jewelry imports.

DETECTIVE—Why do you think he was a drug smuggler?

SALLY—Because he paid cash for his house, and two weeks ago he offered me a couple of marijuana cigarettes. Another time, my husband saw Bob sitting in his car snorting coke, so I put two and two together.

DETECTIVE—That's interesting. Did you know about Mr. Lane's peanut allergy?

SALLY—No, he never mentioned that to me. I'm a realtor and I sold him a house. Most of our discussions were about houses. Do you mean to tell me that peanuts killed him?

DETECTIVE—We won't know that until we get the autopsy and lab reports. Do you know if Mr. Lane had any enemies or if anyone was stalking him?

SALLY--Everyone seemed to like him around here. If he had any enemies, they were probably connected to his business.

DETECTIVE—Here's my card. If you think of anything else to tell me about Mr. Lane, please call me. Would you send your husband in to talk to me now?

SALLY—Certainly.

DETECTIVE—Write and sign your statement. Thank you for your time and information.

SALLY—You're welcome. (She exits).

NARRATOR #1.—Dr. Ashley walked into the room and sat down.

BART—Hello. I'm Bart Ashley. My wife told me you wanted to see me.

DETECTIVE—Yes, I do. How well did you know Mr. Lane?

BART—We volunteered here at the Wornall House together and we played golf a couple of times. My wife sold him a house. That's the extent of it.

DETECTIVE—Was there anything about Lane's life that wasn't above board?

BART—My wife thinks he's involved in drug trafficking.

DETECTIVE—Do you think she's right?

BART—I think she has a good imagination. (Grins). Actually, she's right every once in awhile!

DETECTIVE—Your wife said you saw Mr. Lane snorting coke.

BART—That's what it looked like.

DETECTIVE—Could you swear in a court of law that you saw the coke he was snorting?

BART—No.

DETECTIVE--I'm conducting short interviews tonight, but I'll want to talk to you again. Here's my card. Please call if you think of something else to tell me about Mr. Lane. Thanks for your time. Would you please ask Rhonda Winters to come in?

BART—I'll be glad to. Good night.

NARRATOR—Rhonda entered the parlor with a big smile on her face. She was always happy to see her son-in-law, Homicide Detective John Preston.

DETECTIVE—Well, Mom, it looks like you've gotten yourself mixed up in another murder!

RHONDA—Oh? So you think Bob was murdered?

DETECTIVE—Somebody who knew he had a peanut allergy must've dropped peanuts in his cider. His ex-wife said he wouldn't have had the reactions he had unless there were peanuts or peanut oil in his drink.

RHONDA—Well, just about everybody in this house had the opportunity. Anyone could've slipped into the kitchen when the cooks were bringing the food into the dining room. As for means, anyone could've had a few peanuts in his pocket. But the motive is the puzzler! Who had a motive? And what was the motive? Who had an ax to grind with Bob?

DETECTIVE—You're right, everyone had the opportunity and could've had the means.

RHONDA—The scary thing is that one of the volunteers must be a murderer. I guess your main suspects are the diners and the cooks, which unfortunately, means that Rick and I are suspects!

DETECTIVE—Even one of the witnesses in the tour group could've done it, which makes them suspects, too. I think the cider was just setting there in plain view in the kitchen, so it would've been easy to flip a few peanuts in it. Well, now let's think about motives.

RHONDA—I wonder who Bob's beneficiary is? Who stands to profit from his death? Some other motives are jealousy, hatred, greed, anger, money, fear, and revenge. Maybe Bob ditched an old flame when he met Marianna. That could cover anger, jealousy, and revenge. As Shakespeare once said, 'Hell hath no fury like a woman scorned.'

DETECTIVE—(Laughing) Mom, you're pretty good! Are you going to help me solve this case?

RHONDA—I'd love to help you. Can I?

DETECTIVE—Officially, no. Unofficially, yes! This has to be our secret. I don't want to get in trouble with the chief of police.

RHONDA—What do you want me to do first?

DETECTIVE—You can talk to the suspects. Just take them to lunch one at a time or invite them to dinner. You can bet the conversation will soon turn to Bob's death. The suspects will probably tell you things they won't tell the police.

RHONDA—No problema! I can do that.

DETECTIVE—Use that mini tape recorder you have and tape every conversation that pertains to Bob.

RHONDA --I'll do it, then I'll call and tell you everything I hear and I'll give you the tapes, too. Hey! I'm starting to feel like Mata Hari!

DETECTIVE—(Laughs) Also, would you Google 'peanut allergy' and fax the information to me?

RHONDA—Sure. I'll do it as soon as I get home tonight. I'll FAX you the FACTS!

DETECTIVE—(Grins).Great!

RHONDA—This case is going to be a tough nut to crack! Pun intended!

DETECTIVE—(Laughs) Oh, Mom, you're funny! The first thing we have to do is prove that Bob was murdered. We have a big puzzle to solve.

RHONDA—Do you think there's anything helpful on the surveillance camera?

DETECTIVE—We'll make a DVD of it and find out. We'll download everything from the time the volunteers arrived until now. In the morning, I'll run background checks, find out who Bob's beneficiary is, interview his friends and relatives, and search his house.

RHONDA—Oh, good grief! You've got your work cut out for you. I guess you're planning to check out Bob's import-export business, too?

DETECTIVE—Absolutely. I'll also contact the DEA. If Bob was involved in drugs, the DEA should have some information about him. I'll talk to you tomorrow. Write your statement and sign it, but first send Dad in here. I'll talk to him for five minutes, then you can go home and start Googling! Thanks for your help. Goodnight, Mom.

RHONDA—Goodnight, John, and good luck with the case.

DETECTIVE—Thanks. (Rhonda exits. John looks up to see Rick enter). Hi Dad, what do you know about Bob?

RICK—I played golf with him one day last week. His cell phone rang and I heard a woman screaming that she ought to kill him for ditching her for another woman!

DETECTIVE—Do you have any idea who the woman was?

RICK—No, but I heard he might be mixed up with drugs. I don't know any details.

DETECTIVE—I guess Sally or Bart told you that. Right?

RICK—(Grins) How did you guess?

DETECTIVE—That's what they told me. Thanks for the info. Please tell Mandy to come in here. Write your statement, sign it, and you're free to leave. See you later, Dad. (Rick exits).

MANDY—(Enters) Hello, Detective. My name is Mandy Todd. I helped cook the dinner.

DETECTIVE—Hello. Please have a seat. Who made the spiced punch?

MANDY—I did. I just poured cider into the pitcher and stirred a package of spices for cider into it. The spices came in a sealed package.

DETECTIVE—Could you get me a package of the spices to send to the lab? Were there any peanuts in the spice package?

MANDY—There's an extra spice packet in the kitchen. *I'll get it for you. I'm sure there aren't any peanuts in it. I've never heard of peanuts in spiced cider.*

DETECTIVE—Did you know that Bob Lane had a deadly food allergy?

MANDY—No, I didn't.

DETECTIVE—Did Mr. Lane have any enemies or anyone stalking him?

MANDY—I doubt it. People liked him.

DETECTIVE—My time is short tonight, but I'd like to talk to you again. I'll call you. Would you ask Mrs. Murphy to come in next? Maybe she could bring one of those spice packets to me. Don't forget to write and sign your statement. Thanks for your time.

Mandy—(Nods) I'll do that. (She exits).

JEAN MURPHY—(Enters) Hello! I'm Jean Murphy. Mandy said you wanted this spice packet. (She handed it to him).

DETECTIVE—Yes. Thank you. (Takes it and puts it on a table). Have a seat, please. Did you make the spiced cider?

JEAN—(Sits). No, Mandy prepared it.

DETECTIVE—Did you know Mr. Lane had a food allergy?

JEAN—No, but if he did, he should've told us about it.

DETECTIVE—Was there anyone else besides you and Mrs. Todd in the kitchen today?

JEAN—No, not to my knowledge.

DETECTIVE—Was Mr. Lane involved in drug trafficking?

JEAN—Absolutely not! Where did you hear such a lie? He was a nice man.

DETECTIVE—I'm glad to hear that. I'd like to talk to you longer, but I'm in a rush. I'll call you soon for another chat. Here's my card. If you think of anything that might help us with our investigation, please call me. Write and sign your statement. Thanks for your time, Mrs. Murphy.

SCENE II

(Note: This scene takes place in the parlor of the Wornall House. Jamie has stopped by Rhonda's home to talk to her).

NARRATOR #1.--The next morning Rhonda had a visit from Jamie, the director at the Wornall House Museum.

RHONDA—Hi, Jamie. How nice to see you. Come in and have a seat.

JAMIE—Hi, Rhonda. I have an idea I want to discuss with you. I heard you're a sleuth, and that you've helped solve three murder cases when you were in Mexico. My assistant, Anna, and I were wondering if you'd do a little sleuthing on the case of the MURDER AT THE JOHN WORNALL HOUSE MUSEUM?

RHONDA—I'm flattered you asked me, but I doubt the police would want me meddling in their murder case.

JAMIE—Couldn't you do some unofficial sleuthing? (She grins) We won't tell!

RHONDA—Maybe I could, if it's kept a secret.

JAMIE—Thanks. What do you know about that new detective who's assigned to Bob's case?

RHONDA—I heard he'd had ten years experience in San Antonio as a homicide detective, and that he has an excellent record of solving murder cases.

JAMIE—No kidding? Well, we'd still like for you to do some snooping. Okay?

RHONDA—Okay, I'll snoop unless I'm told to stay out of it.

JAMIE—It will be our little secret!

RHONDA—Then you've got yourselves a snoop!

JAMIE—Thank you. Talk to you later. I have to run. Goodbye.

RHONDA—You're welcome. Bye. (Jamie exits, and Rhonda's son-in-law stops by).

DETECTIVE--(Enters) Hi, Mom. I was in the neighborhood so I stopped by for five minutes.

RHONDA—I'm always glad to see you. Would you like some coffee?

DETECTIVE—No, thanks. I have a couple of things to tell you. By the way, thanks for the peanut allergy info you faxed to me. You must've checked out several web sites to get all of that information.

RHONDA--I did.

DETECTIVE—Good work. I received the autopsy report and one lab result this morning. Thought you'd like to know there wasn't any poison in Bob's stomach, but he had a swollen throat, which indicated an allergic reaction. He died of an anaphylactic shock from a peanut allergy. Just what we thought! According to the lab report, peanut residue was found in the pitcher and glasses, which proves that somebody put peanuts in the cider.

Also, I thought you'd like to know that after everyone left the Wornall House last night, we conducted a thorough search of the house, and we found one peanut in the kitchen. That one peanut was a pretty good clue. It proved to us that peanuts had been in the kitchen. The lab report and that peanut indicates that Bob was murdered.

RHONDA—Good work, John. What do you do now? Focus on the six suspects? Sally, Bart, Marianna, Mandy, Jean, and Karen? You notice I didn't include Rick and me!

DETECTIVE—Of course, and I've talked to all six. I interviewed Karen, Bob's ex-wife, today, and I plan to search Bob's house tomorrow. Karen is still Bob's beneficiary since he hadn't changed his will. She inherits his house, car, business, and everything he has.

RHONDA—She sounds like a prime suspect to me. Was she in the Wornall House the night Bob died?

DETECTIVE—She said she and her boyfriend went to Houlihans for dinner that night, and that she hadn't been to the Wornall House in over a year.

RHONDA—Do you believe her?

DETECTIVE—I don't know. I called her friend, and he told me the same story. So maybe...

RHONDA—Well, she's probably telling the truth. By the way, Jamie called and asked me to sleuth and snoop.

DETECTIVE—Did you tell her you'd do it?

RHONDA—Yes, and she agreed to keep it a secret. I'm meeting Marianna for lunch today, and we're having Sally and Bart over for barbecue tomorrow night. My mini tape recorder will be in my pocket. Every word they say about Bob will be recorded.

DETECTIVE—Good work!

RHONDA-- By the way, did you know Jamie thinks the Wornall House is haunted?

DETECTIVE—You're kidding!

RHONDA—Did you ever see a ghost?

DETECTIVE—No, I never did, but when my mother was dying, she said my step dad came to see her several times. She said she also saw one of her friends who had recently died. When my Granny was dying, she said Grandpa came to see her everyday and sat in the rocking chair next to hers. She said she wanted to go to heaven and be with him. I talked to her doctor and nurse about it. The doctor said her medicine caused her to have delusions, but the nurse said she believes God sends a loved one to be with Christians when they're dying to prepare them for death.

RHONDA—I prefer the nurse's story. Once when I delivered books to the Wornall House Gift Shop for them to sell, Jamie heard somebody walking up the steps. When we couldn't see anyone there, Jamie said it must be their resident ghost. She said they hear him walking up and down the stairs quite often! She also said there's a ghost soldier who stands on the stairway landing above the entrance hall and guards the front door. Apparently, several people have seen a ghost in a long white flowing gown and ghosts of small children who are thought to be John and Eliza's children who died before they were three years old. Perhaps their most famous ghost is the Lady in Blue who is seen in the parlor playing the piano. Many people believe she's John's wife, Eliza, who died when she was only twenty nine years old!

DETECTIVE—I have an appointment to go to the Wornall House tomorrow. Do you want to go with me? Maybe we'll see a ghost! I want to double check something I saw in the kitchen when I was searching it the night of Bob's death.

RHONDA—Sure, I'll go with you. Perhaps we'll see the Lady in Blue!

SCENE III

(Takes place in the kitchen)

NARRATOR--John picked up Rhonda the next morning, and they went to the Wornall House. Jamie had given him permission to re-check something he'd seen in the kitchen ceiling of the Wornall House. When they arrived, Jamie and Anna took them to the kitchen and showed him where the step ladder was kept.

JAMIE—Take your time. We'll be in the office if you need us. (They exit).

RHONDA—John, what are you looking for? I hope there's a hidden camera in here. If so, I have an idea about how you might catch the killer.

DETECTIVE—Maybe that's what I'll find. I noticed something odd in one of the detectors, and I wanted to check it out. If there is a hidden camera, what's your idea?

RHONDA—Tell your prime suspect that there's a hidden camera in the kitchen and you have a clear picture of him or her stirring peanuts into the cider. With "proof" like that, you're bound to get a confession!

DETECTIVE—(Laughing) Is this an example of your tricky ideas that I've heard about?

RHONDA—Well, it might not be a great idea, but it's the best I can come up with at the moment.

DETECTIVE--(Pointing to the ceiling) Look! I see something in that detector? (He used a ladder to reach it and pulled it out). Well, what do you know! It's a tiny covert camera!

(He used his cell phone to call Jamie upstairs) Hi, Jamie, are there hidden cameras in any other rooms beside the kitchen? Oh, there's one in the parlor? Why is one in there? (He listened to her explanation and laughed). Well, that's interesting. Will you give me permission to take the two cameras back to the station to get the film developed? Thank you. I'll give you a receipt. There's always a chance that we'll get a picture of the killer 'doctoring' the cider. Yes, maybe there'll be a picture of a ghost, too! (Chuckles). Thanks.

RHONDA—Why did Jamie say a camera was installed in the parlor?

DETECTIVE—She said the man who installed the cameras owned a security company. He was interested in ghosts and he was hoping the camera would take a picture of the ghost of the 'Lady in Blue'!

NARRATOR—Before they were ready to leave, Jamie came downstairs to the kitchen.

DETECTIVE—(Hands her a receipt) Here's the receipt for the cameras and film.

JAMIE—I'd like to invite you both to attend the ghost tour tonight at seven and see a short skit afterwards titled, "The Ghosts of John and Eliza Wornall."

RHONDA—I'd love to. Can we bring Rick and Nikki, too?

JAMIE—Of course.

DETECTIVE—Then we'll be here at seven o'clock sharp. Thank you. As soon as the film from these cameras is developed, I'll let you know if there's a picture of the "Lady in Blue"!

ACT TWO

SCENE I

NARRATOR #1.—In Act Two, Rhonda went on a school tour to the Wornall House with her grandson, Jeremy. A docent led the children on a short tour through all of the rooms of the house and told them stories about the family who lived here. She told them that John Wornall would rise every morning singing Christian hymns, and that during the Civil War, his son, Frank's childish prank almost caused some soldiers to shoot him.

After the storytelling was over, the tour guide took the tour to the kitchen where Mandy was baking cookies in the fireplace. Mandy told them that Eliza and Roma Wornall had baked cookies in this same fireplace about one hundred and fifty years ago, then she gave each child a cookie.

After they ate the cookies, they were taken to the entrance hall and some volunteers presented a play for the children about the life of the Wornall family during the Civil War era.

NARRATOR-#2. John Wornall built this house in 1858 for his family. The Civil War started about three years later, and the Wornalls suffered many trials and tribulations during this time. In 1863, their house was taken over by Colonel Jennison and his two hundred Kansas Jayhawkers, another time, the Bushwhackers tried to hang Mr. Wornall, and later he was marched off by soldiers with rifles who threatened to shoot him. In 1864, the family was forced to leave their home because of Order Number eleven. That same year, the Battle of Westport was fought nearby and their home was turned into a hospital for wounded soldiers. Besides all of this, five of John and Eliza's children died before they were three years old. In 1864. John's father died, and six months later. His father-in-law was murdered on his front porch, then a few months later, his wife, Eliza, died from childbirth complications when she was only twenty nine years old.

The SECOND ACT begins when Colonel Jennison takes possession of Mr. Wornall's home.

COLONEL JENNISON—(Knocks at door and John and Eliza go to the door. John opened it). Mr. Wornall, I'm Colonel Jennison of the Union Army. I'm taking possession of your house to use as my headquarters. Your parlor will become my office and I'll sleep in your bedroom. I have two hundred Kansas Jayhawkers with me who will camp out on your grounds. You'll need to feed all of us. I realize I have a reputation as a harsh officer, but if you cooperate with me, I won't kill you or your family nor burn down your house.

JOHN WORNALL—In time of war, all men must make sacrifices. My family and I will do whatever you ask to make you and your soldiers comfortable. Welcome to my home. You're lucky that my wife is an excellent cook!

ELIZA—I'll be glad to prepare your meals. I enjoy cooking.

NARRATOR—The Wornalls treated Jennison and his men with courtesy and kindness, and Eliza never complained about cooking for them. When Jennison was ready to leave, he called John Wornall into the parlor.

JENNISON—Mr.Wornall, I'd heard rumors that you were a southern sympathizer, but I've investigated you quite thoroughly and questioned your loyalty to the Union, and I'm now convinced of your loyalty. Because I appreciate the good food your wife prepared, the accommodations, and the courtesy your family has shown us, I'm going to pay you what I owe you for the damages my troops did to your farm. Here's $2,880 dollars. My men and I will be leaving your home tomorrow morning.

WORNALL—Thank you, Colonel. You're a fair man. (Takes the money and counts it, then puts it in his pocket).

JENNISON—I normally do not pay for food and damages when I use homes. As you are probably aware, in the past I've burned down homes and killed some of the owners. I know your family feared for your life because on several occasions I heard you and your wife praying to God for safety. I probably would've killed you if it hadn't been for the Christian kindness you showed to us. I want you to know that God has answered your prayers.

SCENE II

NARRATOR #1.—After the Lawrence Massacre, led by William Quantrill and his Missouri Bushwhackers in 1863, General Thomas Ewing issued Order Number Eleven, which forced many Missouri farmers to leave their homes. Only those farmers who could prove that they were Union sympathizers and who took an Oath of Loyalty to the Union could stay in the region, but they still had to leave their farms. Those who didn't take the oath had to leave the area and many of their homes were burned to the ground. Ewing issued this order to prevent the farmers from providing food to the Confederates. Because of Order Number Eleven, John Wornall was forced to move his family out of their home. He moved them to downtown Kansas City. They did not spend Christmas of 1863 in the Wornall House, but they were allowed to return to their home in March, 1864, after part of Order Number Eleven was repealed, and they were allowed to plant crops.

NARRATOR # 2.—One Sunday morning when Mr. Wornall and his family were in their carriage on their way to church, some Bushwhackers stopped them, pointed guns at them, and told them to turn their carriage around, go home, and unlock their front door. As the Wornalls rode home they prayed for safety.

(This scene takes place on the lawn in front of the Wornall House.) After John Wornall unlocked his door, the Bushwhackers looted his house and stole everything they could pack in their saddlebags.

When Wornall's hired hand, Hans, saw the family was in danger, he sneaked away without being seen and raced to a nearby unit of soldiers for help.

BUSHWHACKER—Mr. Wornall, I know you've buried money in your garden. Get a shovel and start digging it up.

WORNALL—I don't have any buried treasure.

BUSHWHACKER I don't believe you. Dig up your money and give it to me.

WORNALL—I have NEVER buried any money in the garden or anywhere else.

BUSHWHACKER--You're a liar, and if you want to have another birthday, you'd better start digging.

WORNALL--My money is in a bank, not in the ground. I'll go to the bank and get money for you.

BUSHWHACKER—We don't have time to wait around for that. We've heard all about your buried money, and we want all of it! Start digging!

WORNALL—I'll dig, but there's no money to be found. I'm telling you the truth. There's NO buried money.

BUSHWHACKER—I'm tired of fooling with you. Since you refuse to dig up your money, I'm going to hang you from the top of your balcony. (He grabbed a rope and made a noose while another man pointed a gun at Wornall). Lean your head down so I can get this noose around your neck. (He slipped it over Wornall's head).

ELIZA—Oh, please don't hang John. He hasn't done anything wrong. Please don't hurt him. His family needs him. (She's crying).

BUSHWHACKER—Get out of the way, woman! Okay, boys, tie this noose to that balcony and let's string him up!

NARRATOR—Just as the Bushwhackers started to tie the rope to the iron balcony over the front porch so they could hang Wornall, here came Hans to the rescue! Several soldiers on horseback accompanied him. The soldiers were waving shotguns as they rode up to the front porch.

SOLDIER—(to Bushwackers) Get that noose off of Mr. Wornall's neck! (One of the Bushwhackers removed the rope).

SOLDIER—Now, hit the road, boys, or we'll shoot every one of you smack dab between your eyes. And I ain't a'whistlin' Dixie!

NARRATOR--The Bushwhackers jumped on their horses and took off as fast as they could go! Wornall profusely thanked Hans and the soldiers, then his family gathered around him, hugging him and rejoicing that his life had been spared.

SCENE III

(The scene takes place with Frank and Mittie standing on the balcony).

NARRATOR #1—A third incident that happened during the Civil War was instigated by John Wornall's young son, Frank. He and a girl named Mittie Pigg were standing on the balcony, watching some Union troops riding up the lane in front of their house.

MITTIE—Frank, I dare you to yell, 'Hurrah for Jefferson Davis!'

FRANK—I'll take that dare. (Yells) Hurrah for Jefferson Davis!

NARRATOR #2—Frank shouted it as loud as he could. The soldiers stopped and looked at him for a minute, then they decided to ride on. But later that day, they returned to John Wornall's home and asked to speak to him. He went outside and talked to them on the porch. Eliza joined them.

SOLDIER—Your son stood on the balcony there in front of your house and he shouted 'HURRAH FOR JEFFERSON DAVIS'. Now, we know for sure you're a Southern sympathizer.

WORNALL—That's not true.

SOLDIER—Then why did your son yell 'Hurrah for Jefferson Davis' when we rode past your home this morning?

WORNALL—He's a young boy and he was dared to do it. It was just a childish prank. He didn't know he was doing wrong.

SOLDIER—I don't believe you. I think he's heard you praise Jefferson Davis, and he just repeated what he's heard.

WORNALL—I've never praised Davis.

SOLDIER—I don't believe you. (Points gun at Wornall). You're going with us. Start marching. You'll have to do some mighty fast talking to keep from being shot before sun down.

ELIZA—Please don't take my husband away. He hasn't done anything wrong. You must be hungry. If you won't take him, I'll cook a good dinner for you. Do you like fried ham and cheese grits?

FRANK (Crying)—Please don't take Father away. It was just a dare! It was just a dare!

SOLDIER—Get out of the way. Wornall deserves to be shot.

NARRATOR #1—The soldiers marched Wornall out the door and up the lane. Frank and Eliza were crying, afraid they'd never see him again. They prayed the entire time he was gone. About one hour later, they heard somebody knock at the door.

ELIZA—(She went to the door, and there stood her husband. She and Frank hugged him tightly). Oh, John, I'm so thankful you're home. How did you escape?

WORNALL—The captain told me to go back home. He didn't give a reason.

FRANK—We know the reason. God answered our prayers!

NARRATOR #2—In 1864, John had been forced to join a Minutemen militia unit to help defend the area, and while the Battle of Westport was raging near his home in October, 1864, Eliza and ten-year old Frank were HOME ALONE. When John was finally allowed to come home, Eliza and Frank told him what had happened.

FRANK—Mother and I hid in the cellar under the kitchen floor until some soldiers forced open the front door and found us. They told us to get out of that hole and get to work.

ELIZA—The soldiers informed us that our house would be used as a hospital for the wounded soldiers of both the Union and the Confederacy. I've been working as a nurse and bandaging their wounds. Also, I've been cooking for those poor soldiers. I feel so sorry for them. Surgeries are being performed in our family room, and so many soldiers have died, they are stacking their bodies in the dining room by the window. The bodies are passed out through the window and loaded on wagons to be carted away for burial.

JOHN WORNALL—How sad. I'm thankful you two are safe.

ELIZA--At one point during the battle, when I went to the smokehouse for a ham, a cannonball whizzed past me. It came so close to me that the bun on the back of my head was knocked down.

FRANK—Mother said I was very brave.

JOHN—I think you were both very brave.

NARRATOR #2--Christmas of 1864 was the last Christmas celebrated in the Wornall House for ten years. The Civil War finally ended in April, 1865. Both Eliza's father, Rev. Johnson, and John's wife, Eliza Wornall, died in 1865. Eliza's father was murdered on his front porch, and Eliza died from childbirth complications. John was left with two sons to raise alone, one was a tiny baby.

The following year, in September, 1866, John married Eliza's cousin, Roma Johnson and they moved to a house at Ninth and Delaware in Kansas City, Missouri.

Roma took care of John and Eliza's two sons and she said she loved them like her own. Later, Roma and John had two more sons named John Bristow Wornall Junior and Charles Hardin. In 1870, John Wornall became the president of Kansas City National Bank and was also elected as a Missouri senator that year. There was some talk of electing him Governor.

In 1874, John and Roma moved back to the Wornall House and lived there thirteen years. John built a new house for Roma in downtown Kansas City and moved his family there. They lived there until John's death in 1892, then Roma sold her home and bought back the Wornall House. She said that was the house she loved, that it felt like home. She lived there until she died in 1933. Roma and John Wornall were buried side-by-side at Forest Hills Cemetery, in Kansas City, Missouri. Altogether, Roma had lived in the Wornall house for over fifty years.

In 1962, after the death of John Bristow Wornall's son, John B. Wornall Jr., the family sold the Wornall House to the Jackson County Historical Society for $25,000.00. The Wornall House

Museum now supports itself through tours and various other activities, plus sales from its gift shop, its herb garden, donations, and its membership fees.

NARRATOR #1: After this play was over, the children applauded, then their teacher led them back to the school bus and they returned to their school.

Six year old Jeremy hugged his Nana, Rhonda Winters, and thanked her for coming on the school tour with him.

ACT THREE

SCENE I

NARRATOR—Amateur sleuth, Rhonda Winters and her son-in-law, homicide detective John Preston, have worked together for one week trying to solve the Bob Lane murder case. So far, after all the suspects had been interviewed at least twice, after they'd taken polygraph examinations, after one had been tailed by the police, after several clues had been gathered, and after Preston had searched four homes, they've finally narrowed the prime suspects down to two people.

(John knocked at the door. This scene takes place in the family room of the Wornall House).

RHONDA—(Opens door). Hello, John. Come in and have a seat.

DETECTIVE—Hello, Mom. (He sits). I have some news for you.

RHONDA—Good! I want to hear it, but first I want to tell you that Rick and I have been invited to Sally and Bart's party tonight. They've invited all six suspects. When the conversation turns to Bob Lane's death, you can bet I'll have my tape recorder turned on.

DETECTIVE—I hope you find out 'whodunit' tonight! My news is that the lab finally sent me the fingerprint reports and the DNA analysis. You won't believe this, but all of the suspects had a clean record. None had prior convictions!

RHONDA--That's a shocker! I'm hoping to flush out the killer tonight.

DETECTIVE—Now, Mom, don't do anything foolish.

RHONDA—Oh, John, you know me.

DETECTIVE—Yes, I do, that's why I'm starting to worry! Call me if you need me. I've got to run. I have an appointment with one of our suspects. See you later. (John exits).

NARRATOR—When Rick and Rhonda arrived at the gathering, they joined the others in the family room and nibbled on appetizers while they talked. After a delicious Italian feast of lasagna, spaghetti and meatballs, salad, and garlic bread, they were served Tiramisu for dessert with coffee and hot tea.

Rhonda carried a mini tape recorder in her pocket. When she heard Bob's name mentioned, she flipped the switch. As expected, the conversation turned to the subject of Bob's death and continued for most of the evening.

MANDY—Why would anyone want to kill Bob? Everyone seemed to like him.

BART--We've heard some gossip that Bob might've been smuggling drugs over the border in his import-export trucks. He might've been killed due a drug deal that went bad.

JEAN—Do you have proof of that?

BART—Well...

JEAN--I don't believe Bob was involved in drug trafficking. He was a good man.

SALLY—I'm not so sure about that. When I was leading a tour through the Wornall House, I heard Bob and some woman arguing. She told him to get his drugs out of her house. And I don't think she was talking about Bayer Aspirin.

MARIANNA—One night when I was in Bob's car, he got a call on his cell from a woman who was talking so loudly I could hear everything she said. She told him she was in Nuevo Laredo, Mexico, and that she was bringing back one hundred pounds of coke. And I don't think she meant Coca Cola! Why would anyone tell him they were bringing coke to KC unless he was mixed up in the drug trade?

RHONDA—Since the call came from the Mexican border, it might've been from Bob's partner in his import-export business. I heard he had a silent partner who owned the trucks and the plane. Do any of you know who his partner was?

(They all looked at each other and shook their heads).

BART--I have no idea. I didn't even know he had a partner.

SALLY--I'm getting tired of being questioned by those detectives. Let's pool all the information we know about Bob, and try to solve his murder ourselves.

MANDY—That's a good idea. Just call us the "Crime Solvers!" I heard the killer is usually someone the victim knows, often a relative or a friend.

RHONDA—I've heard the killer is usually the last person you'd ever expect.

SALLY—I overheard Bob talking to someone on his cell and he said, "Will you get out of my life and stay out?" That sounded like he was talking to a former girlfriend. If she killed him, her motive could've been jealousy, revenge, and anger. All three.

RHONDA—So far, four motives for killing Bob have been mentioned. A bad drug deal, revenge, jealousy, and anger. To find the killer, we need to know who had motive, means, and opportunity.

MANDY—Jean and I had an opportunity because we were in the kitchen where the cider was setting, but we didn't have the means, which in this case was a peanut, and we didn't have a motive, either.

MARIANNA—Mandy, nobody suspects you or Jean just because you were in the kitchen. I was in the car with Bob one night when he got a call on his cell phone from a woman who was yelling at him. She said, 'After all I've done for you, I ought to kill you for dropping me like a hot potato!"

RICK—That woman probably had three of the motives—anger, revenge, and jealousy.

SALLY—I overheard another conversation when I was at the Wornall House, and it's a real puzzler! I don't know if Bob was on the phone or whether he was talking to a volunteer there, but I heard him ask somebody, 'Am I supposed to take the coke out of the cookies and put it in the shoeboxes?' What on earth do you think he was talking about?

BART—Take coke out of cookies? That one has me stumped! Well, I saw Bob sitting in his car one day and it looked to me like he was snorting coke.

JEAN—Do you have proof he was snorting coke?

BART—No, but that's what it looked like he was doing. Maybe I just have a good imagination.

(The group laughed.)

MARIANNA—Does anyone know if the police are close to finding Bob's killer?

RHONDA—I know who killed Bob, but I can't tell you until after I talk to the police.

MANDY—YOU know who killed him? Who was it? Do you mean the police don't know?

RHONDA—I mean I can't tell you until I ask the police if it's okay to tell you. I've called that detective twice, but he was out of the office both times.

MANDY—What makes you think you know who the killer is?

RHONDA—On the night of the Christmas Candlelight Tour, I saw the killer sprinkle peanuts over the cider and stir them in. I didn't tell the police because at that time I didn't realize the significance of what I saw.

SALLY—Rhonda, you can't drop a bombshell like that on us and not tell us Whodunit! Come on, who's the killer?

RHONDA—I'm sorry, but I can't tell you yet.

SALLY—Is it one of the six of us?

RHONDA—I can't say.

MANDY—Well, it's getting close to my bedtime. I have to go to work early in the morning.

JEAN (yawned) I'm tired, too. Sally and Bart, thanks for the lovely dinner. I really enjoyed it. (She picked up her purse, and said) Goodnight everybody. (They exit).

NARRATOR—After they left, Rhonda stepped into the kitchen, and took her cell out of her pocket. She dialed her son-in-law's number. When he answered, she told him what she'd done.

RHONDA—John, I told everyone I know who the killer is.

DETECTIVE—Oh, no! Mom, why on earth do you do these things? You stay there until I arrive. I'm going to follow you home.

RHONDA—Sorry to be a bother, but I'll feel safer if you do.

DETECTIVE—I'll be there in less than ten minutes.

NARRATOR #2—When Rhonda returned to the living room, Bart said…

BART--Rhonda, be very careful. If the killer is here tonight, you've put your life in danger.

RHONDA—I'll be careful. Thanks for the warning.

NARRATOR #2—John followed Rhonda and Rick home, then insisted on coming inside to search their house. He checked every nook and cranny, from the attic to the basement.

DETECTIVE—Mom, don't go out of this house by yourself, and keep all the doors locked, with the door jambs under the knobs. Do you promise?

RHONDA—You know we have an alarm system, and I wear a Life Alert pendant around my neck when I'm home, day and night, so I'll be safe. I'll call you if there's a problem.

DETECTIVE—You're always up to something. I expect I'll be hearing from you!

SCENE II

(This scene takes place in the
family room at the Wornall House.
They're sitting on the sofa).

RHONDA—Rick, I'm going to call John about my adventures today. Can you hand me the cell phone? (She dialed his number) Hi, John, I thought I'd tell you that the suspect has tried twice today to send me to the Happy Hunting Ground! First, I stopped at the Wornall House for a minute and went upstairs to the gift shop. As I started back down, somebody tried to push me over the banister. Then after that, Rick took me to lunch at a restaurant. He dropped me off, then drove on to park the car. When I started to cross the street, someone tried to hit me with their car. I guess she followed us from the Wornall House. I'm okay, though. God sent His angels to protect me, and I was able to jump out of the way. (She listened to his reply, then said). Okay. Thanks, John. Goodbye.

RICK—What did John say?

RHONDA—He said he's coming over to talk to us about the push and the attempted hit-and run.

RICK—I guess he'll tell me I shouldn't have dropped you off. From now on, I'll stick with you like Elmer's Glue. Well, the doors are locked and John is on his way, so I'm going downstairs to my office.

RHONDA—(Petted the dogs) Do you guys want to go outside? I'll put you out in the back yard. We'll go through the garage.

NARRATOR #1.—When Rhonda heard the dogs bark, she went out to let them in, and the dogs ran inside. Before she could go back inside the kitchen, she felt a hard object poked against her back and she heard a falsetto voice saying…

SUSPECT-- Raise your hands or I'll shoot!

NARRATOR #1.Rhonda turned to see who was there, and saw a woman wearing a ski mask pulled down over her face. She knew this was the same person who had tried to push her over the railing at the Wornall House.

SUSPECT--Get inside, but keep those hands in the air." (Rhonda went inside, as directed, and the dogs began to bark furiously at the suspect).

SUSPECT—Make those mutts shut up.

NARRATOR #1—The suspect kicked them, and they both rushed at her and jumped on her, causing her to drop her gun. Rhonda scrambled to pick it up, then she pointed the gun at the suspect.

RHONDA—Get out of my house or I'll shoot you, and don't think I can't do it! I'm an expert marksman!

NARRATOR--The suspect raced out of the door, got into her car, and took off. Rhonda locked the door. About the time, the suspect was leaving, John pulled into the driveway and Rick came up from downstairs.

RICK—What's been going on up here? I had the TV on, but I could still hear the dogs barking.

RHONDA—The dogs were protecting me from the intruder.

RICK—From what? What did you say?

RHONDA—From an intruder. I think it was the woman who killed Bob.

RICK—Thank goodness, you're okay. I shouldn't have gone downstairs. (The doorbell rang.

Rick went to the door to see who was there. It was John).

DETECTIVE--Rhonda, are you okay? I saw the suspect yank off her ski mask and drive away. I didn't try to arrest her because I want to catch her in a couple of deals an informant told me about. I called the dispatcher and told him her location and license tags number. He said there's a cop in this area who's following her. She's being tailed as we speak.

RHONDA—She should've been tailed all day.

DETECTIVE—Yes, she should've been. My fault. Tell me what happened just now.

RHONDA—In a nutshell, I had put the dogs out. When I was in the garage putting them back inside, someone wearing a ski mask over her face, stuck her gun to my back and threatened to shoot me. The dogs barked at her, and when she kicked them, they both attacked her, causing her to drop her gun. I scrambled for it, grabbed it, and pointed it at her. I told her to hit the road or I'd shoot her. When I told her I was an expert marksman, she got the heck out of Dodge!

DETECTIVE—Well, good for you! I didn't know you were an expert marksman.

RHONDA—(Laughed). I've never shot a gun in my life!

DETECTIVE—Oh, Mom, you're something! (He laughed and sat down at the kitchen table). Well, you and the dogs handled the situation just fine without our help.

RICK--Rhonda, why didn't you keep the suspect here at gun point until John arrived?

RHONDA—Are you kidding? I was up here by myself. I wanted her out of the house before she could take the gun away from me and shoot me.

DETECTIVE—You did the right thing. Now, If you'll give me a cup of coffee, I'll tell you what I found today. And it's a big story!

RHONDA—Coffee coming up. (She poured a cup and set it on the table for him).

DETECTIVE--Another detective and I searched Bob's home. In a locked storage area in his basement, we found nearly half a ton of cocaine hidden in pallets of Mexican cookies!

RHONDA—Coke in cookies! Well, Sally was right about Bob.

DETECTIVE—She sure was. After the DEA were called to do a search and seizure at Bob's home, one of the agents said, "When I write up my report tonight, I'm going to call this OPERATION COOKIE CAPER!"

(The three of them laughed.

JOHN—Well, I have to go. I have several appointments . Don't worry about that killer who just left. We'll keep a tail on her. Don't leave the house and keep your doors locked.

RHONDA—Who are you going to interview?

DETECTIVE—I'll tell you later. I've got search warrants, too, just in case.

RHONDA—Search their homes! You never know what you might find. Thanks for coming.

DETECTIVE—I'll call you this evening if I learn anything interesting. Keep your doors locked.

NARRATOR—Rhonda didn't hear from John until the next day about noon when he phoned. This time, he really had big news!

DETECTIVE—Hello, Mom. Sorry I was tied up and couldn't call last night. Can you and Dad meet me at the police station? I'm going to be interrogating the killer and ringleader of the cocaine drug smuggling operation. I thought you'd like to sit in on it. Of course she won't know you're there. The killer and I will be in the interrogation room which has two way mirrors. You two will sit in the adjoining room on the other side of the mirrors, and you can hear and see everything that's said and done.

RHONDA—Oh, John, I'm so proud of you! You've solved Bob's murder and cracked the drug smuggling ring at the same time! How soon do you want us to be there?

DETECTIVE—Can you be here in thirty minutes?

RHONDA—You bet!

NARRATOR—When they arrived, John met them in his office and took them to the room next to the interrogation room.

DETECTIVE—Look through the mirrors and you can see our suspect sweating it out in there while she waits for me. I'll join her now. (Her face is turned away from the audience).

RHONDA—Thanks for letting us come, John. This will be exciting!

RICK—Look, there's your suspect. Not looking too happy, is she?

DETECTIVE—(Entering the interrogation room) Hello.

SUSPECT—Hello, Detective Preston.

DETECTIVE—Before I ask you any questions, I want to tell you what I've been doing since I searched your house. When my partner and I were in your basement, he was able to crack your locked safe which was filled with hollowed out books full of hundred dollar bills. We also moved your sofa and found hidden beneath it a narrow door, which opened into your secret cellar. I guess you got the idea for that cellar from the one in the kitchen of the Wornall House. Woods picked your lock, forced the door open, and we found dozens of shoe boxes packed with cocaine packages. We took pictures of the cash-filled books and the cocaine-filled shoeboxes. We assumed if we left early, you'd think we hadn't seen either the cash or the coke. We thought you'd arrange to have it all hauled away that night, so we staked out your house. About midnight, we saw two men park a van in your driveway, and we watched them fill the van with the books and shoeboxes. We followed the van as it left your house. When it turned onto the freeway, we notified the state patrol and asked them to stop it and search it. They seized the contents of the shoeboxes and books. The two men turned out to be your two truckers.

SUSPECT—The books and boxes were things Bob had left in my basement.

DETECTIVE—That's not true. You see, we also have filmed you paying two drug couriers this week with the cash-filled books in exchange for shoeboxes of cocaine. In fact, your most recent transaction took place this morning at Loose Park where you were arrested. The courier was an undercover agent who will testify against you in court. So, what do you have to say?

SUSPECT—Read me my Miranda rights and let me call my lawyer.

DETECTIVE—(Reads the Miranda and hands her a phone). I won't ask you any questions until your attorney arrives, but instead of sitting here for thirty minutes twiddling our thumbs while we wait for him, I'll tell you what else we know about you.

You were tailed and filmed when you drove to the Forest Hills Cemetery, dug a hole beside John Wornall's tombstone, and buried a key in it. We arrested your pilot who came to pick up the key. He took us to the storage locker that was packed with boxes of cocaine, and the narcotics agents picked up the coke.

I was curious why you put the key in a hole instead of just giving it to your pilot, then it dawned on me that Bob Lane had dealt with him and he had never seen you. You didn't want him to know your identity.

The two truck drivers and the pilot who worked for you have been arrested, and they've sung like canaries! They told us you're the mastermind behind the drug trafficking operation that smuggled cocaine from the Mexican border to Kansas City.

If that's not enough proof of your guilt, we have you on film, wearing a ski mask, and forcing your way into Rhonda's house, armed with a forty-five automatic. Rhonda had a sophisticated alarm system and a type of surveillance camera which filmed every move you made. You threatened to shoot her and probably would have if her dogs hadn't attacked you, causing you to drop your gun. She picked it up and told you to get out, which you did. I was parked outside her house and I saw you jump in your car and yank off your ski mask. I'll testify in court that I saw your face. I also took a picture of your car and a close up of your license plates. I have no sympathy for you whatsoever. Rhonda is very dear to me. She's my mother-in-law. You'd better be thankful that you didn't harm a hair on her head.

LAWYER—(Escorted to the room) Was Preston interrogating you?

SUSPECT—No. He was explaining the charges against me.

LAWYER—Do you wish to answer questions at this time?

SUSPECT—Yes, we might as well get it over and done with.

DETECTIVE--There's a hidden camera in the kitchen at the Wornall House, and we have you on film stirring peanuts into the cider. Don't tell me there were no peanuts in that kitchen. We found one lying on the floor. Why did you kill Bob Lane?

LAWYER—You don't need to answer that!

DETECTIVE—I think she does.

SUSPECT—(Ignores lawyer) I didn't mean to kill Bob. I just wanted to punish him for ditching me for Marianna, and for threatening to turn me into the police.

LAWYER—You just confessed. What's this all about?

DETECTIVE—It's about murder and drugs! (He turned to Jean) How long have you been a drug smuggler?

LAWYER—Don't answer that! I wonder why you called me. You're ignoring my advice and you're confessing to this detective.

SUSPECT—He caught me red handed. I want you to make a deal with him. I need a plea bargain. I did not mean to kill Bob. He never told me his allergy was life threatening. It boggles my mind that a few little peanuts could've killed him. Death by peanuts is not exactly a typical gangland killing.

DETECTIVE—Who's the ringleader of your drug trafficking operation?

SUSPECT—(Replies proudly) I'm the ringleader and I have been for ten years.

DETECTIVE—I suspect the DA will charge you with Murder One, drug trafficking, and the attempted murder of Rhonda Winters.

LAWYER—I realize the seriousness of these charges, and I'd like to cut a deal. I believe she was sincere when she said she did not mean to kill Mr. Lane. Since she's been cooperative, don't you think the charge could be reduced from Murder One to manslaughter?

DETECTIVE—That depends on what the DA and the judge have to say. But before we call it a day, I want to know why you got involved in drugs?

SUSPECT—My ex-husband got me involved, then he left me for another woman. By that time, I was in too deep to get out. I wish I'd never met that man.

DETECTIVE—Our lives are the result of our choices.

SUSPECT—I suppose that's true.

DETECTIVE--What's your ex-husband doing now?

SUSPECT—He's married to the other woman and they're both involved in the drug trade.

DETECTIVE—If you want to get even with them, give me their names and address. We'll get them for you!

SUSPECT—That thought's cheered me up! (She grins). What a wonderful suggestion! Their names are Gary and Earlene Murphy, and they live in Savannah, Georgia. I know their birth dates and his social security number. That will help you catch them, won't it?

DETECTIVE—Yes it will. Yes, it sure will! (Big grin).

SUSPECT—Don't put them in the same prison with me. That would be double jeopardy!

SCENE III

(This scene can take place in the family room of the Wornall House).

NARRATOR#2.—On her way home from the police station, she made a stop at the Wornall House. Jamie and Anna met her at the door.

JAMIE—Hello.

RHONDA—Hi! I can't come in. I'm sorry this is the last minute, but can you both come to my house for pizza, salad, and spumoni ice cream tonight at six? Bob's killer's in custody. I'm in a rush now, but you'll learn all about it when you get there.

JAMIE—Wild horses couldn't keep us away!

RHONDA—I'll see you at six. (She waved, then turned and hurried back to her car. She took out her cell and called Sally, Bart, Marianna, Mandy, and Karen). I'm calling to invite you for Pizza, Pepsi, and Spumoni ice cream tonight at six. I'm sorry this is a last minute invitation, but if you can come to our house, Detective Preston will tell you who killed Bob and why. We'll also find out whether or not Bob was involved in drug smuggling.

NARRATOR #2.—Everyone Rhonda called accepted her invitation, and they all arrived on time. Rhonda had set out a platters of grapes, cheddar cheese, crackers, and fresh vegetables. Detective Preston arrived and Rhonda invited him to the front of the room. She stood behind a makeshift podium and...

RHONDA—I'd like to introduce you to our son-in-law, Homicide Detective John Preston.

SALLY—You sure can keep a secret! We had no idea he was your son-in law.

RHONDA—He is, and we're proud of him. He'll tell you about Bob's killer.(She sits down).

DETECTIVE—(goes to the podium). Hello, everybody. This is going to be short and sweet because I have an appointment in forty five minutes. I'm here to tell you that Jean Murphy couldn't come to the meeting because she's locked up in jail. Not only did she kill Bob, but she's made three attempts on Rhonda's life. Also, she's been the ringleader of a cocaine smuggling operation in Kansas City for ten years! If you have any questions, I'll be glad to answer them.

MARIANNA—I can't believe Jean did it. She seemed so nice and she was such an excellent cook. Was Bob involved in drugs?

DETECTIVE—Yes, he was. When I searched his house I found nearly one half ton of cocaine hidden in pallets of cookies.

SALLY—So the coke was in the cookies?

DETECTIVE—Yes, and he took the coke out of the cookies and put it in shoeboxes!

BART—Well, Sally, was right about Bob. I told you she was often right!

ANNA—I'm shocked! I'd thought Bob and Jean were so nice. People can sure surprise you!

JAMIE—They certainly can! How did you find out that Jean killed Bob?

DETECTIVE—When I told Jean about the hidden camera in the kitchen of the Wornall House, and said there were clear pictures of her stirring peanuts into the spiced cider, she confessed. That was Rhonda's idea. Rhonda tricked her, and it worked!

RHONDA—It was actually a lie, and I feel guilty about it. The film only showed someone's back, but they were stirring the cider.

DETECTIVE—The police are allowed to stretch the truth if that's what it takes to solve a crime.

RHONDA—That makes me feel better.

DETECTIVE—Do you remember when Rhonda told everyone at Sally and Bart's party that she knew who killed Bob? After that, Jean tried to kill Rhonda three times. Not only did she try to push her over the banister at the Wornall House and hit her with her car at a restaurant, but she broke into Rhonda's house yesterday and threatened her with a forty five automatic. Jean would probably have shot Rhonda if the dogs hadn't attacked her first. Rhonda's dogs saved her life!

SALLY—Rhonda, Bart and I had worried about you. I'm thankful you're safe. Though it put you in danger, I think your comment at our party helped break the case.

DETECTIVE—Yes, it did. Jean was an evil lady who involved Bob in the drug trade, ruined his life, then killed him. Her motives for killing him were jealousy, revenge, and fear. Bob wanted out of the drug business, but Jean wouldn't allow it, so he threatened to turn her in to the police. That's when he signed his death warrant. She couldn't let that happen, so she killed him.

MARIANNA—Did Jean know about Bob's peanut allergy?

DETECTIVE—Yes, she knew about his peanut allergy, but she said she didn't know how serious it was, which may or may not have been the truth.

MARIANNA—Did Jean know the peanuts would kill Bob?

DETECTIVE—She swore she did not, that she only wanted to make him sick because he'd ditched her and she was afraid he'd turn her in to the police. Frankly, I think she knew.

MARIANNA—How did Jean involve Bob in the drug trade?

DETECTIVE—He'd been out of work for quite awhile, so she offered to set him up in the import-export business. She became his silent partner and she gradually began shipping cocaine in his imports.

JAMIE—Did you see any ghosts in that film taken at the Wornall House?

DETECTIVE—Not a one. Not even the "Lady in Blue"!

RICK—What did Jean say when she realized she was on her way to prison?

DETECTIVE—All she said was, 'My goose is cooked'!

Note: (The actors leave the stage. Only the narrator is left to end the play).

NARRATOR—(Stands in the front of the stage). Jean Murphy's court date has come and gone. She was found guilty of Second Degree Murder in Bob's death, attempted murder of Rhonda Winters, and conspiracy to possess and distribute cocaine as ringleader of a drug trafficking operation for ten years. She received a combined sentence of thirty years in prison.

The three co-defendants, the two truckers and the pilot, also received sentences for conspiracy to possess and distribute cocaine, and they each got ten years in prison.

The police chief stated, "This successful operation has dealt a blow to cocaine trafficking in Kansas City, Missouri."

In a television interview, Detective Preston gave credit to an amateur sleuth who wished to remain anonymous. He said, "Without her help we wouldn't have had a GHOST *of a chance of solving THE MURDER AT THE JOHN WORNALL HOUSE MUSEUM in ten days!"*

THE END

THE GHOSTS OF JOHN AND ELIZA WORNALL

(A one-act skit)

BY

RUTHIE WORNALL

NARRATOR—It was Halloween night. After the Ghost Tour of haunted Wornall was over and the Wornall House museum was locked up for the night, the ghosts of John and Eliza Wornall met in the parlor of their former home. They sat on the green Empire sofa and reminisced about their life in this house during the Civil War.

ELIZA—Well, John, it's good to see you and to be here in my home again after all these years. I haven't been here since 1865.

JOHN—You're as beautiful as ever, Eliza. I like the blue dress you're wearing.

ELIZA—Thank you. Do you remember buying it for me to wear to our party celebrating the end of the Civil War?

JOHN—Yes, I remember, even though the Civil War has been over for 150 years. We had some scary times during those war years.

ELIZA—That's for sure. Do you remember the day Colonel Jennison came to our house and took possession of it to use as his headquarters?

JOHN—I certainly do. He turned this parlor into his office, he slept in our bedroom, and his two hundred soldiers camped out on our land.

ELIZA—I was petrified because I'd heard that sometimes he'd killed people who had not accommodated him and his men and that he'd burned down their homes. It was quite a chore to cook for all of those men. I remember the morning Jennison told you he was leaving, and he paid you for the damages his men had done to our property. He told you he might've killed you if we hadn't treated them with kindness and courtesy and fed them so well.

JOHN—It was your good cooking that saved us! Do you remember that Sunday morning when we were in our carriage on the way to the Baptist Church when the Bushwhackers stopped us and forced us to return to our house and unlock it?

ELIZA--They looted the house and stole whatever they could pack into their saddlebags. I remember as soon as we pulled up to the house, our hired hand, Hans, realized we were in trouble, and he ran to a nearby army unit for help.

JOHN—Yes, Hans was a great guy. The Bushwhackers had heard a rumor that I'd buried money in the garden and they kept telling me to dig it up. I told them repeatedly that I had NOT buried money anywhere. Why would I bury money in the ground when I could put it in a bank? I offered to go to the bank on Monday and get some money for them, but they said they didn't have time to wait around for that. They continued to harass me about digging up my supposed buried treasure. When I didn't start digging, the leader said he was going to hang me from the balcony. He put a noose around my neck, and I thought my last day on this earth had come.

ELIZA—Just as the men were getting ready to tie the rope around the balcony and string you up, here came Hans to the rescue! He brought several soldiers on horseback with him. The soldiers pointed their guns at the Bushwhackers and told them to hit the road and not come back!

JOHN—Hans saved my life!

ELIZA—You had divine help, too. I was praying non-stop!

JOHN—Thanks for praying. God works in mysterious ways! He sent Hans for the soldiers to save our lives. Do you remember how angry we were when Ewings's Order Number Eleven forced us to move out of our home in 1863?

ELIZA—Yes, but you rented a nice home for us to live in, so it wasn't so bad. I was happy when part of the Order #11 was repealed the following March, and we were allowed to return home and plant our crops.

JOHN—Not long after that, I was forced into a Minuteman unit. I was really worried about leaving you and Frank alone in the house.

While I was gone, the Battle of Westport was fought almost in our front yard.

ELIZA—Frank and I hid in the cellar under the kitchen floor, where we thought we'd be safe. Soldiers forced their way into our house and found us. They told us they were turning this house into a military hospital. They brought all the wounded soldiers inside and laid them on pallets on the floor. They told me I had to cook for everyone. I didn't mind cooking for those poor wounded guys. The worst part was all of those surgeries. I can still hear the poor men screaming with pain. So many soldiers died, and they stacked their bodies in our dining room.

JOHN—You were brave and so good to the men. When you weren't cooking, you were bandaging their wounds. I remember you told me about going outside to the smokehouse for a ham, and how a cannonball came so close to you, it knocked your bun down from the back of your head.

ELIZA—One of the soldiers told me he was sure glad I wasn't hurt because he loved my cooking!

JOHN--I loved your cooking, too.

ELIZA—Thank you.

JOHN—Do you remember the morning that Frank and Mittie were standing on the balcony, watching some Union soldiers ride past our house? When Mittie dared Frank to yell 'Hurrah for Jefferson Davis', he took the dare and yelled it as loud as he could! He said the soldiers stopped and glared at him, but then rode on. I'd hoped that was the end of the incident, but later that day, the soldiers returned to talk to me about it. I tried to convince them that it was just a childish prank, but they were so angry about it, they marched me away at gunpoint, and threatened to kill me.

ELIZA—Frank and I were so scared. We prayed the entire time you were gone that God would save your life, and then you returned home! The captain had a small boy that age, and understood how mischievous kids can be! We were so thankful he sent you home!

JOHN—I believe in the power of prayer! Frank was a pill, wasn't he? He was the best son any father could ever want, except when he was up to mischief! Remember the day the builders were putting the roof on this house, and Frank climbed up on top of the roof where they were working?

ELIZA—(Laughing) That little rascal nearly scared me to death! Though we had many trials and tribulations during our eleven years of marriage, the saddest things that happened were the deaths of our five little children and the day my father was murdered.

JOHN—(Took her hand). There was one thing that happened that was even sadder. It was the day you died.

ELIZA—But I left you two sweet sons, Frank and Tom, and my kind Cousin Roma, who took good care of all of you.

JOHN—Yes, you did. Roma was a good mother to the boys and a good wife to me. She said she loved your boys as much as her own. Roma and I were lucky to have two more sons, John Junior and Charles. I'm proud of my four boys.

ELIZA—(Laughing) I couldn't believe you took your entire wedding party along to Baltimore on your honeymoon with Roma! If I were her, I would've been so upset with you, but I guess she was too nice to complain. I hope you were as good a husband to her as you were to me.

JOHN—I tried to treat you equally. I hired George Caleb Bingham to paint her portrait, just as he painted yours. I also built her a house that was as the nice as the one I built for you.

ELIZA—Well, John, I've enjoyed visiting with you this evening.

JOHN—I've also enjoyed seeing you, my dear.

ELIZA—Let's don't wait another one hundred and fifty years to meet here again. Let's invite Roma and the boys to join us next time.

JOHN—What an excellent idea! I know they'd enjoy getting together. I'll play the piano, they'll all gather around it, and we'll all sing just like we used to. Why don't we start visiting this house each time Jamie conducts a ghost tour?

ELIZA—That's a grand idea!

JOHN—Be sure to wear your blue dress to our next rendevouz.

THE END!

NOTE: Some people believe the ghost known as the "Lady in Blue", who supposedly haunts the Wornall House, is Eliza Wornall.

ABOUT THE AUTHOR

Ruthie Wornall, a former history teacher, has written four culinary murder mystery novels starring sleuth Rhonda Winters, and a series of seventeen "Three Ingredient Cookbooks." She has prepared quick and easy 3-ingredient recipes on television stations in Missouri and Arkansas. For eighteen years, she has written a weekly newspaper food column, "The Reluctant Chef", for the Weston Chronicle. She has owned a publishing and distribution business since 1988. She volunteered at nursing homes for twelve years. Ruthie and her husband, Jim, live in Overland Park, Kansas, with their two poodles. They have two children and three young grandchildren. They are members of Wornall Road Baptist Church. Ruthie earned three college degrees and was listed in Who's Who of of America in 2006 and 2007 and in Who's Who of the World in 2009.

LaVergne, TN USA
27 May 2010

184091LV00002B/10/P

9 781449 073251